MARGIN PLAY

ERIC PLUME

This book is for my family, who never stopped believing I could

Acknowledgments

First, to Barbara, Jose and the rest of my personal Chicago Outfit, for all your consulting, fact-finding and testing...this book might have come into being without your help but it would not have ended up nearly as good. And to my lady Faye, who was many things; sounding board, consultant on ladies' fashion, editor, format guru, internet wizard, cover artist, whip-cracking motivator...Oh, the many hats you wore. A writer could ask for a better partner, but I doubt any has ever been lucky enough to find one.

As for the rest of you...how this novel came to be would make an epic story all on its own, complete with cast of thousands; to thank each of you personally would require a book longer than the one I wrote. I'll have to get away with simply saying I appreciate every gesture which helped me along, no matter how small.

I can do whatever I want. I'm rich, I'm famous, and I'm bigger than you.

-Don Johnson

Chapter 1

It was eleven in the morning when I finally closed the Cullen case. Getting to that point had been a three-week effort but I did not mind that much; three weeks of billing was exactly what my firm needed. The trick would be getting the Andersen law firm to pay up. Most lawyers didn't fully appreciate how long a proper skip-trace could take, and Thomas Cullen had been a tough one to nail down.

Three weeks of tracking had brought me to a cheap neighborhood on the north end of Everett along old Highway 99; plenty of water, lots of trees and a set of houses long past their prime. I had parked my little Golf just behind a stand of fir trees, through which I could see the house where Cullen had chosen to hole up - or at least where my investigative efforts put him. The house was a low-slung rectangle clad in moldy white vinyl, shingles missing here and there. The house belonged to Thom Cullen's half-brother; apparently Frank Cullen wasn't all that into home repair.

Thomas himself was a thoroughly unpleasant man, going by what I had found in his record. Thom Cullen was a two-time loser on the felony scoreboard, with a few lesser offenses like DUIs, domestic restraining orders thrown in for flavor. Then there was what had brought me to look for him; a lawsuit involving a truck full of tools that Cullen had made off with courtesy of a business partnership gone sour. The argument which had ended the partnership had left one Mr. Levon Jones in Harborview Medical, with a broken nose and two cracked ribs. Cullen probably needed to go to jail...but Jones wanted his truck and tools more than he wanted justice, so he had hired Andersen Law to serve Cullen some papers. Cullen skipped town, and Andersen Law had given me a ring. I remained surprised that a law firm would give a hard case like Thom Cullen to a small-timer like me - female too, natch - but money is money and my little business needs a steady supply of it.

The papers for the court case sat on the passenger seat of my VW Golf, next to a camera case and a set of binoculars, both of which were too obvious for use at the moment. A cooling Starbucks mocha was wedged into the drink holder. I sat in the driver's seat with a copy of the *Wall Street Journal* held in front of my face. I'd adjusted my rear-view mirror so I could see Cullen's driveway and stare at it without appearing too interested. To an observer, I was just reading the paper in the car. Every ten seconds my eyes flicked to the mirror; no action, but patience was always part of the game.

Outside, rain leaked out of the low clouds in the petulant drizzle endemic to the Pacific Northwest, a sort of lazy downpour that soaked a person caught out in it much faster than it seemed like it should. I was glad to be doing my stakeout from the comfort of my car. I took another sip of my mocha and decided against finishing it. My bladder had already started complaining, and my lack of outdoor-compatible plumbing could make that problematic. I snacked on some carrot sticks instead; they weren't the cinnamon roll I wanted but they were something, an IOU to my body. My pants had gotten tight again. Sacrifices had to be made.

A rumbling sound came from down the road behind me. A truck, a big one from the sound of the engine. I wanted to look but disciplined myself to wait. Nothing spoils a stakeout like rubbernecking. Sure enough, a big red Dodge pickup came ambling down the road. I waited until it passed by, then snapped a picture with my phone and texted it to my assistant.

Run those plates Izzy, I sent along with the photo. In less than twenty seconds my phone buzzed with her response.

Got it and done, boss. That's our client's truck. Make model color and plates all match.

I watched a big man in dirty denim get out of the

truck and amble up the steps to the house, toting a plastic grocery bag. I recognized Thom Cullen from photographs; a greasy brown ponytail gave him away. Even at forty yards I could see the pale patch on his scalp where his hair had thinned. His gait was a little off, the sort of lazy stagger that usually resulted from booze for breakfast. As I watched a ragged Doberman came around the side of the house, tail wagging. Cullen gave it a few scratches on the head and let it lick his hand. I sighed.

Wish me luck, I texted to Izzy. **There's a big ugly dog on the porch.**

There was another buzz. **Don't get eaten XD** glowed on my phone's screen. I checked my face in the mirror. A makeup free thirty- something with crow's feet looked back. "Game time," I muttered. I rolled up the newspaper as tight as I could get it and stepped out of the car.

The rain had soaked through the shoulders of my pea coat by the time I got to Cullen's yard. The dog fixed its eyes on me as I opened the gate.

"Nice doggie," I muttered under my breath. "Good doggie."

The Doberman launched itself at me.

"Or not."

I came up on the balls of my feet, pinpricks of sweat breaking out along my spine. The dog got to within arm's length and I whacked it with my newspaper.

Rolled up and wet the Sunday *Journal* weighed as much as a blackjack; state law mandated that process servers couldn't carry weapons on duty but I'd found nothing in the statutes which prohibited the aggressive use of journalism. The dog's growls became a yip of pain as I smacked it on the side of its snout. I stepped aside as it blundered past me and gave it another shot for good measure, this one on the ear. It bolted towards the side yard and disappeared around the corner of the house.

I felt guilty for hitting him. Likely his owner deserved it more. I continued up the walk, keeping the paper balanced in my left hand.

The yard looked like a wheat field just after harvest time. Cigarette butts littered the cracked concrete of the walkway. The porch sagged in the middle and creaked when I put my weight on it, the planking slimy with mold. A big pile of empty tallboys sat to the left of the door; Steel Reserve, the skid-row malt liquor of choice. I could just see the recycling bin they were supposed to fit into. Just above that a sign had been nailed to the siding, a stylized picture of a 9mm Glock below the words WE DON'T DIAL 911 spelled out in blocky red capitals.

There was no doorbell, just an empty hole where one used to be. I gave the door three firm raps and waited. No one answered. I knocked again, hard enough to make my knuckles sting a little. This time I heard movement inside the house. I dusted off my professional smile as the door opened a crack.

A leather-faced man in a dirty undershirt peered out, lank gray hair falling over one bloodshot eye. He had a soft middle but wiry arms; the build of a laborer. I recognized Frank Cullen from photographs. "Yeah?"

"I'm looking for Thom Cullen," I said.

"He isn't here," the old man growled in the thick wet voice of a chain-smoker.

"Funny, I saw him come in," I said.

"Fuck off, lady." Frank went to shut the door. I managed to get my hiking boot in the crack first.

"That truck is stolen property, Mister Cullen," I said. "Now, there are two ways this can go. Your brother comes back to settle his problems in Seattle, or you and him can split a cell here in Everett. Your call."

He glared at me and I smiled back at him. Sticking my foot in the door was pushing my luck but sometimes that is what you have to do.

"What the fuck's going on out there?" An angry

voice, male and slurred, came from somewhere in the house. Thom Cullen, I guessed.

Frank looked over his shoulder and stiffened. "Aw, Jesus," He said.

There was a flurry of movement on the other side of the door and Frank Cullen moved aside. In his place came an unwashed piece of work with a beer gut and a five o'clock shadow; Thomas Cullen, in the flesh and not at all happy about it. What really got my attention was the AR-15 rifle he held.

"Get the fuck out of here," he snarled. I found myself staring at the little black eye of the AR's muzzle. It was less little sitting two inches from my nose. My heart rate found a higher gear.

"Thomas Cullen," I said, "you are being served." I held out the plastic document case. My voice came out steady and I took a second to be proud of the fact. The back of my neck was hot and damp and my stomach had crawled behind my backbone, but the drunk with the rifle didn't know it and that's what counted.

"Izzat so?" The barrel swayed back and forth. I did my best to ignore it and focus on Cullen. His eyes were glazed and I could smell the sickly-sweet stench of beer on him. His finger was on the trigger and the safety was off but the bolt was still forward.

"Yes it is," I said. "If you would just sign the documents, I'll be on my way."

Cullen yanked at his rifle's charging handle with a clumsy take on action-hero panache and leveled it at me again. "What now, you fuckin' cunt?"

I glanced at the AR's receiver. "Now it appears you're having performance issues," I said.

He blinked and looked at the AR's action. The bolt was halfway back. "Shit," he mumbled.

It was work not to giggle. Adrenaline always made me a bit goofy. "We can wait a half hour and you can try again," I said, "but in the meantime, sign the documents?"

The look on his face was somewhere between anger and embarrassment. He fumbled with the charging handle.

"Jesus, Tommy, put that goddamn thing down," I heard from inside. Frank stepped up next to him and reached for the rifle.

"Not till this fuckin' cunt leaves me alone," he yelled. They struggled over the rifle, and I did my best to keep the muzzle away from my face while they did. Jammed like it was it probably wouldn't go off, but I didn't want to end up perforated by a statistical anomaly. Frank snatched the documents out of my hand; I let him while I thought about the level of incompetence required to jam an Armalite like that.

"I ain't doing time for you, you fucking idiot," Frank snarled as he pushed the documents into Thomas' gut. "You didn't tell me that truck was stolen. Now go deal with your shit like a man."

I held up a pen. Thom Cullen gave me a sullen glare but took the pen and signed the forms where I pointed out he needed to. "The court case is scheduled for two weeks from Friday," I said. "Failure to appear means that you will be held in contempt and a warrant will be issued for your arrest."

"Yeah, yeah," he said.

I handed him his copy and touched two fingers to the brim of my stocking cap. "Have yourself a nice day," I said.

"Fuck you," he said.

"Under no circumstances." I turned around and walked out of the yard. The spot where my bra straps came together itched with sweat. I made sure my steps were leisurely despite a sudden increased need to pee.

"Hey," I heard from behind me. Frank's voice,

sounding quiet and guilty. I turned around.

He had his hands in the pockets of his jeans; out of habit I checked for the bulge of a weapon but saw none. His shoulders hunched low, either against the cold or from a lifetime of hard labor. His back had a bend in it that suggested the latter more than the former.

"Look, I'm sorry 'bout my brother," he said. "He's a fuckup."

"No argument here," I said.

"Been takin' care of him since we were kids, I have."

I shrugged. "Well, he has to take care of himself this time."

Frank nodded. "I guess so. Maybe it'll do him some good. You gonna call the cops?"

"Nope," I said.

"Thanks," he said.

"Thank the client wanting your brother to actually pay him," I said. "He can't do that from inside a jail cell."

"And the gun?"

I shrugged. "What gun?"

He smiled. "Thanks again," he said.

I did not smile back. "If you want to thank me, go back inside and get that damn rifle away from that dumbass brother of yours before he hurts himself."

Frank's eyes narrowed. "What the do you care if he does?"

"He can't pay his dues from under a tombstone either." I turned around and walked back to my car before he could respond. The adrenaline rush had ebbed away and left jitters in its wake; basic professional pride meant that I didn't want Frank to see me sweat.

By the time I dug my keys out, the shakes had fully kicked in; it took me three tries to get my door unlocked. The little black eye of the AR-15's business end danced in my head. I sat in my car and closed my eyes and waited for my hands to stop quivering. "One," I said to the inside of my car, "Two, three, four..."

My pocket buzzed. I jumped before I realized it was my phone. I dug it out and looked at it.

You get him served okay? :) Izzy again.

There were complications, I typed, thanking AutoCorrect for making it easier. **I'll tell you about it when I get back.**

'KK. What should I tell the client?

My fingers paused over the screen. **Tell them they'll be getting a bill soon. Total everything up and add 8%.**

Why the 8%??

I smiled slightly before answering. **Complications :)**

Izzy didn't respond. I sat and took deep breaths until my heart rate was normal and my hands were steady. It took about three minutes. I spent the time watching Cullen's front door to make sure no one came looking for me in a fit of alcoholic bravado. No one did, so I started my car, put it in gear and pointed it in the direction of my office.

Chapter 2

I caught a meal at a Shari's near Southcenter on the way back; club sandwich, seasoned fries and four cups of passable coffee. It wasn't the healthiest way to feed myself but I figured getting a gun shoved in my face had burned a few calories. That made as good an excuse as any other for ordering a slice of pie. The receipt for dinner went into my purse; I debated whether or not to pass the cost on to Andersen Law and decided against. I'd racked up more hours than expected already; when it came to billing one charged what was expected, not what one spent. A customer's expectation of cost typically enjoyed only a flexible relationship with reality. I cut around the back of Southcenter after likewise feeding my car, doing my best to avoid the worst of the traffic and almost succeeding.

Kent looked as it always did when I drove through it. Kent is one of those towns that thinks it's a city, but everyone who lives there or spends any time there knows better. It's a filing cabinet for strip malls and auto dealerships, though less of the latter and more of the former since the economy took a nosedive. I kept my practice in Kent because the rent was cheap compared to Seattle proper. Thanks to a nosediving economy there were plenty of vacant business properties.

My firm rented one of those spaces, a sprawling collection of subdivided warehouses painted institutional dirty-white, fronted by scraggly beds of juniper and beauty bark. My left-hand neighbor was a struggling steel distributor; the right was empty, vacated three weeks ago by a tech startup that had thrown in the towel. Watching them close their doors had been an unwelcome reminder of how close I was to the same fate.

It was early afternoon when I pulled into my parking space. The rain had stopped but the sky had started to turn dark, not dusk or evening, just the dimming that occurred at the tail end of daytime. In the wash of my headlights I noticed our sign had started to peel again. I made a mental note to get it repaired; a ratty sign spoke of a shoestring operation. Since I was exactly that, I couldn't afford to resemble it. The wind bit through my damp coat as I walked inside.

"Hiya boss," my secretary said as I closed the door, looking up from his screen to give me a gleaming smile. Julian Wu was pretty in that way boys around twenty sometimes manage, all pale skin and languid green eyes and cheekbones like cut crystal; luck of the draw had spared him from both adolescent awkwardness and acne. He augmented nature's bounty with longish black hair, tight denim and an ever-expanding collection of piercings. I could hear something clicking against his teeth when he spoke, along with a slight slurring of his Ss.

"Julian," I said with a smile, "what did I say about the tongue stud?"

"Uh...that it was artistic and arousing?" He turned up the wattage on his grin. It might've lit a city block but I'd long since been acclimated.

"Thus why I don't want you wearing it in the office," I said.

He had the good grace to wince. "I know, boss...sorry, I forgot. I have a date tonight."

I laughed. "Who's the lucky girl this evening?" A good many people who met him thought Julian was gay; I never failed to find that mistake amusing. Anyone who tried to track his feminine entanglements would've needed a spreadsheet.

"Shelly," he said. "She likes a guy with a tongue stud. You see, it's good for -"

I held up a hand. "I know what a tongue stud is good for."

He blinked. "How?"

"I used to have one."

His cheeks reddened; it was work not to laugh. Julian had always been under the impression that since I was ten years older than him, I'd always been a prude. I hung up my coat while he wrestled with his awkwardness.

"How'd the Cullen thing turn out?"

"Sticks and stones may break your bones, but guns are tons more fun," I said. He raised his eyebrows in surprise. I gave him a quick rundown of the serving.

"Wow," he said. "Did you call the police?"

"Nope," I said.

He sat back. "Cullen stuck a gun in your face and stuff. That's illegal."

"Extremely," I said.

"So...why didn't you?"

I smiled at him. "I don't know, Julian. Why didn't I?"

His face scrunched up in thought, teeth working at his lower lip; I fetched myself cup of coffee from the machine while the wheels in his head went round and round. I had just finished doctoring my cup with cream and sugar when he sighed in defeat.

"I give up, boss," he said.

I sat on the edge of his desk. "Remember, Julian...Cullen's got two priors, and felons aren't supposed to own guns. So where does a third conviction put him?"

"Away for a long time," Julian said. "Well, I guess he would have a hard time paying back that Jones guy from jail...but we were just hired to find Cullen, right?"

"True," I said, "but putting him behind bars serves Jones' interests pretty poorly. Jones would get mad at his lawyer, who would in turn be mad at us. Remember also that Jones didn't hire us, Andersen Law did."

Julian put it together; he was young and naive but there was nothing wrong with his brain. "Getting Cullen arrested makes the lawyer look bad...and then they don't want to pay us?"

"Pretty much," I said. "Also, poor Levon Jones has to wait for the courts in Everett to get done with Cullen before he can get his truck and tools back. He can't work without them, so maybe Andersen Law doesn't get paid at all."

"So Cullen going to jail screws everything up?"

"That's about the size of it," I said.

"But he could have killed you," Julian said.

"He could have," I said, "but he didn't, so I'm not going to fret about it." My coffee had cooled to drinkable temperature so I sipped some. "Enforcing the law isn't our job, Julian. We're supposed to serve the client - and if the client walks away mad, they tell all their friends what screwups we are and we don't get work. It isn't like the movies."

"I guess not," he said. "Sorry for not getting it."

"Don't be sorry, just keep learning," I said with a smile.

"Boss," he said pensively, "how did you know Cullen wouldn't shoot you?"

"He didn't," I said.

"Huh?"

I sipped at my coffee. "My father always said that if someone with a gun means to use it they use it right off. If they whip one out but start talking, they don't have the stomach to pull the trigger. At that point, as long as you don't back them into a corner you'll be okay," I said. "My dad never got shot following that advice, and neither have I."

"Oh," he said.

"Cullen was a bully. Bullies are cowards. You plant

your feet and stay calm, they don't know what to do." I smiled. "Now, back to work. You get any calls?"

"Crichton Corp sent us a couple more due-diligence things," he said. "Izzy's on them."

"Good. Anything else?"

He looked faintly mournful. "Nope. Sorry."

I made sure not to let my disappointment show. "Not your fault. Anyway, I'd better go and do battle with Andersen Law over monies owed."

He quirked his eyebrows. I usually passed off phone work to Julian on account of his charm, taking it only when the situation required a dose of starch. Julian was pleasant as a summer's day, but about as mutable. Fortunately he knew it and was working to fix it. "You think they'll give us trouble about the bill?"

"If the Pearly Gates had a two-dollar cover, Kevin Andersen would give Saint Peter trouble about it," I said as I walked back to my office.

We kept most of our space neat and tidy, the better to impress would-be customers with, but my actual working space was clutter approaching chaos six days out of seven. Today was not my lucky day; papers, burnable DVDs, file folders and bits of random tech filled every available surface. The room was barely big enough for the two desks we had crammed into it. About the only empty spot in the room was the office chair in front of the right-hand desk.

The other was occupied by Izzy Alphabet, my research assistant. She didn't look up as I came in, instead remaining hunched over a multi-tabbed Google Chrome session. "'Sup," she said, twin reflections of the screen printed on the lenses of her steel-rimmed glasses. She was a stump-legged five foot two, eighty-odd pounds overweight and bright as a fresh dime. If there was a limit to her technical skills, I had yet to discover it. Her real name was a tongue-twisting Polish epic I couldn't get right for love or money; I'd called her Izzy since she started on with me three years ago, and Julian had made the 'Alphabet Soup' reference. It had stuck, but Izzy didn't mind.

"I got the report all ready for the Cullen case," she said, tapping a neat stack of paper that sat to the right of her mouse pad. "I didn't email it yet...figured you'd want to be here."

"You figured right." I sipped some coffee.

"I'm also figuring they're going to drag their feet and complain a lot," she said.

"Two for two." I kept at my coffee cup. Sleep was for the weak.

Izzy looked up and grinned. "If they weren't lawyers, we'd call them humans instead."

She caught me midway through the sip, and her monitor came within an inch of wearing it. "Dammit, Izzy," I said when I could speak. She batted her eyelashes at me and tried to look innocent. I couldn't help but smile.

"So," she said, "what were the complications you had me charge the client for?"

I repeated my tale of the dog, the rifle and the two drunken fools. She shook her head. "Jeez," she said once I was done, "I'd have gone over eight percent for *that.*"

"About all I can get away with squeezing them for," I said as I sat down at my desk. "Speaking of, how are the finances?"

"Same as the last time you asked me," she said. "Those freaking loan payments are eating us alive."

I'd had to borrow money two years ago to keep my firm afloat. The interest rate was murder and the loan was government backed, which added multiple complications to our lives...not the least of which was how if I found myself in default, I'd lose my permits to operate.

I sighed. "Tell me we'll at least finish the month in the black."

"We'll finish the month in the black," she said.

"You mean that?"

"Nope."

I could feel a headache coming on. I rubbed the bridge of my nose in an effort to stave it off. "How much?"

She told me. I winced, and my headache grew larger. "I guess I should've gone over eight percent," I said.

"Totally. By the way, payroll's in your box to sign off on."

I nodded and did so while covering another wince. I could afford to pay my employees but there wasn't a whole lot left for me to take home. In fact, unless some greater work came down the pike before month's end I'd be sleeping in the filing room by November. Still, I hadn't shorted an employee or a supplier in five years of doing business and I didn't plan to start.

I got the Cullen case all off to Andersen Law via email along with a bill and put in a call to Kevin

Andersen's private line. His secretary informed me that he was with a client. I waited thirty minutes and called again, and this time a familiar tenor voice answered.

"Good afternoon, Ms. Eckart," Andersen said. His tone was full of friendliness, the manufactured warmth of his profession.

"And to you, Mister Andersen," I said. "You got my report I assume."

"I did, and let me just pass on congratulations at dealing with such a difficult case. My client will be thrilled." He was still all warm and fuzzy. "I did have a question about this eight percent surcharge..."

"There were complications," I said.

"Involving?"

"Cullen set a dog on me," I said, "and then pointed a rifle at me when I came to the door."

"Oh my," he said. "Are you all right?" The concern in his voice was positively artful.

"Peachy," I said. "I'll be perfect when I receive payment for services rendered."

"Just as soon as my client pays the remainder of their bill, I'll cut a check for yours," he said.

Levon Jones wouldn't have to settle up until the court proceedings were done, and that could be well into next year. Andersen knew that, and so did I. "Our contract stipulates payment on completion of services, Mister Andersen. It says so on the first page, right above your signature."

The warmth in his voice changed, became a chummy sort of patronizing. "Here now, Ms. Eckart...I would like to remind you that this firm does a good deal of business in the Seattle area -"

"-Then there should be plenty in your accounts to cover my bill," I said before he could continue handing me his snow-job.

"I'll speak to Accounting about the matter," he said after a moment.

I leaned back in my chair and swiveled left and right, just like the gumshoes in the movies do. It helped me feel tough. "Mister Andersen," I said, "I wonder how Everett's finest would feel about Cullen's AR-15."

"You didn't report it to them." Some of the friendliness had left his tone.

"Not yet," I said.

"Are you planning to?"

"I haven't decided," I said. Everything I'd told Julian

cut both ways. Implied threats were always the best threats.

Silence reigned on the line for a few seconds. I waited. "All right, Ms. Eckart," Andersen said. "I'll make sure the check is in the mail tomorrow morning, first thing."

"I'll be looking for it Monday morning then, first thing." I kept my tone friendly. His no longer was.

"Pleasure doing business with you," he said.

"Likewise," I said.

We exchanged good-byes and I hung up. Izzy cocked an eyebrow at me. "Was it a good idea to lean on him like that?"

I sighed. "No," I said, "but waiting for him to get paid so we can get paid is definitely a worse one. If I let him run that game on me, we'll be lucky to see the money before next Easter. Andersen Law is into us for five thousand above retainer...I'm willing get a little butch for that. You know my maxim on getting paid."

She grinned and nodded. "In full, on time, without complaint..."

"Pick any two," we said together.

Even without too many contracts there was always

a good deal of busywork in any office, and mine was no exception. I slogged through my share and delegated as much to my two employees as my conscience would let me get away with. At five Julian made noises like he wanted to leave. I let him so he could have his date. I could brew my own coffee and the chances of someone interrupting our work with a call at that hour were slim to none. Izzy finished the two due-diligence reports and left at six-thirty, giving my shoulder an encouraging squeeze before she walked out. I kept at it for another half-hour before I realized there wasn't anything for me to do. I shut off everything and locked all the doors. The place was creepy after hours anyway. I made sure my pepper spray was in my coat pocket before I headed out.

Home was an aging apartment complex tucked in the woods off Kent-Des Moines Road, all peeling paint and wanna-be rusticity. It would have been a nice place if the owners put some time into the idea of making it so, but they didn't, so it wasn't.

The pavement of the parking lot was half-hidden by a crust of dead needles. My feet made crunching sounds as I got out of the car. I gave the parking lot my habitual scan for vehicles I did not recognize. There were none, as well as a lack of people loitering in the parking lot. My apartment was on the lower floor and the stairs creaked their welcome as I walked down them.

Zork the cat waited at the foot of the stairs for me as he always did, over twenty pounds of flame-point Siamese tom I'd rescued from a nearby Dumpster. His blue eyes shone red in the fading light.

"Been out making the lady cats sigh, eh good buddy?" I said.

He put his paws on my knee and stretched, reaching nearly to my waist when he did it. I smiled and gave him a scratch behind the ears. He *mrowled* and moved aside so I could unlock the door. I never worried about letting him roam; he was better than my last three boyfriends had been about coming home reliably. He was also bigger than the raccoons who lived in the nearby woods and smart enough to avoid cars. Once I got the door open he darted in, followed by me.

My apartment stayed mostly tidy because I was seldom home to mess it up, but there was always clutter on surfaces and dishes in the sink. Tonight was no exception. I'd not been able to afford new furniture in a while, and the result was an apartment anyone in their early twenties would have recognized as home; A couch sporting eighties-vintage ugliness that was nonetheless quite comfortable to sit in, coffee table from IKEA, posters tacked to the walls, and a few layers of dust I never found time to get rid of.

More than half the living room was dominated by my book collection, most of it contained on an enameled metal monstrosity of a bookshelf I'd also rescued from the Dumpster out back. My complex is populated by college students and every June at graduation was better than a furniture sale. I'd added to the insanity by hanging shelves above all the windows and doors. Reading is my only hobby outside of work, as books from Goodwill are about all I can afford. Most of it was pulp paperbacks; Robert B. Parker, Sarah Paretsky, Tanya Huff, Daniel Keys Moran, Mercedes Lackey and others jumbled up with more weighty literature by the likes of C.S. Lewis and Raymond Chandler. The only valuable book was a first-edition copy of Tolkien's *The Simarillion,* a gift from my first serious boyfriend.

I hung my coat up on the wire rack near the door, in the open space between my college-vintage leather jacket and trench coat. The trench coat fit. The leather didn't, but sentiment refused to let me get rid of it. Or maybe that was the hope that it would fit again someday. Gravity and age were rendering that possibility more unlikely with each passing day. There was a black fedora hanging there also, brand new and never worn; a gag gift from Izzy and Julian two Christmases ago.

I put Bonnie Raitt on the stereo to keep the silence at bay and made dinner, a basic poverty-fry of chicken and onions over rice. My cooking skills could charitably be described as "utilitarian". There was a box of wine in the fridge and I started in on that. The first glass went down rough, but after two more it didn't taste so bad. The trick with cheap wine is slipping the first few sips past your palate.

The buzz came on as I wrapped up dinner; that warm-blanket feeling every drinker knows and loves. I let it hang between my mind and my day, humming along with the tunes as I alternated between forkfuls of poverty-fry and sips of Franzia Merlot. Zork tried to help me with my dinner and I let him. He purred when I petted him. The fur felt good under my fingertips. That might have been the wine.

"Just another day in paradise," I said to no one in particular, as my big cat rumbled and Bonnie sang about angels from Montgomery. I'd never been to Montgomery. Or seen an angel, for that matter. Couldn't really find the time for either. But I could have another glass of wine, so that's what I did.

It's amazing how glasses of wine tend to have children. I had three more after what I'd intended to be my last, and by then the lonely signal I drank to avoid was buried in warm, agreeable static.

Sleep wasn't too hard to find after that.

Chapter 3

I awoke the next morning with a medium-strength hangover. I dealt with it by popping some extra-strength ibuprofen and hopping in the shower, hanging my head under the shower nozzle and running the water ice cold to bring my headache into line. My stomach petulantly informed me breakfast was out of the question, but eventually I negotiated a settlement which allowed for coffee and antacids. It was a common discussion of late.

Julian's black Kawasaki and Izzy's bicycle were already present when I pulled into the lot. I told the guilty feelings in the back of my head that I was the boss, therefore I was allowed to show up a little late. It sort of worked.

I mumbled a greeting at Julian on my way through the door. He waved but did not speak due to the phone being pressed against his ear. I wondered how he could sound so cheerful at this hour and figured that barely being old enough to drink had something to do with it.

"Morning, Boss." Izzy was neck deep in something, our finances from the look of what was on her screen.

"Mmmph."

"Hangover?"

"Yeah," I said. There were sticky notes on my monitor courtesy of Julian; possible clients I needed to get back to. Another batch of due-diligence work from an insurance firm downtown and a possible skip-trace. I started on a response email.

"That's the third time this week," Izzy said. "So?"

"So it's Thursday, boss." Her voice was strained.

I was spared from replying by Julian sticking his head through the door. "I've got a live one."

I looked up. "Talk to me."

"A lawyer from that firm we did that thing for last year," Julian said. "He has a fraud investigation he needs done."

I dredged up a smile. "Julian, I did lots of things for law firms last year. Lay off the Buffy-speak and give me a name."

"Burton, Cameron and Clive," he said. "Guy's name is Hastings. Said he wanted to meet with you as soon as possible."

I smiled. "Best news I've heard in a while." I remembered the firm; hardly anyone who had even a peripheral connection to the judicial system hadn't heard of BC & C. They had given us a big divorce case, lots of leg-work and photography, high profile and at the end of the day quite lucrative for all concerned. They had been pleased with our work and perhaps more relevant, they had been kind enough to pay us without much prodding. "What did you tell this Mister Hastings?"

"That you were available. He'll be here in a half-hour or so."

I nodded. "Give the conference room a good once-over. I'll go make myself presentable." I looked down at the jeans and wrinkled green blouse I'd thrown on that morning and winced. "Well, more presentable anyway."

Izzy gave me a look that was eloquent in its silence. I pretended not to see it as I got up to head to the bathroom.

Modern cosmetics can do wonders for hiding things; by the time I was done it was a good deal less obvious that I'd spent last night drinking cheap wine. Covering flaws in my complexion was something I had plenty of practice at, thanks to how my face had moved straight from acne and freckles to crow's feet and worry lines. When I heard the door open and Julian's voice I gave it a five-count before walking out to the front.

Standing by Julian's desk was a square-faced man in

his middle forties, trim and crisp in a brand name suit; Hugo Boss, maybe something more expensive. His dark hair was full and neatly barbered, and he lacked the roll at the waist most men that age acquire. We traded handshakes and professional smiles. His was neat and white as a fresh picket fence, and his grip told me he worked out.

"John Hastings," he said. He had a rich voice, full of warm authority. It likely served him well in the courtroom.

"Amber Eckart," I replied.

"Yes. I've heard good things about you." His tone suggested that he wasn't quite convinced of them.

"Always nice to hear," I said. "We've got a conference room if you'd like privacy. Coffee?"

"Yes to both," he said.

I turned to Julian. "Two cups," I said. He nodded.

I led Hastings back to our conference room, a cramped space with a plastic laminate table and six Ikea chairs. I was pleased to see that everything was clean and squared away like I asked Julian to make it. I took a seat. Hastings did likewise. "So how is Joseph Clive these days?"

"Doing just fine," he said. His face took on a closed look. I shut down the friendly patter and went straight for business.

"What can we do for you, Mister Hastings?"

He set his briefcase on the table and opened it. "First, I must inform you that this matter is extremely sensitive."

"I understand," I said. "Everyone in my office is a licensed investigator and they all know the rules."

He nodded in acceptance. "Also, my client would appreciate being left out of the proceedings."

"Well, on a case like this the work-product rule is crucial -"

"No," he said. "My client wants to be completely left out of it."

I blinked in surprise. "They won't meet with me at all? Not even with you present?"

Hastings nodded.

"May I ask why?"

He sighed. "I could give you any number of answers, Ms. Eckart...but the truth is that my client is acting irrationally. But they paid my fee, so..." he glanced at the ceiling. I nodded in sympathy.

"That will make my job more difficult," I said.

"It will," he said. "If you aren't interested I can try

someone else."

"I'm interested, Mister Hastings. What can we do for you?"

He steepled his fingers. I grabbed a pad of paper and a pencil and prepared to take notes.

"The client I represent is in difficulty with their bank over a mortgage," he said. "My client and I both believe the bank has committed fraudulent behavior, but we have no proof."

"Does the bank have an attorney I should be aware of?"

Hastings gave me a grim look. "They have as many as they need," he said. "It's First American."

"David versus Goliath," I muttered with a wince.

He nodded, but did not continue to speak. Julian came in with two cups of coffee and the accessories to doctor them on a tray, set it between us and left without a word. I took mine. Hastings did likewise. From the smell I could tell Julian used the good coffee, and I made a note to thank him.

"You can speak freely in front of Julian," I said. "I'll be using him for phone work so he'll know whatever you tell me later on anyway."

"He's licensed?"

"Apprentice," I said. "Not ready for fieldwork quite yet, but he's got his certifications."

Hastings eyed the door again, this time with a smile. "Does his mother know what he's doing after school?"

I laughed. "She's acclimated," I said. "If this bothers you, I can recommend another firm."

His smile deepened. "I'm still interested, Ms. Eckart."

"Then by all means, please continue."

He took a thick file folder out of his briefcase and opened it. "The problem began about a month ago. My client came home from the store one morning to find bulldozers parked in her cul-de-sac. They produced documents stating that her property had been purchased and they were there to demolish it."

I held up a hand. "What time in the morning, what day, and who did the men say they worked for?"

"Eleven o'clock on a Tuesday," he said. He rattled off the exact date and I wrote it down. "The men worked for a company called Drevin Earthmovers - when I pressed the owner, he passed me up to a general contractor, Ironhorse Construction."

I wrote down both names. "Go on."

"My client of course phoned the police as well as a son, who in turn phoned my law firm. I managed to acquire a temporary injunction, but that will run out in another two weeks."

More scribbling. "What's the bank's story?"

Hastings gave me a wry look. "That everything is in order. They handed me a huge stack of documents that supposedly proves it." He held up the file. "This is a summary." The file was two inches thick.

"And while you dig through their Mount Everest of paper, the temporary injunction runs out and your case suffers death by bureaucracy," I said.

His eyes glittered with what looked like respect. "Which brings us to you, Ms. Eckart."

"You want me to short-circuit the bank's paper pile and find proof of fraud," I said. He nodded. "How long would I have?"

"A little less than two weeks. I can try to get you more, but realistically that's all I can guarantee."

"Going to be tight," I said.

"Can you do it?"

"That depends," I said, "how good your client's been about paying her mortgage. Your client is a woman, isn't she?"

He blinked.

"I mean, staying on top of a mortgage can be tough to do for a retired widow."

The second time his blink was much slower. "How'd you guess all that?"

"For starters, you've been careful not to mention your client's gender this whole time," I said. "In my experience, men don't protect other men that way. Since you are dealing with her rather than her husband I guessed widow. And as to the retired thing...considering all the other aspects, who but a retiree would do her grocery shopping at eleven on a Tuesday?" I kept a smile off my face. It never hurt to drag out a little Conan Doyle for the customers, but only if one could avoid being smug about it.

"Correct on all cards," he said. "They told me back at the office you were sharp. I'm glad to see it's true."

I made more notes, glad my hungover brain had added two and two correctly. "I take it I'm hired."

"You have the skills and the price is right. I haven't the time to keep shopping," he said.

I leaned back and opened the door. "Julian, get me a contract form."

"I assume you'll be wanting a retainer," said

Hastings.

"Indeed." I named a figure. It was higher than I usually went due to the potential work involved, but Hastings didn't flinch one bit. He took out a gold Cross pen and a checkbook and scribbled for ten seconds just as Julian came in with a sheaf of papers. I went over the contract. Hastings signed it and handed me the check. I tried to keep my eyes from bugging out when I saw what he'd written on it.

"This is twice the amount I named," I said.

"So it is," he said.

If I ended up working through all of it, Hastings' check would put me in the black for this month and part of next in the bargain. I made sure those facts didn't show on my face as I folded it and tucked it in a pocket. "Thank you," I said instead.

Hastings passed me the thick file and two other thinner ones; all three were stamped with the BC & C logo. "My business card is in the file. Call me any time if you have a question."

"You said something about a mountain of documents..."

"A metaphorical mountain," he said. "There's a DVD in the file with all the bank's paperwork on it. Email correspondences as well."

"Technology at work," I said.

We completed the minutiae of setting up a deal; it did not take long. After we finished I showed Hastings to the door. As he slid into his overcoat he turned back to me.

"One more thing, Ms. Eckart."

"Yes?"

"Are your investigators licensed to carry?"

I blinked. "I am," I said.

"Good," he said.

My automatic was at home in the hall closet; carrying a pistol on the job often caused more problems than it prevented. I hadn't touched it except to go to the range, and the last time for that was over a month ago. Thanks to politics within the gun community ammunition had grown too expensive for regular practice, and between that and the extra insurance and permits an armed investigator's license required I'd toyed with the notion of letting it lapse. Clients had asked me about whether I carried a gun before, but never a lawyer. They knew better.

"Is there something you aren't telling me, Mister

Hastings?"

He finished adjusting his coat. "Ms. Eckart, my client is eighty-five years old, blind in one eye and walks with a cane. She's lived in the same house since before you were born...the only reason she's still paying on it is a second mortgage I do believe some sleazy banker tricked her into signing up for. Now, that same bank is willing to toss her out of her home in order to make some big development group happy."

"That's all very unfortunate," I said, "but not a reason to play Dirty Harry."

"Until it is," he said.

He walked out the door before I could frame a response, but not before favoring me with a chill little smile.

"Boss," Julian said, his face split in a wide grin, "is it my imagination or did we just win the lottery?"

I took out the check and looked at it. It felt heavier than it had a second ago. Not too heavy to hold, but heavier than I liked. I felt like I should've asked more questions before taking it, but there was no turning back now that my signature was on the dotted line. Besides, we needed the money.

"I'm not sure about that," I said. "Not yet."

Chapter 4

I moved into the conference room and brought Izzy and Julian up to speed. I could afford to put everyone on the same case for once; Hastings had certainly paid me enough, and from the sound of things I'd need the help if I wanted to bust the case open in the time allotted me.

"Wow," Julian said after I was done explaining. "That's messed up."

"That's modern banking," I said.

"Yuck," said Julian. "So where do we start?"

I tossed Izzy the DVD. "You go through that," I said. "There will be a lot of chaff, so your first job is to strain out what's relevant from what's just in there to distract. We need to establish a chain of events."

"Gotcha." Izzy opened the DVD case and plugged the disk into her laptop.

"And me?"

I held up the file folder Hastings had provided. "You help me with the paper end of things."

"What are we looking for?"

"Clues," I said.

We spread out all the documents in the file and sorted them. There was a lot paper to work through, but as we sifted through it all out we found very few facts to build a case on. Everything Hastings had told me was true; all the bank's paperwork was in order but I found it damnably odd how the old lady could have been kept completely in the dark until bulldozers showed up to claim her house. Suspicious, even.

On the bank's end the problems had begun when the mortgagee, one Cordelia Anne Kitsmiller by name, had given the bank a short payment – which was in turn caused by the bank raising her escrow fees by $4.52. That had caused all her successive payments to be placed in what the bank termed a "holding account", from which late fees and full payments had been deducted. From the payment schedules the bank had provided to her attorney, it appeared that Kitsmiller had been notified of the situation...but her behavior as documented by the paper trail suggested that she hadn't known of it.

According to the bank documents they had sent numerous letters notifying her of the change and the need for consultation. Everything was postmarked, and all the dates were correct...but no responses from Mrs. Kitsmiller were on file. Thus had she had ended up four months in arrears and the bank had begun foreclosure proceedings. Six days after the foreclosure had been finalized Ironhorse's backers had swooped in with a cold offer on the property. The bank had accepted less than twenty-four hours later.

After four hours of chasing paper we broke for lunch. I called down the street for Thai food, and once it showed up we sat slurping noodles and comparing notes.

"Okay," I said after popping a shrimp in my mouth, "it looks like our client is on a fixed income and just kept sending the same check every month. Only the bank needed more money and somehow the old lady missed the memo."

"...And she keeps missing the memos for four whole months?" Izzy made a face. "Yeah, that's not suspicious at all."

"Suspicious, yes," I said, "but not proof of any wrongdoing on the bank's end. Maybe the old lady threw the notices away, buried her head in the sand."

"Don't tell me you believe that," Izzy said.

"No, but a judge might," I said.

"Hey now," said Julian. "Banks can't just take a person's house out from under them like this. I mean it belongs to you, right?"

"They can, they will and they do," I said. "All the time."

"Are you serious?"

I sighed. "Julian, before you got hired on here Izzy and I worked some cases that'd turn your stomach." I turned to Izzy. "Remember the Williamson case a year ago?"

"I remember it," said Izzy. "Where they went on vacation and come back to find their house had been sold? When they'd already paid off their mortgage six years before?"

"That's the one," I said.

"Jesus," Julian said. "Don't tell me the bank got away with that."

"They didn't," I said, "but our clients never did get all their stuff back. Most of it ended up in a landfill during the sale - what didn't get auctioned off or five-fingered by the various people who went through the house, that is. Oh, they got a settlement for it from the insurance company...but you can't replace family heirlooms by writing a check, now can you?"

Julian turned pale. "Yuck," he said.

"Yeah. And the same thing will happen to this little old lady unless we can prove fraud before someone drives a bulldozer through her front room."

"Speaking of that," Izzy said, "I Googled that development Hastings mentioned."

"And?"

She grabbed her laptop and switched tabs on her browser. "It's huge, boss. Take a look."

I did, and Izzy was right; it was a massive mixed-use affair, shops and stores below and apartments above them. It went on for blocks and was being touted by the press as the model of sustainable building. It was also worth three-quarters of a billion dollars. I sat back from the computer and chewed my lip in thought. I didn't look as cute as Julian, but I was slightly better at putting facts together while I did it.

"Izzy," I said, "I want you to find out everything that is in the public record about this development. I want to know who the financial backers are, who the contractors are, when they bought the properties, who sold them and for how much, that kind of thing. The area was mostly houses before they got started...if you can, get me a list of the former homeowners."

"Got it, boss...you want the size in millimeters." She

spun her computer back around and buried herself in the Internet.

Julian glanced at me. "What do I do?"

"When Izzy digs up a list of homeowners, I want you to get on the phone and call each and every one of them. Turn on your famous charm and see if you can get them to spill their story about selling their house. If you find any bad ones, get their name, number and current address. Make a list."

He nodded. "What should I use as a pretext?"

"Nothing," I said. "I want the homeowners to know who we are and what we're doing. Don't give out Hastings' name or Kitsmiller's, but other than that just tell them the truth - we're digging for bad bank behavior."

"Okay," he said. "You think someone else got scammed too?"

"I'd bet sex to doughnuts on the fact," I said, standing up so I could pace. It was a habit I'd picked up since I'd quit cigarettes. "And, while one disgruntled former homeowner can be easily ignored, we call a whole bunch of disgruntled former homeowners with a lawyer out in front of them something else entirely."

Izzy looked up from her computer. "A class-action

lawsuit," she said.

"Yep," I said.

"But there's no suit," she said.

I grinned. "Not yet."

Behind her glasses I saw Izzy get it. Her face lit up like the Cheshire cat's. "Boss, you're freaking awesome."

I sketched a bow. "*Gracias.*"

Julian looked from Izzy to me. "Am I a ditz for being totally lost?"

"Yes," Izzy said.

Julian flicked a paper clip at her. She stuck her tongue out at him.

"Decorum, people," I said.

Julian gave Izzy a sour look before returning his attention to me. "So what *are* you talking about, boss?"

"Burton, Cameron and Clive is the largest, most-respected law firm in Seattle," I said. "They're cool enough to make even a multinational financial institution like First American come down with a case of nerves. Everyone knows that the banks have been up to shady shenanigans in the mortgage industry but no one can prove it...at least not well enough to put any serious hurt on them."

Julian toyed with his earing, eyebrows scrunched up in thought. "Okay."

I paced back and forth, laying out the final details as they came to me. "Now, lawyers like Hastings love big profits and a good rep just as much as we do. If in the course of digging up dirt on Kitsmiller's behalf we *just happen* to stumble across a wider problem and *just happen* to pass it on to him – "

"- And since we're already on his firm's payroll, familiar with the case and oh-so-handy -" Izzy chimed in.

Julian's face lit up with comprehension. "You...you figure we can get a big-ass contract out of this?"

"Not just a pretty face," I said.

"Okay," he said. "One question...how?"

"Class-action lawsuits," I said, "can half of forever to resolve. If we play our cards right we can work this matter into the next decade. All we need to do is find Hastings enough proof of a bigger problem. If he's half the lawyer I think he is, he'll be all over it."

Julian pushed his hands through his hair, not noticeably neatening it. "That sounds cool," he said, "but what's the catch?"

I patted him on the shoulder. "I was just getting to that. It wouldn't be ethical or even all that legal for us to waste our current client's billing hours on something for our own benefit. Which means if we find something interesting that doesn't help Kitsmiller *directly*, we have to chase it on our own time." I looked at Izzy and Julian in turn. "Are you two okay with that?"

Izzy nodded. "Let's burninate some bankers," she said.

"I'll take that as a yes," I said.

Julian grinned. "I'm down, too."

"Just so you know, the second catch is that there may be no class-action suit to stir up," I said. "Either we don't find enough proof or we do and BC & C doesn't want to risk it. We could put in a lot of off-the-books work and wind up with nothing to show for it."

Julian looked at me. "Couldn't we take what we find to another law office?"

I shook my head. There was a reason Julian was still an apprentice. "That," I said, "would be revealing confidential client information. Thus breach of contract, loss of permits, that kind of thing."

Julian winced. "Oops. Right. Sorry boss."

"See how easy it is to screw up while playing in gray areas?"

"Point taken," he said. "I'll remember."

"We'll all need to," I said. "But I think this is one of those rare times where we can do the right thing and profit off the result, if we're careful and smart about how we do it."

"Last question," Izzy said. "Didn't you just have to twist a lawyer's arm to collect on a bill? What's to say Hastings' firm won't just ditch us and hire somebody else?"

"On the surface, nothing," I said. "But I've met both Carter Burton and Joseph Clive, and they aren't bottom-feeders like Kevin Andersen. They're old school...they grok the concept of professional courtesy, and if we give them something that's of use to them, they'll reciprocate."

Julian spoke up. "So what's the first move?"

"Same as I described before," I said. "Izzy, you'll be first up. You up for pulling an all-nighter?"

She batted her eyelashes at me. "Do I get bribed?"

I dug out the petty-cash box, took out two twenties and handed them to her. "All the junk food and Monster you can handle," I said, "on the company."

She cracked her knuckles. "I'm on it."

"And me?"

I smiled at Julian. "We finish out the day. You go get laid and then get plenty of sleep. Izzy will have a list for you by tomorrow...I want you here early, working the safe phone."

He nodded. "What are you going to do?"

"Tomorrow I'll case Kitsmiller's neighborhood," I said. "You know, knock on doors, take some pictures, see what's there. I can't talk to the client but I can get to know where she lives." I started sifting through the stack of bank documents again. "I won't be in the office tomorrow...Kitsmiller lives in West Seattle, so there's hardly any point in me coming in before I go there. You guys understand your marching orders?"

They both nodded.

"Okay then," I said. "Let's do it."

We all returned to sorting through the documents. I could feel an old familiar tingling heat in my chest as I sifted through the trail of paper. I hadn't gotten the feeling in a while, but I liked it; the sense of a case, getting good and hot and profitable.

Eric Plume

Chapter 5

I put in a full day of phone calls and Google searches before I called it quits at six. Izzy promised to keep in touch; I told her she could have the first half of the next day off since she'd be up all night on my behalf. I'd found it always paid dividends when I kept my employees happy. Julian spent a few minutes slicking himself up before hopping on his bike and heading out for his latest conquest. Watching him peel out on his black rice rocket, it wasn't hard for me to see why the girls went for him.

"You have fun," I said to his retreating back.

I got in my car and pointed it towards Des Moines, my mind three-quarters occupied by the events of the day. What I'd told Izzy and Julian had been more or less true; if we handled the Kitsmiller case right we could earn enough scratch to push the loans off our back...and maybe, just maybe, Eckart Investigations could become something more than just another ragged PI firm on the brink of collapse.

Halfway home, my phone buzzed. I grinned as I saw the number and popped it over to speaker phone.

"Hey, Candi," I said.

"Evening, *cherie.*" Candace's voice was soft and warm, like sun-struck velvet. "What are you doing this evening?"

"Having a drink with you?"

She chuckled. "Good guess. How soon can you be here?"

"I'll catch the train," I said. "See you soon."

"Excellent. There is a bottle of wine that cannot wait to make your acquaintance."

"Tell it I feel the same way," I said, making sure I changed course. Conversation with an old friend sounded a hell of a lot better than one more night of cheap drink and empty rooms.

I parked my car at the Kent Metro station and bought a ticket for downtown. No way would I deal with downtown traffic and parking if I could avoid it.

 The Metro station was a soaring edifice of concrete and sheet glass; I'd always waited for some Hollywood director to use it as the setting for a shootout. Something about the place just screamed for gunplay. Who knew why?

The car was full of people ending their workday or heading towards their work night. I found some standing room between a middle-aged lady and a hipster boy in skinny jeans. Neither looked at me. It was like that on the train. I remembered when I was in high school and people actually talked to one another. Now we all pulled out phones and talked to people we already knew. Progress, I guess.

The train dropped me off near the layer-cake craziness that was Pike Place Market, and I hiked the rest of the way to Candi's bar, keeping my collar turned up against the rain. The weather wasn't bad, but then again it wasn't the sort anyone would want to hang out in for the fun of it. There were the usual collection of skinny club kids and tourists to thread my way through.

The Pegasus Rest was tucked into the crook of Pike Place, under the main part of the market in a location one had to know existed before it could be found. Anyone glancing down towards it would see a good place for a mugging and not much else. I walked down and found the door without much fear. It was a black metal rectangle wedged into a brick wall. For some reason passers-by had decided that the wall was a good place to stick their used gum. After thirty years of this the brick underneath could barely be seen.

Inside it was quite a bit warmer but only slightly brighter than outside. I could smell wine and the faint ghost of burning cloves. Smooth jazz came out of the jukebox in the corner; Nina Simone, from the sound of the vocals. I nodded to the bartender and headed towards the back corner booth, where a question mark of blue smoke rose above the divider.

Candace Andrea-Marie Estermont was one of those lucky women for whom aging had meant trading a pinch of youth for a pound of dignity. Forty-two years had only added a few faint lines to her cheeks and a dusting of silver in her hair; otherwise she was as glossy and sleek as a witch's cat, the same incisive beauty I had met sixteen years ago. She sat with a glass at her elbow and a Kindle under her fingers, black Djarum cigarette smoldering in the ashtray before her.

"Evening," I said.

She looked up and smiled in a way that made her face light up. "Amber!" She flowed out of the booth. Her greeting was pure Old World; a firm hug and a soft kiss for both cheeks. I returned it with a smile.

"You're looking well," she said as we sat. Ten years of living across the Atlantic had put a smattering of accents in her voice; most people assumed Candi was French, but I knew better.

"You're looking like you always do," I said. "How do you manage that?"

She arched one eyebrow. "Black magic and the

blood of virgins," she said.

"I'd believe it," I said. She laughed.

The *sommelier* appeared at the table. "A glass for your guest, Miss Estermont?" He was a polished young man about Julian's age with the same pretty-boy good looks, only blond.

"Yes. And bring the bottle." She held up her half-empty glass. He nodded and disappeared.

She held the glass out to me. "Try this and tell me what you think."

I took a sip. For as dark as it was the wine was light and airy, carrying the bite of a proper red without the heavy finish. I closed my eyes "I think that's freaking delicious. French?"

She took the glass back. "Your palate is slipping, *cherie.*"

"My palate," I said, "is currently on strike. One too many glasses of boxed Merlot."

Candi gave me a look of horror that was only half-exaggerated. "Oh honey, the first round is on me. No one should have to drink that swill."

The *sommelier* came back with a bottle and a glass. He poured one for me and left the bottle on the table. I took another sip. It was nice not to have to get buzzed before the wine in my glass tasted good. I tried to sneak a look at the bottle, but Candi kept it turned around. After one more sip I gave up. "Okay, you win...where *is* this from?"

"Hungary, believe it or not." Candi turned the label around so I could read it. "Donausonne, 2010. A fine red." She took a sip to illustrate her point.

"Is that a screw top I see?"

Candi laughed. "You know I've never been a traditionalist about anything."

"I seem to remember a certain girl who wouldn't drink anything without a cork," I said.

"That was then, this is now."

"Very Zen."

We shared a laugh. Candi was an easy person to laugh with, mostly because she laughed often...and when she did it, she always meant it.

I looked around. The bar was more than half full and had that pleasantly lazy flow a proper drinking establishment ought to have. Some of the other patrons smoked; that wasn't legal, but Candi kept the law at bay by technically being a 'members only' establishment so no one ever complained. I had never figured out her metric for deciding who rated entry and who did not, but it worked; the Rest was always lively without being obnoxious. "I take it business is good," I said.

She shrugged. "As good as it always is. People like to drink, especially when times are bad. I ought to be tending bar, but Martin is coming along nicely."

"Easy on the eyes, too," I said, giving her a playful smile.

"He is that," she said. "How is your firm doing?"

"Pretty terrible, up until this morning."

"A good client?"

"An opportunity," I said, and explained for several minutes. I left all the names out of the explanation; Candi might have been my oldest and dearest friend but rules were still rules. If you got in the habit of breaking them it was tough to know when to stop. Fortunately Candi knew better than to ask. The Hungarian red went quite well with our discussion; by the time I had finished my explanation more than half the bottle was gone.

"This sounds like something you ought to be careful with," she said.

"I know," I said.

"The rich," Candi intoned, "have a habit of guarding their wealth quite closely."

"I know that too," I said.

She poured out the last of the wine between our two glasses. "Oh, I forgot to tell you...I ran into Phillip at a party the other week."

"My ex?"

"The very same."

"My condolences," I said. Phil had been a lousy life decision even by my relationship standards; he'd cheated on me all over town, which was doubly humiliating when one considered my profession. "Let me guess...he hit on you."

"Of course he did. I told him I was seeing someone, but I promised to introduce him."

"Okay, I'm waiting for the punchline..."

The curve of her smile made her look like the Devil's own handmaiden. "I introduced him to Layla," she said.

I almost gagged on my wine. "Oh snap," I said. Layla was a local legend; a drag queen who took the stereotype of the ugly she-male and blew it right to flinders. Layla was better at women's fashion than most women and took a delight in widening the paradigm of the narrow-minded; my ex certainly qualified there.

"Tell me...how badly did Layla break him?"

"Consider yourself avenged," Candi said.

I laughed as much as sweet justice and two glasses of strong wine allowed for, and once again Candi joined me.

"So," Candi said once we had calmed down, "is there anyone new?"

"What do you think I'm going to say?" My sip of wine was more like a swallow; the vintage deserved better. "I suck at dating, and we both know it."

"Practice makes perfect, *cherie.*"

"No time for practice," I said.

"For some things one should make time." She refilled both our glasses with practiced ease.

"How about you?"

She smiled and let me change the subject. "I met a lovely couple the other month. I saw them last night, actually."

"How'd that go?" Candi's dating life had long since stopped shocking me; she was bisexual, polyamorous, open about both and totally unconcerned with what the world thought of her choices. I admired her for her lifestyle but knew better than to try and emulate it. I sipped some more wine while she elaborated.

"Pleasant, but problematic." She toyed with her glass. "Anne wants to experiment, but Joseph is...not sure about the whole thing. I'm not certain I should pursue it any further, to be honest."

"Some people don't like to share," I said.

"Well I know it," she said after another sip.

I nodded.

"She loves him very much, but I doubt it will last between them."

We drank in silence for a bit. It was the presence of pleasant quiet rather than the absence of talking. I enjoyed it. We passed the clove back and forth; the things burned for half of forever, and were better shared because of it. I was warm with a pleasant buzz and had a good friend to share it with.

"Break it off," I said into the silence. Candi looked at me.

"Sure," I continued, "you'd have fun, and they'd have fun...and I don't doubt that you could talk this Joe guy into forgetting about not wanting to share for a few hours. But then they'll wake up, get dressed and be the same people they were when they climbed into your bed." I stubbed out the cigarette. "They'll split up and you'll feel like crap about causing it. Break it off. Stay friends. Don't talk yourself into doing something you'll regret."

Candi smiled, the warm secret one she saved for her friends. "I suppose I just had to hear someone else say it," she said.

"So I'm not butting in?"

She shook her head. "You never do," she said.

"Maybe I'm better at this relationship stuff when I've had a bit to drink," I said.

"Most people are. Then again, maybe you just know me."

I held up my glass. "Sixteen years, I should hope so."

We clinked glasses. "To sixteen years," she said.

We drained our glasses. Candi went to refill them and then looked at the bottle.

"We appear to be empty," I said.

She gave me a questioning look. "Open another?"

"We'd be fools not to," I said.

She waved to the bartender. "It's a pity," she said as another bottle was delivered, "Anne tempts me sorely."

"Other fish in the sea," I said, stealing another of Candi's cigarettes.

"That is good advice," she said. "Plan on taking it anytime soon?"

I lit the clove with Candi's silver Calibri torch, watching her over the hissing flame. In the soft lighting of the bar, her eyes were the blue-green of a Mediterranean sea.

"Maybe once I learn how to properly throw a net," I said.

Chapter 6

Candi kept me longer than I'd planned on, but not longer than I wanted to stay. We parted with a mutual promise to meet again soon. I left a twenty and a ten with the bartender for my share of the wine and a tip for his work. Candi would never ask for it, but it would've been rude of me not to leave it for her.

By the time the train got me back to my car I was pretty much sober and looking forward to my bed. The rain had finally let up and the puddles on the pavement were still, reflecting moonlight in shades of quicksilver and oil. There were a pair of texts in my phone; Izzy had already found a host of interesting information on our burgeoning case. I answered her before climbing behind the wheel.

Good work, I sent back. It took her about twenty seconds to respond.

The more I look, the dirtier it gets boss.

Once again, AutoCorrect was my friend. **Keep at it. I look forward to reading it all tomorrow once I'm done casing Kitsmiller's neighborhood.**

I got into my car and started for home

My phone buzzed once on the way home. **I is on da case :D**

"I know you are," I said to the screen. Izzy couldn't hear it but she probably knew anyhow. If our play worked out I told myself I would give both her and Julian raises; they'd been good employees and I had been forced by economic reality to suspend any wage increases.

I pulled into my apartment complex around eleven, thoroughly ready for bed. I hoped Zork wasn't too mad at me for being late. I looked for him as I walked through the parking lot.

I found my cat at the base of the stairs, being petted by someone I did not recognize; a rangy man about my age with a head of sun-bleached dreadlocks. He looked up as I came down the stairs. I kept one hand on my pepper spray.

"Evening," I said.

"Been waiting for you," he said. "This your cat?"

"Yeah," I said. "Can I help you?"

The stranger grinned. "I figured you wouldn't recognize me."

I looked him over. Six feet and change, slim at the hips but a wedge of muscle from the waist up. Skin the color of aged oak set off high cheekbones and bright hazel eyes, while a soft smile touched a memory of mine. I knew him, but I couldn't place from where. "Should I?"

"Drake Albie," he said.

The memory came all the way back; study sessions deep in the stacks with a skinny soft-spoken geek much smarter than me.

"Western Washington U, class of 2004," I said. "You squeaked me through chemistry and physics." I tried to reconcile the awkward boy in my memories with the muscled-up slice of hippie beefcake in my present.

He grinned wider. "Actually, *you* squeaked you through chemistry. I just helped."

I smiled. "Come on," I said. "I'd have choked without you holding my hand. Anyhow, what are you doing here?" I relaxed my grip on my pepper spray, but only a little. People change after college.

"Looking for you," he said. "I'm out doors, you see."

He looked it. His clothes showed serious wear. His boots were laced with packing twine, and so worn they resembled ballet slippers. The army-surplus parka he had on was black with rain and road dust. I looked for and spotted a big duffel sitting out of the weather under the staircase. "Any particular reason? For being out doors I mean."

"I'm not on the lam or anything if that's what you're

asking," he said.

"It was," I said, watching as Zork rubbed up against his ankle. Drake reached down to scratch him behind the ears. I could hear him purring.

"It's freezing out here," I heard myself say. "Let's talk inside."

"Jesus, yes, let's." The relief in his voice was palpable.

I walked down past him to open the door. He picked up his duffel. "I didn't think you were going to let me in, there for a second."

I shrugged. "Zork likes you," I said. "He doesn't like anyone, usually."

"Zork's a good judge of character?"

My smile was a sad creature. "Better than I am, sometimes."

I hung my coat up. Drake slipped out of his. Underneath he had on a ratty thermal undershirt, damp at the shoulders. "How long were you waiting out there?"

"A couple of hours, maybe."

I glanced at the thermometer I'd mounted on the kitchen window. It read a little below fifty, plenty cold with a stiff breeze and a good dose of rain; the perfect cocktail for a miserable two hours outdoors. "Damn," I said. "You want a shower, warm up a little?"

He nodded. "Thanks," he said.

I pointed towards the bathroom door. He picked up his duffel and went that way, closing the door behind him. I went to the fridge and started setting out dinner for two. Zork watched me from the arm of the couch.

"You'd better be right about this," I told Zork. He ignored me, being more focused on grooming his paw to perfection. I dug my pepper spray out of my jacket and tucked it into my pants pocket, just in case my cat was incorrect.

By the time the sound of the water stopped and the bathroom door opened I had something resembling dinner worked out; chicken and rice, along with a couple of bottles of Kilt Lifter scavenged from a six-pack I'd forgotten about. Drake came back, much less dirty and cold. He saw the food and got a look on his face one usually saw on religious converts.

"Thanks," he said softly.

"Least I can do," I said. "Sit, eat, have a beer. After that you can tell me what's going on."

He sat, and ate. Not quick the way casually hungry

people do, but slow, savoring every bite, chewing for flavor in the fashion of the truly starved. I went to work on my own portion.

"When's the last time you ate?"

He sipped some beer. "Yesterday, I think."

"I thought so," I said. "My cooking isn't *that* good."

"It's good enough," he said. I could tell he meant it. I let him finish without further distraction.

He helped me gather the plates and washed dishes while I dried them and put them away. I took the time to sort through the weird mess of feelings his arrival had brought on. College hadn't been the happiest time in my life. Drake hadn't had anything to do with that, but I couldn't help but think about a few times and places I did not wish to return to. I also couldn't help but think about the fifteen pounds I'd gained, or the fashion sense I'd let decay. Or maybe it was the fact that I was still living like a college student at thirty three. Maybe I didn't like the pepper spray in my pocket, there because I was paranoid about someone who used to be a friend.

My insecurities weren't sorted by the time we finished the dishes so I shoved them aside instead. We dug the last two beers out of the six-pack and sat down at the kitchen table.

"Okay," I said, "tell me a story."

"First off, you probably aren't going to believe this."

I shrugged. "Try me," I said. *Don't lie,* I thought.

He sipped at his beer. "After grad school I got a job back East with a big advertising firm, just out of nowhere. I mean, I had sent them a resume and shit but I hadn't seriously expected to get anything out of it. They paid for the move, the plane ticket...hell, they even sent a car to the airport. Six figure salary, my own office. It was unbelievable."

"I figured you'd go far," I said.

"Heh, I didn't. Anyhow. So, I'm under a lot of stress. I do a couple of slogans – I think one was for diapers of all things. But it sells. So does the next one, and the next one. Pretty soon everyone's looking at me."

"You cracked?"

He took a pull on his beer, bigger than before. "No, I goofed. Office Christmas party, I get a little too drunk...I wasn't really used to booze and they had a huge bar there, all this expensive liquor. I ended up in a closet with an intern." He smiled, but there wasn't much humor to it.

"Uh-oh," I said. Several of my more chaotic cases had started while investigating that sort of indiscretion.

"It gets better. She was my boss's niece."

"Oops," I said.

"I didn't know," he said. "She didn't tell me. Anyhow, it gets better still. We were both drunk and she falls against the door and it opens, right as a bunch of higher-ups come around the corner. It couldn't have been more perfect if someone had scripted it."

"And her uncle was right there?"

He nodded. "He saw who I was with and came after me with a champagne bottle. He was way, *way* drunker than I was. We tangled. He ended up face-planting the bottle. Hard."

"How hard?"

Drake's face was stony. "It took two rounds of surgery to get all the shards out of his face."

"Jesus." I took another sip. "So, you got arrested?"

"Yeah, but the cops ruled it self-defense. I mean, there were a dozen witnesses to say he came after me with the bottle...and Nadine was of age and everything. There was no reason for him to do what he did. You can look it up if you want. The *New York Post* did a piece on it."

I made a mental note to do exactly that. "So, why are you the one who's out doors?"

Drake's face took a hard set. "First, Halcourt got me fired. Then, he called up all his buddies and got me blackballed. Finally, he hauled me into civil court and took me for everything I had and then some."

There wasn't much I could say to that. I figured he'd told me the truth. I'd seen similar things happen before.

"He didn't stop there, either. He kept up with the lawsuits...emotional damages, surgery costs, you name it. Finally, I just took off. They can't get you into court if they can't serve you."

My mouth went off on reflex. "What about service by publication?"

Drake shrugged. "Halcourt tried. Judge denied the motion, basically said that if Halcourt wanted me he had to find me first. So he keeps hiring private investigators to track me down. I can't keep a job, I can't get an apartment. Every time I do, some investigator finds me. I've climbed out of more windows because of those punk fucks..." He took another sip of beer. "Sorry. It's been a tough couple of years."

"No worries. It sounds that way."

He smiled. "So, what have you been up to?"

I dug in my purse, found my PI license and tossed it on the table. Drake looked at the square of plastic like it might bite him. I didn't blame him one bit.

"It's okay," I said. "I hadn't heard Halcourt's name until you mentioned it."

His shoulders slumped; I had not noticed how tense he'd gotten until he relaxed.

I shrugged. "You didn't know. I didn't know. No harm, no foul. Besides, inviting you in to trap you into getting served violates your right to due process."

"I've gotten used to having my rights violated," he said. "What happens now?"

"You mean if Halcourt calls me, or if some other process server knocks on my door?"

"Both."

"If Halcourt calls me, I tell him to go fuck himself, politely." I was starting to feel the beer. "Crushing people isn't what the legal system is for. If someone else shows up I tell them I've never heard of you, and you leave by the back door once they're gone."

He looked at me like he didn't know what to say.

I smiled. "I meant what I said earlier. I would have

failed at least two classes without your help, and...well, I had a lot going on back then. I never really thanked you properly. I can put you up for a while, unless you want to leave."

"I don't. I'm out of places to go." He held up his bottle. "I consider myself properly thanked."

I held up mine. "What should we drink to?"

He clinked his bottle against mine. "To assholes," he said, grinning.

"To assholes?"

"Without them we never find out who our real friends are."

That made me laugh. We drained our beers and set the bottles on the table.

"There's a blanket and pillows on the couch," I said. "Feel free to raid the fridge, just leave me some coffee or I'll get homicidal. We'll work the rest of it out tomorrow."

"Like I said, properly thanked."

We shook hands and said goodnight. By the time I finished my before-bed rituals I was nearly asleep on my feet. Zork came in and curled up on the pillow next to mine. I struggled into some sweats and an old Queensryche t-shirt, set my alarm and crawled into bed. Zork nosed my face and I petted him.

"Like I said...you'd better be right about this."

The pepper spray went under my pillow, just in case he wasn't.

Chapter 7

I awoke next morning to my alarm - and the smell of cooking bacon. I came all the way around in a moment of startled confusion before my brain reminded me of the events last night, of my old friend and me agreeing to let him sleep on my couch. I relaxed, found my robe and wandered out into the kitchen.

Drake was at the stove, wearing a pair of faded black track pants, no shirt or socks, minding a pan of bacon slices. There was a full pot of coffee and two portions of scrambled eggs on plates.

"Morning," he said. "Thought you might want breakfast."

"You," I said, "can stay as long as you like."

He grinned and gave the bacon a flip. The muscles in his shoulders rippled with the motion. I could see the pale stripes of several scars on his back and arms, as well as a puckered circle on his lower chest. I got myself a cup of coffee and tried not to stare too much; Drake had a build most often seen in cage fighters and on romance novel covers. It was an eyeball magnet.

"You've seen some rough use," I said.

"Living on the street isn't a picnic," he said.

I gave the scars an appraising glance. "I'd guess knife."

"Two of them are. One was a broken bottle."

I pointed at the round scar. "And that?"

He shrugged. "Termites."

I stirred cream and sugar into my cup. "I didn't know termites carried nine-millimeter handguns."

"A thirty-eight, actually." He divided up the bacon between the plates. "I tried to sleep in a lumber yard. The security guy on his rounds didn't like it. He shot at me on my way out."

 "That isn't legal," I said.

"No," he said. "It isn't."

We sat at the table. Drake started in on his breakfast and I started in on mine. It wasn't the best for my waistline but it smelled too good to say no to. "You end up in the hospital?"

Drake shrugged. "A veterinarian. I couldn't afford a trip to the ER."

"Jesus, I'm sorry."

"You didn't do it." He smiled. "That's life at the bottom, I guess."

I focused on finishing my breakfast. The coffee was perfect; black as mortal sin and just as invigorating. "This is great...and how did you get so big? Last time I saw you, a stiff breeze would have knocked you over."

He laughed. "I worked nine months at a lumber mill down near Portland, tossing six-by-sixes for eight hours straight on the green-chain. You either build up to it or quit doing it."

"Sounds like my job," I said.

We finished our breakfasts and I went to take a shower. I took a bit more time with my grooming, on the theory that I might have to talk to strangers later; a pair of slacks, a new-ish white blouse and some of my nicer jewelry. I wrestled my hair into a decent French braid and actually put on makeup. By the time I slipped back out into the living room the kitchen was clean. Drake sat at the kitchen table, typing on a battered laptop.

He looked up, saw the questions on my face and smiled. "This thing was too damn useful to sell. I can check weather patterns, look for jobs, stay up on Halcourt's shit, you name it. Better than the fifty bucks I'd get for it at a pawnshop, and there's free wi-fi almost everywhere."

"I wasn't going to ask, but that makes sense." I

crossed into the kitchen and peeked out the window at the parking lot. No vehicles I did not recognize. I walked back to the kitchen table and sat down. "Okay, here are the rules if you don't want to get found."

I ticked them off on my fingers. "Rule one; don't go outside, not even at night. Rule two, check the street from the northwest window in my office and the parking lot through the kitchen window here. Don't bother checking the parking spots, watch the line of curb beyond them. If you see a vehicle there for longer than an hour, the place is being watched."

He closed the laptop. "Why those places?"

I smiled. "Because If I were a PI casing my apartment, that is where I'd be. From there it *looks* like a vehicle can't be seen. But it can be and there's no way to know that short of being on the inside looking out."

He nodded. "Anything else?"

"Don't answer the phone. Let it go to voice mail, I'll check it when I get home. My home number's unlisted but that wouldn't slow a PI down all that much." I paused as a thought struck me. "How did *you* find me, anyway?"

"I Googled you and got your address."

I nodded. "Well, there you go. It isn't hard to find people these days. Anyway, I need to get to work. Try not to go stir-crazy."

"Four walls, a roof, hot food and a shower," he said, "plus free internet and plenty of books. I'll be just fine."

"I believe it," I said. I left him at his laptop, collected my coat and headed out.

I gave the parking lot a scan once I got up to it; there was a battered red Ford parked in 24 G's spot, but I knew the girl who lived there. The car likely belonged to her boyfriend-of-the-month, and no PI would take a reserved parking spot for surveillance purposes. I discounted it and got into my own car.

The sun was out but the clouds were low and solid, turning the sky overhead a dull shade of pewter. I threaded my way through the streets to West Seattle, where Kitsmiller's neighborhood was. Traffic was typical for a Friday morning, which is to say not homicide-inducing. I got where I was going around ten; I noticed that as I neared the neighborhood the traffic thinned out a good deal. It was gone completely once I came within eleven blocks of Kitsmiller's address.

There is a fair measure of both art and science to casing a neighborhood; too much pushing and you get nothing. Too little, same deal. I had practiced my three favorite cover stories on the way over, but as I rounded the corner into my target neighborhood I saw that I needn't have bothered. Nearly every house had a FOR SALE-SOLD sign out in front of it.

I pulled over to the sidewalk and looked around. Yards were overgrown. Siding was streaked with dirt where it wasn't attracting mold. Most occupied houses have stuff out front like potted plants and kid's bikes. These didn't. I spotted a half-mangled doll sitting against the curb.

"Damn," I muttered. I got out and locked my car.

My original plan had been to do a rough circle around Kitsmiller's cul-de-sac, with the idea that staying as far away from a paranoid client as the investigation would permit was both wise and polite. But as I walked the streets and took in the sights I started to wonder if this was even going to be possible.

For want of anything more productive to do, I took pictures of what I saw. The act of lining up the shots distracted me from how unsettling the deserted neighborhood was. And it truly was deserted; about all that was missing was a tumbleweed blowing along the street. But it was raining and the lazy wind was too weak to lift the masses of damp leaves off the pavement.

I tried the door at every house without a realtor's sign that I came across, but no one answered. I wrote down all the addresses of the ones which did have signs, making lists of which agents had sold what house. Most of that was easily accessible online but it was always nice to confirm it by going on-site. By noon, however, I was ready to concede defeat. I pulled out my phone and punched up the office, settling my Bluetooth headset in the crook of my ear.

I got Julian after two rings. "Hi there," he said.

"That how you answer the phone?"

"It is when the caller ID says it's you," he said.

I chuckled. "Fair enough."

"How goes it?" I heard keys tapping in the background.

"It doesn't," I said. "This neighborhood's deserted...I'm talking eleven square blocks that look like the prelude to a zombie flick."

"Creepy," Julian said.

I buttoned up my pea coat as I walked; the wind had picked up. "Tell me about it. You having any luck?"

"Yeah," he said. "I think you were right about other people having the same problem...I've got about fifteen different versions of the same story - you know, from those who were actually willing to talk to me."

"I'll take a look at them when I get in," I said. "What's the story?"

"It's like you said it would be," he said. "People got into it with the bank all of a sudden and couldn't seem to get out. At that point, they got a call from a realtor with an offer on the house...for less than it would have normally been worth, but most of them took it anyway."

"And those that didn't?"

"Foreclosed on and tossed out," he said. His voice sounded disbelieving.

I snapped another picture of a realtor's sign. In the background, a basketball hoop stood netless and worn over the garage; the hoop left rust streaks down the backboard like old blood.

"Let me guess," I said. "All the nifty federal assistance the banks are supposed to offer never materialized."

"Gee, how'd you guess?" I heard papers shuffling, followed by a pause.

"You've got a thought," I said.

"I'm not sure it means anything," he said.

"Nothing means nothing, Julian. Spill."

"You know how most of the time when people don't want to talk to you, they get annoyed, maybe just blow you off?"

"Yeah," I said.

"Everyone sounded...scared. A couple just hung up on me. Even the people who did want to talk, most of them have moved out of town. You've been doing this longer than I have...is that weird?"

I heard a car approaching and turned around; it was a white sedan, the surplus police model. It had a security logo on the door. It passed me, slowed down and flashed its lights.

"It is," I said. "And it just got weirder."

"You okay?"

"I might have found someone to talk to," I said as the car pulled over to the curb and a figure in a tan uniform got out. "Stay on the line and hit 'RECORD'." I plastered a smile on my face as the driver approached me.

"Hi," I said when he got within earshot.

"Can I help you," he said. It wasn't a question. He was a beefy kid barely old enough to get into a bar, with soft pink features and a peroxide crew cut. A gold earring went well with the shiny badge on his chest but clashed with the black nylon duty belt heavy with nightstick, flashlight and Smith & Wesson automatic.

"Oh, I'm just looking around," I said, giving him my sunniest expression.

"No," he said, "you aren't." His jaw took on a tough-guy set. With his baby face he looked like the overgrown version of a sandlot bully.

"I'm not?"

"No, you were just leaving."

"This is a public street," I said. "I've a right to be here."

"That's a nice camera," he said, putting one hand on his nightstick. "It'd be a shame if it got broken."

"That's a slick badge," I said, "It'd be a shame if it got revoked."

His pale skin flushed red. He grabbed the microphone on his collar and muttered alphabet soup into his radio. I wondered if his company had a radio code for 'wiseass bitch' and whether or not he'd used it. "Look lady," he said, "this is private property. You need to leave."

"If this is private property, who owns it all?"

"None of your damn business," he said.

"Did your boss tell you to be rude, or did you come up with that on your own?"

The color in his cheeks got darker. "You want to get smacked around, you just keep standing there," he growled. "But one way or the other you need to leave."

I shrugged. "I guess you're just too persuasive for me," I said. I walked back in the direction of my car.

He moved towards his security cruiser. "I'll follow you out."

"Such a gentleman," I said.

Once he was inside his car I spoke again. "Did you get that?"

"Most of it," Julian said. "Jesus boss, what was that guy's damage?"

"Penis envy," I said.

Julian laughed. I kept walking. "I'm going to go get some lunch," I said. "I'll phone you once I'm not in danger of being braced by a rent-a-cop."

"What do you want me to do with the recording? I

mean, we can't use it right?"

I smiled. "I'm about to get gray-legal on your ass," I said. "The recording itself cannot be used in court...I had you get it so that we can both remember exactly what was said, so we can testify against the security company for harassment and abuse if we want. And you witnessed it...seeing as you did the electronic equivalent of being a bystander."

"And for the case?"

"We'll play it for Hastings, let him know we're taking risks."

I kept walking. The security car was about fifteen feet behind me, cruising at the same pace I walked. I went slow. It might've made his job harder, but I didn't care much. "I'll be in the office in a few hours," I said. "I've got a few more leads to follow."

"Watch your step, boss," Julian said.

"Apparently I need to," I said.

The rent-a-cop followed me all the way back to my vehicle. As I got into my car I saw him scribbling in a pad, no doubt recording an altercation with Caucasian female, early thirties, five-five, brown and blue, no name given, driving a 2000 Volkswagen Golf. I wondered why the double dose of attitude; private security could be coarse and sometimes discriminatory but usually not quite so pathologically hostile. I pulled out my phone and went back over the recording. No doubt about it, he had started out rude and gone straight for cheesy threats.

"What's your damage indeed," I muttered.

There was a honking sound behind me; I turned and saw Cujo Junior pointing at me with his finger. I smiled at him, put my car in gear and started driving. He followed me for five blocks before turning away. I waved. He didn't wave back. I headed downtown, to try my luck with the real estate agents.

My luck remained consistent; a few hours of hitting them up proved fruitless. I pretended to be a reporter doing a story on the big development, playing to their egos and hoping one of them would want to talk about themselves. They either blew me off, or talked a lot and said nothing. I even tried flirting with one who gave me the eye; all I got was a dirty look from his secretary. From the look of things I was poaching on her turf. Too bad the wedding ring he wore said she was on the poach as well.

 I took a late lunch at a Subway, sticking to one of the low-calorie options and reviewed my notes. There wasn't much to go over, since very few people wanted to talk to me. I wondered about all the stonewalling I was getting. First the security guard, and now the realtors. I sighed and called up the office.

I got Julian again. "How goes, boss?"

"Again, it doesn't. Either there's no one to talk to or no one wants to talk. You found anyone willing to speak in person?"

I heard paper shuffling. "Maybe. I couldn't get a call through - her phone's disconnected - but I found someone who was foreclosed on who didn't leave town."

I grabbed a pad and pencil. "Talk to me."

"Her name's Tiera Weston. Her and her husband bought a house three streets down from Kitsmiller five years ago. Foreclosure procedures just ended last month...they took a while, I guess the Westons decided to make a fight out of it. Anyway, she wouldn't talk to me at all. I think she might know something."

I found my car and opened the door. "What makes you say that?"

"Call it a hunch I guess. I read into the case a little...it looks like the Westons got a divorce while the foreclosure stuff was happening, and then the husband shot himself two months after the divorce went through."

"I'll take it." I was already scribbling notes. "Give me her current address." He did and I scribbled that down too. Weston hadn't gone far from her home; her new address put her in White Center. "In the meantime find out everything the internet will tell you about her."

"Uh...I'm not Izzy."

"You'll have to pretend," I said.

"Okay, boss."

I signed off and tossed my trash and got back into my car, hoping that this time I could find someone who would talk to me. Silence was evidence all by itself.

I sure didn't like the implications.

Eric Plume

Chapter 8

Sprawl is a common feature in the Seattle area; the various named towns don't have borders so much as they have low-density semi-urban buffer zones. Filing cabinets for strip-malls and low cost apartments, places to begin an otherwise promising life or end a failing one. White Center was one such place; I suspected that it only had its own name because neither Burien nor West Seattle wanted to claim the neighborhood as their own. I'd been there a few times working various cases and was always glad to leave. Seattle natives called the place "Rat City", though not to the faces of the residents.

Tiera Weston's apartment complex looked a good deal like my own, a comparison I could have done without noticing; peeling paint, overgrown landscaping, a cracked parking lot strewn with litter. The complex was on a corner, a wide L of brown wooden siding and postage-stamp balconies. I drove by slow once, caught a couple of door numbers and estimated where Weston's apartment would be. I parked at a gas station across the street from that leg of the L and pulled out my iPhone.

You find anything on Weston, I texted to Julian.

About a minute later I got a response. **A little she**

works parttime at a hardware store gets foodstamps and doesnt do much else, I read. **Izzys here shes looking at it more.**

What shift does Weston pull at the store?

Days looks like she should be at work right now she gets off in an hour maybe. I glanced at the clock on the dash; plenty of time to do a little sleuthing.

Good work, keep me posted I sent back before getting out of the car.

According to Julian's research Weston lived in apartment 104, which meant ground floor, fourth from one end. I glanced at the parking space for 104 and it was empty; either Weston didn't drive or she was at work. I found apartment 104 and rang the bell. No answer. I walked around to the other side of the complex, careful to keep my stride nonchalant and unconcerned. People cut through apartment front lawns all the time, but those doing it with a furtive manner tended to worry the residents.

I found Weston's patio by counting the windows. There was nothing on it except a chair and an overturned plastic bucket serving as a table. An ashtray was perched on that, overflowing with butts. I looked at one. From the white paper and filter length it was a light 100, and I spied a white-

and-gold cigarette pack crumpled in one corner of the patio. A quick glance through the glass on the sliding door didn't tell me much. There was clutter and dimness and not much else. I walked back to the gas station and bought a newspaper and a pack of Marlboro Light 100s along with a pack of gum. I sat and waited and read the newspaper, ignoring the cigarettes which sat in the center console.

Forty-five minutes later a beat up 90s Toyota sedan pulled into 104's slot and a woman about my height got out. She had on dark slacks, a white blouse and a brown leather jacket three sizes too big for her. A thick sable braid reached to her hips. She locked her car and walked straight into her apartment without looking around. I broke open the pack of cigarettes, pulled out three and then stuffed the pack into my pocket. After that I got out of my car and crossed the street.

I was nervous, and with good reason; interviewing subjects is always a unique experience and sometimes a dangerous one. One never knew what sort of life you were intruding on by ringing a stranger's doorbell. I'd heard horror stories at conventions of PIs blundering into everything from fistfights to drug deals to murder cover-ups; my own personal best was accidentally interrupting a swinger's party in full...well, swing, but I knew it could get far worse than middle-aged nudity. None of that was likely here, but it was just as unlikely anywhere else and it still happened. I made sure my pepper spray was handy as I rang Weston's doorbell.

"Pretext or the truth," I muttered to myself. "Which will you be, Tiera?" Always a coin toss in my line of work; some people liked cooperating with investigators, other people saw us as the scum of the earth.

The lock clacked and the door opened as far as a night chain would permit. Beyond it was half a pale face and one tired, suspicious brown eye. "Yeah?" her voice was brittle and raspy, heavy with a smoker's wet rattle.

"Tiera Weston?"

She nodded but flinched back, as if her own name had bit her.

I decided to go with the truth. Instinct told me it was right. "My name is Amber Eckart, Ms. Weston." I pulled out one of my business cards and handed it to her. "I'm a private investigator, and I'm looking into something I think might benefit you."

She took the card with the careful wariness one generally reserved for poisonous snakes and sharp objects. "You aren't a cop?"

I shook my head. "Nope. You're under no obligation to talk to me. I'd just like a few minutes of your time."

She looked at the card and then at me. "Do you have some ID?"

I had already dug my PI license out; people always asked to see it. When I handed it to her she examined it carefully, and then my face.

"Sure, whatever. Come on in." She lifted the chain and stepped aside to let me through. "I've got nothing better to do."

Weston's apartment had been partially unpacked and then lived in for six months. Boxes were everywhere; an ironing board had been set across two of them in front of the couch to serve as a makeshift coffee table. Six empty bottles of Arbor Mist sat on it along with a water glass, stained purple at the bottom. Clothes, trinkets and dust were scattered across the floor. I could smell stale food, pot smoke and sour wine.

Weston was twenty-eight going on forty, with frown lines and a chin blurred by fat. She wasn't heavy but her figure had that lumpy bulgy look skinny people get when they don't exercise or eat right. She watched me carefully and kept out of arm's reach. She had changed into jean cutoffs and a pale green t-shirt, and her feet were bare.

"Sorry about the mess," she said.

"Did you just move?"

"Yeah. Look, I hate to be rude but could you just tell me what you want?" She tucked her hands into the back pocket of her shorts, probably to avoid fidgeting with them.

"I'm looking into the foreclosure practices of First American Bank," I said.

"Who sent you?" she took her hands out of her pockets.

"Not the bank," I said.

"And why're you asking me?" She played with her braid. She had nice hair, or would have if she took better care of it.

"According to records, your house in West Seattle was foreclosed on by them," I said.

"Maybe they did," she said, not looking at me.

I got out my small notepad and pen. "Care to tell me about it?"

"Why should I?"

I tossed the dice. "Well..." I made myself appear to hesitate. "Look, I probably shouldn't be telling you this...but there's a class-action lawsuit that might be brewing. A big one."

"Yeah?" I saw her perk up. Hope edged out from behind the cynicism in her eyes. She wanted justice - and money. That was easy to work with.

"Yeah. Like I said, you didn't hear this from me." I looked around. "Is there someplace I can smoke?"

She nodded. "Balcony. Let me get my coat."

"Thank you," I said.

Weston slipped into the big leather jacket I'd seen before. It was a man's coat; I guessed it had belonged to her ex-husband. We stepped out onto the porch. She dug a crumpled pack of Marlboros out of her pocket. "So, there's like a lawsuit? Going after the people who took my house?" She pulled the last cigarette out of her pack. It was bent double, broken in the middle. "Shit," she said.

"Here, have one of mine." I pulled the pack out of my pocket and handed her one. She took it.

"Thanks," she said.

I stuck one in my mouth and patted my pockets. "Tell me you have a lighter," I said. "I left mine in the car."

"Sure." She passed me a powder-blue Bic.

I used it. "With our powers combined," I muttered. It made her smile.

We made small talk for a few minutes after that while we smoked. I listened more than I talked, let her direct the conversation to herself and her plight, how hard it was to make rent on a store clerk's wages. I made sympathetic noises and offered anecdotes of my own. I'd worked as both a waitress and apprentice investigator for two years before I'd started my practice; there was plenty of story-worthy black comedy to be had.

The cigarette tasted terrible after several years of not smoking them, but I made it look like I enjoyed myself and only inhaled as much as necessary. It still made me dizzy and filled my vision with little white sparkles. I was glad to put it out. It was worth it, though. By the time the cigarettes were gone Tiera and I were friends, at least in her eyes. And, a little in mine as well. The tricky part about empathizing with people is that one needs to mean it. Anything less gets sniffed out.

We went back inside. She offered me coffee and I accepted. There was more small talk while the coffee brewed. It was cheap stuff but I thanked her for it all the same.

"So, this lawsuit thing," she said as we found seats on her couch. "Would I, like, need a lawyer or something?"

I shook my head. "There isn't a lawsuit *yet,*" I said. "Really, I shouldn't be talking about it at all...but I need answers. These big guys are good at covering their tracks."

"Don't I fuckin' know it," she said. "I mean, sure we were late a few times but the bank *told* us everything was fine. Stupid me for trusting them, because next thing I fucking know there's a sheriff on our doorstep telling us we have to get out. I couldn't believe it!"

"Jesus, really?" I said. It wasn't hard to feign disgust.

I let her rant for a little while longer. After a bit she went and got a box of documents and showed them to me; all the foreclosure information the bank had given her. I looked it over. I was no mortgage expert but I could see the similarities to the Kitsmiller file. One name stuck out at me; HANSEN, BRADLEY J was the senior loan officer. The same senior official who had signed off on Kitsmiller's paperwork.

"Do you need any of this? I mean, should I get it all together or something?"

I tried not to wince. Apparently my friend approach had worked too well. Tiera Weston was desperate. I shook my head. "No, and I'd be careful who you show that stuff to. But yeah, get it all together and get it as organized as you can. Like I said, there's no lawsuit yet..."

She looked at me. "Square with me, Amber. How likely is it?"

"Honestly, you can never tell. And..." I hesitated. "Again, I didn't say this, but sometimes the people in class-action suits don't really get anything. The only people who reliably get rich are the lawyers."

"But it hurts the people getting sued?"

"As much as losing a lot of money hurts anyone. Look, I can't promise anything," I said. I wondered which one of us I was speaking to.

"If you promised me something I wouldn't trust it," Tiera said.

We talked a bit longer. I took notes this time. The story was pretty similar; one day everything was fine, the next Weston and her husband were getting thrown out of their house. By the time we wrapped up I had two pages of notes. Time would tell if any of it was going to help.

"One last question," I said. "This Bradley Hansen guy...did you ever meet him?"

"Yeah, once. He told us that everything would be okay, that he was on our side, all that feel-good bullshit." Her voice was a bit slurred. She had doctored her second cup of coffee with a generous measure of Black Velvet.

"Can you describe him?"

She shrugged. "He was cute. Tall, blond, tan, always smiling. Looked like a million bucks. Danny didn't like him one bit." She smiled, and then winced. "I believed him. I shouldn't have." She took a big gulp of whiskey-laced coffee.

"Where did you meet him at?"

She shrugged again, more fluidly this time. Her eyes were dull with booze and old anger. "At the big branch, downtown. We went in there to yell at them about what was going on, but the guy was just so smooth, he calmed us right down." She finished off her cup. "I should've kicked him in the fucking dick."

"I don't blame you," I said.

"I want my house back, Amber," she slurred. "I want my house back and I want my husband back and I want my life back." Her eyes were wet. "I didn't *do* anything to these people, but they just walked up into my fucking world and took everything."

She kept talking. I sat for one final rant session, refusing her offers of something stronger than coffee. After she wound down I said my goodbyes and left. It was good to get out. She didn't want to let me leave; I could tell because she hugged me. I wondered how many people came to visit. I guessed not many.

I walked down the hallway, pausing to smile neutrally at a rough-looking man my own age as he held the door for me on the way out. He did the same as I passed him, giving me a lingering glance. I just kept walking; I wasn't in the mood to be ogled. Visiting Tiera Weston's apartment had left a sick feeling in my stomach.

My phone buzzed. It was Izzy.

"This is a first," I said. "You calling instead of texting."

"Yeah well, too complicated for text," she said. "I've got the background done on the development deal."

"Talk to me," I said.

"It's huge, boss."

I looked both ways before darting across the street. "We knew that already."

"No, we didn't. I kept digging last night...every time I thought I'd found the end of it there was another layer of contractors and investors and stuff. Seriously boss, if I printed all the articles I have tagged for the report, you'd have to take it to a bookbinding service."

"Okay. Give me the principal names." I unlocked my car.

"The name I kept coming across most often was this guy Govrolev," she said. "He owns the big construction company running all the others. He's been interviewed a whole bunch about the development too...it's supposed to be, like, all environmentally friendly."

I thought of Tiera Weston, rotting in her apartment. "Yeah, as long as you aren't a human in the way." I told Izzy about my interview.

"Wow."

"Yeah." I got in my car and fired it up. "Anyway, I'm on my way back to the office now. We can compare notes."

"Think we've got enough for a class-action yet, boss?"

I grinned. "Not yet," I said, "but we're close. Get on the phone with Hastings, tell him about our progress."

"I'll have Julian do it," she said.

We signed off. I popped a piece of gum in my mouth to get rid of the smoke taste; it didn't do anything for the smell in my hair and clothes but that'd have to wait. I thought about throwing away the rest of the cigarettes but figured I might have to visit Weston again, so I stashed them in the center console instead.

My belly gurgled as I neared towards the West Seattle Bridge; the half-sandwich was long gone, and my stomach declared its unhappiness with the situation. I sighed and pulled off onto Marginal Way, managing to find a bar that served food. I compromised by ordering a salad, even though my metabolism would've preferred grease and meat.

While I waited for my food I nursed a Red Hook and went over the interview with Weston, dragging out my notes from the last two days and comparing them. Sure enough, the same patterns and strategies emerged. Weston's case was complicated by a few late payments...but last I checked being five days late on one occasion was not grounds for complete removal of property. When I stacked up the experiences of Weston and Kitsmiller next to a big development and a bunch of other people too scared to talk, the pile said conspiracy.

Problem was, not much I'd found would prove it in court.

I finished off my beer, had another one with my salad -the meal needed the help -, paid and left. The bartender didn't look at me twice.

I decided to take a turn around the block to walk off the beer, on the notion that getting a DUI was a bad career move. I was just turning back onto the street where my car was parked when my phone buzzed. It was the office.

"Hey, how-"

"Boss, we've got problems." It was Julian. His voice was tight with tension.

I stopped walking. "What is it?"

"Nobody knows who Hastings is."

Eric Plume

Chapter 9

"What the hell do you mean, 'nobody knows'?"

Julian spoke rapidly. "I couldn't find the business card he left, so I called the firm directly – we worked for them before so their number's in our files. Only the number wasn't the same."

"Well, that doesn't mean anything, maybe it's a cell."

"Boss, I called the firm. They *didn't know who John Hastings was.* They have no record of anyone by that name ever working there. I even talked to one of the senior partners. No one's heard of him, or even recognized the description I gave."

I closed my eyes. "Oh, fuck me."

"It gets worse. I'll let Izzy explain."

I heard a series of clicks and rustles as Julian punched up a conference call. I was already moving towards my car, quick. The next thing I heard was Izzy's voice.

"Okay. So, we called the Washington Bar Association and did some poking. They had three guys named John Hastings. One's dead, the other's black, and the third retired twenty years ago. He's eighty-five. None of them could possibly be our client."

"What about the money...don't tell me the check bounced." I thought of the two days I'd spent screwing around on the case, two days I could have been doing something that paid.

"The check cleared. But here's the thing; the account was a fake just like the phone number."

I fired up my car and headed for the bridge again. "So where'd the money come from?"

"Cayman Islands," she said. "That's as far as I could trace it with a phone call. What the fuck, boss?"

My mind shifted gears just like my car as I got back on the road. I hoped a cop wouldn't see me with a phone pressed to my ear and add a ticket to my already terrible day. A fake client ranked high on an investigator's list of worst case scenarios; I tried to stay calm and think matters through, but it was difficult. The fallout from something like this could ruin my practice.

"We're being used," I said. "Here's what we do...Izzy, I want you to break Hastings' number. It's probably some bullshit go-phone but if it has a physical address I want you to find it."

Julian sounded chagrined. "Boss, I don't have the card, remember?"

"Then find it," I snapped.

"Gotcha. What else?"

"Lock the door, close the shades, and hang out the "closed" sign. Then arm the security system. Don't leave until I get there."

Julian spoke. "Should I call the cops?"

"No," I said. "No cops. For all we know we just aided and abetted a criminal act. Until we know just what the hell is going on the boys in blue stay out of this."

Izzy, sounding scared. "Boss, I don't -"

"Guys, do what I tell you." I tried to keep the anger out of my voice and didn't manage it.

"Okay," Izzy said. Her voice was small.

"You coming back here?" Julian again, sounding more worried than ever.

"Not yet. First I'm going to see old lady Kitsmiller. Hardly any point in not, considering."

"I guess," Izzy said. "We'll get the place locked down."

"Good." I signed off before I could make my employees any more nervous than they already were.

It was not too far from where I was to Kitsmiller's

house; I drove within the law, kept my eye on the mirrors every five seconds like they teach you in counter-intelligence school. It was all but impossible to pick out a tail in stop-and-go traffic, but it wasn't easy to follow someone that way either. I didn't see anyone, but that didn't mean they weren't there.

Traffic lightened up as I got to the empty neighborhood, then faded out entirely. As I approached Kitsmiller's street it was obvious that this was Ground Zero for the development; I saw more holes in the ground than houses, and a raw metal frame that stretched up two stories, skeletal in the harsh glare of halogen worklights. Billboards were everywhere, but the one that dominated the site was of a massive black horse's head; the letters IRONHORSE CONSTRUCTION were spelled out beneath it.

I looked for a good place to park and found one; a driveway with trees on either side fairly close to Kitsmiller's house. I eased in and shut everything down as quickly as possible. Ordinarily when conducting operations in risky neighborhoods remaining visible was the safe choice; here there was no one to call the police and no police to trust, two good reasons to remain hidden.

The construction site occupying the vanished homes was empty as I walked past it. I could see a small security shack at the other end of the site but the guy inside it was reading a book. I walked on by without staring at him. People had a weird ability to know when they were being stared at and I did not want to risk his attention. I was glad to put some trees between me and him; I'd already dealt with this site's security enough for one day.

Kitsmiller's place was an old ranch-style home, the low rectangle made popular in Eisenhower's America. This one had been redone with cedar shingles and some nice decorative woodwork around the porch. There was a nice square of grass, and flowerbeds along the walls of the house.

All the flowers had been cut down. The lawn was longer than most people who care about their yards let it get. There was a big fence around the property which had the faded look of old wood, but the NO TRESPASSING and NO SOLICITATION signs were a recent addition. The nail heads on both were still shiny. The gate creaked as I opened it.

The windows had those heavy blackout curtains older people sometimes favored, but a faint glow from around the edges told me someone was home. One of the windows had plywood nailed over it; the window had been broken recently enough that there was broken glass in the flowerbed beneath it. An eighties-vintage Buick sedan sat in the driveway, tires sagging into the pavement. I could see the marks were they'd been slashed.

I paused and dug out my phone to text my employees, keeping my hand over the screen as much as possible. The glow from a cell phone screen could carry a surprising distance, even worse than a lit cigarette. **Everything buttoned up tight?**

Izzy answered at once. **Yeah. We're scared, boss. D:**

I know, I typed. **Sorry I snapped at you.**

S'ok, she sent back.

Anyway, email me the names of all of Kitsmiller's children, her husband, her mortgage number, all of it. I think I'll need to prove to her that I'm on the level. If we got a picture of Hastings send me that too.

Why whats going on?

I snapped a picture of the boarded up window and the car with its tires slashed. **This,** I put in beneath the picture.

Holy shit. O.O

Yeah. I kept one eye on the windows. I thought I saw some movement but I couldn't be sure. **I'm going to go talk to her wish me luck.**

Stuffs in your email good luck boss, I read on my

screen. I put the phone back in my pocket and straightened my hair. "Here we go," I said.

The door creaked open before I was halfway up the front walk. "You get out of here," I heard from the crack. There was barely any light behind it.

"Ma'am, I just want to -"

"I don't care what you want. Can't you read the sign? Now, get out of here before I call the police." Her voice was sharp, but it cracked and shook like a building about to fall down. She was scared.

"Please, Mrs. Kitsmiller. I'm not here to hurt you." I kept my hands visible and didn't walk forward.

"Why should I believe you?" I could just make out a white cloudy shape about five feet up the crack. Kitsmiller's hair, most likely.

"I guess you don't have a reason," I said. "May I have a couple minutes of your time? We can talk like this if you'd like."

There was a pause. "I have a gun," she said. From the way she said it I believed her. "If you try anything untoward I will shoot." I believed that too. "Now, tell me your name and who you work for."

"My name is Amber Eckart, ma'am...and up until about an hour ago I thought I was working for you."

Silence. I plowed on.

"Do you know a lawyer named John Hastings, Mrs. Kitsmiller? Claims to work for a firm called Burton, Cameron and Clive? Maybe you hired him, and he said he'd fight the foreclosure proceedings for you, something like that?"

More silence.

"John Hastings doesn't exist, Mrs. Kitsmiller. He isn't licensed to practice law in Washington...I know, I called the bar association. The law firm of Burton, Cameron and Clive hasn't ever heard of him. He's a fraud, ma'am. And I think he's scamming us both."

"How do you know all this? Who are you?"

"I'm a private investigator. Hastings hired me to work your case. That's what I was told. I just found out the rest of it an hour ago."

"Why should I believe any of this?"

"Hastings gave me your file," I said, and proceeded to rattle off everything Izzy had sent me. I got about halfway down the list before she spoke again. Her voice sounded a good deal less sure.

"All right, young lady, that's enough. How do I know *you* are what you say you are?"

I took a deep breath and started to relax. I'd made her listen. That was a start. "I can show you my license, ma'am, right now. I have it in my purse. May I reach for it?"

The porch light came on, and in its backwash I could see a slight figure standing in the doorway. "Don't make any sudden movements."

I opened my purse and held it so she could see inside of it. Then I slid my driver's license out so I could get at my investigator's permit. I keep it there so I always know where it is, and in moments like this I was glad I'd made that call. I slid out the little rectangle and held it up.

"Come up and put it on the porch railing, and then back away."

I did that, with careful steps and keeping both hands visible. Just for good measure I included my driver's license and business card; I placed the cards on the porch railing, then stepped back to where I had been standing.

A slim figure not much more than five feet tall came slowly out of the door. Cordelia Anne Kitsmiller was a doll of a woman who walked with a gray medical cane. In her other hand was a scarred black revolver. She gave the area a wide scan. From where I stood I could see that one of her eyes was milky with cataracts. If she decided to shoot me she wouldn't need both eyes to find her target. Sweat formed on the back of my neck. With the deliberate delicacy of the aged, she leaned forward and picked up the cards. She looked at them. She looked at me.

"Step into the light," she said.

I did so. This close I could see the worry in Kitsmiller's good eye. It was pale blue, like a rare sunny day in winter. I waited. My hands had already gotten cold and I wanted to put them in my pockets. I didn't.

"I don't know if I should trust you."

"I know, ma'am. I bet a lot of people have been lying to you over the past few months." I chanced a step forward. "But I haven't lied to you yet, and I don't intend to start. You have my word on that."

She looked at my cards, and then back at me. She set them down on the railing, and then turned to head back inside. I waited. She got halfway through the door before turning around.

"Wipe your feet before you come in, please."

"I will," I said.

I picked up my cards and stuck them back in my purse. My hands shook from the cold and for a couple of other reasons in the bargain, so it was plenty difficult to get the cards back where they belonged. After that I walked up to the door. I was sure my boots were clean but I gave them a good wiping anyway.

Eric Plume

Chapter 10

Kitsmiller's house was warm and dark, with the peculiar combination of clutter and cleanliness that only the elderly ever get right. I took off my shoes without her asking and hung up my coat while the old lady put her revolver back into a cigar box. I got a good look at it; a five-inch Smith & Wesson, the model cops used to carry back in my father's youth. The thing looked unreal in her hands, wrong somehow.

"I'm terribly sorry about the pistol," she said.

"From the look of your yard I'd say you have reason, ma'am."

"It isn't loaded," she said.

"That won't do you any good," I said.

"My husband never showed me how."

"I can, if you want."

"Maybe later," she said. She closed the box. "Can I get you something, Ms. Eckart? Some tea?"

I nodded and thanked her. She went into the kitchen. I walked into the living room. Pictures dotted the walls; Kitsmiller had a large family. Front and center was a sepia-print from a wedding, her in a satin gown and him in full Marine Corps dress.

They had both smiled for the camera.

Sitting on a small end table was a stack of mail; the top two envelopes were from First American Bank. One had a red URGENT stamp on it. I took note of that as I found a chair. Kitsmiller came back with a tray in less time than I would have expected. The water must have already been hot.

"So, you're a private detective?"

"Yes, ma'am." I kept my long-unused courtesies on full display. Kitsmiller was from a generation that considered such matters important.

"That is an odd career choice for a young lady, if you don't mind my saying so."

"It certainly has its moments." I doctored my tea. It was just cool enough to drink. "Like now."

"Yes, this matter with Mister Hastings." She sipped some tea. "You say he is a fraud?"

"Yes," I said, and proceeded to tell her everything I knew about Hastings. I was less worried about client confidentiality than I was about finding out who my client actually was. She listened and waited and didn't ask questions.

"...and so that's how I ended up at your door," I said. "Like I told you outside, I thought I was working on your behalf until a few hours ago. I'm really just looking for answers at this point."

She digested what I had told her. I let her. Finally she said, "I believe you."

"I appreciate that, ma'am." I set my teacup aside, being sure to find a coaster when I did. "Would you mind telling me your side of the story? I know about the bank stuff...but how does Hastings fit into it?"

Well. After the men with the bulldozers showed up, I called my son, who arranged for me to get an attorney. At first I was dealing with a Marie Rosales, from the firm of Burton, Cameron and Clive. My son said they were the best lawyers in Seattle."

I nodded. "They are known for that," I said. "I've worked for them before."

"After that is when the threats started. Some ugly young men harassed me while I was at the grocer's...and then someone ruined my flower beds. I called the police of course, but they could never find anything. When one of them ruined the tires on my car I dug out my husband's pistol."

"Wait...please, describe the young men to me." I dug out my pad and pen.

She set her teacup aside, her eyebrows knitted up in thought. "They were young...boys, really. All dressed like hoodlums, and they sounded foreign. They kept using language I didn't know, but when they spoke English they were all very foul-mouthed."

I was scribbling notes as fast as my hand would move. "Foreign how?"

"Eastern Europe maybe, not Germany...I don't really know, Ms. Eckart. I've never been outside the country, you see."

I looked up as a thought struck me. "Do you remember any of the words they used?"

"One of them sounded like 'lad', or 'yad', something like that. They kept calling me that."

I smiled grimly. "*Blyad,*" I said. "It's Russian, ma'am."

She blinked. "What does it mean?"

"You don't want to know." The word meant *whore* but I figured there was no reason in offending her. What I wanted to know, and very badly, was why Russian gang kids were harassing her. "I see most of the other houses are empty...did anyone else have an experience like yours?"

The wind made a moaning noise where it got in around the plywood. Both Kitsmiller and I looked at it.

"Some people sold their properties and left," she said after a moment. "I remember there was a real estate agent who stopped by and offered to buy this house, but I did not want to sell. He was very pleasant about it, but quite insistent. I had to ask him to leave three times."

I asked her for the agent's name; she didn't have it, but a short trip over to a massive oak desk netted me his card. The name looked familiar; I flipped my notebook back a couple of pages and compared the name to my list of realtors. He was the third most common.

"What happened to the ones who didn't sell?"

Her face grew hollow. "Some got into difficulties with the bank and had to make a deal. Others were forced out. I was lucky...my son managed to find me a good lawyer, but I don't know if that will be enough."

I could see the fear, and knew I should probably keep the conversation away from it. "When did you first meet John Hastings?"

She thought a moment. "It would have been three weeks ago now, I should think. He had all of my case information, and he said he knew Miss Rosales...I never thought to call and ask. I feel so foolish for that."

"I fell for it too, ma'am," I said, feeling my own embarrassment at getting played for a sucker. "Did he tell you he was hiring me?"

She shook her head. "I don't mind telling you, Miss Eckart...I'm not sure what to believe now."

"I can understand that," I said. "So, you said that some of the other people who lived near you were run off. What happened?"

She shivered. "Two were bought out...my neighbor died in a car accident. A big truck jumped the curb and struck him while was out for a walk one morning."

"What was his name?"

"Roger Wainwright. He lived across from me – I mean, the house that used to be across from me."

I wrote down that name. I was in the process of scribbling when Cordelia suddenly perked up. "Oh! I almost forgot something." She got up and headed over to a big oak desk liberally covered with papers. "About six months ago, a young man came to see me...he said he worked for the paper, that he was doing a story on some big development that was going in around my neighborhood." She walked over to me and handed me a business card. "This is what he gave me."

I looked at it. I recognized the name; Andrew Stark. "I know this man," I said. "Olive skin, black hair, big mustache, real nice smile?"

"That's him," she said. "He was quite charming."

"He's not a reporter. He's a PI like me." I'd met him at a convention in Iowa a few years ago; he'd bought me a drink and flirted with me, made a concerted effort to get me back to his room. I remembered politely declining and I remembered regretting that decision later in the evening. "Did he ever come back?"

"Not that I recall." She looked out her window, the one that did not have plywood over it. "What do I do now?"

I pocketed Stark's business card. "Give me a day to sort this out," I said. "I've got some connections at Burton, Cameron and Clive...I'll find out the status of your case, make sure you haven't been forgotten about somehow."

"Why are you trying to help me?"

I looked at the window, the one with the plywood over it. "This shouldn't happen," I said.

We were both silent a moment. The only sound was the wind. It made a keening noise around the edges of the plywood. I could feel the cold from it.

Kitsmiller fingered the gold cross hanging from her neck. "So what happens now?"

I crossed the room to the cigar box where she had put her pistol. "I show you how to load this," I said.

"The good book says 'thou shalt not kill,'" she said.

I opened the cigar box. The Smith sat in it, next to an old box of military ball ammunition. "A man's home is his castle," I said, "and God's law as well as Man's sets a guard upon it." I took the pistol and cartridges out of the box and looked up at her. "' He that assaults it does so at his peril."

She simply watched me, fear in her one good eye.

"Ma'am, a gun isn't a negotiation tool. I've had plenty of people stick them in my face over the years, people who wanted me to back down...and guess what, it's never worked. There's a big step between waving a piece and pulling the trigger. I know that. So will anyone serious who comes to hurt you. With all due respect, ma'am...either put this away or be prepared to use it. I'm sorry, but that's how it has to be."

She took two slow, careful steps towards the mantel, leaning on her cane. She studied the photographs, then at a spot on the floor between herself and me.

"I watched my son take his first steps," she said, "where you are standing now. I taught my daughter to cook in this kitchen."

I didn't say anything. I watched a sad sort of resolve surface in her good eye. It was the courage of a martyr. "Show me, please...about the gun. It would seem I need to know."

I did. It didn't take long. I gave her the same basic lecture my father had given me almost twenty years ago, and she listened. I showed her how the cylinder opened, how the shells went in and how they came out, how to hold it, and told her what to expect when it went off. I trusted that she knew the gravity of pointing a weapon at someone.

She put the pistol back in the box; loaded with the safety on, hammer down on an empty chamber. "So you will be in touch?"

"Either I'll call you tomorrow or somebody from my office will," I said. I gave her one of my cards. "If anything happens, call the police first and then me. " I rummaged in my purse and came up with my spare cell phone. "Here. There's fifty minutes on this. If the bad guys cut your phone line, you can still call. Keep it charged and close by."

She took the phone and charger. "Thank you," she said.

"You're welcome," I said. "I need to go now. I've got work to do."

"I'll pray for you," she said.

"Thanks," I said.

I hadn't seen the inside of a church since before my eighteenth birthday but at this point I would take all the help I could get. I put my boots and coat back on and said my good-byes to Kitsmiller. She watched me go, that same martyr's courage in her good eye.

Full dark had come on while I'd been inside; I kept my head on a swivel and my hand on my pepper spray, wishing against sense that I'd brought my pistol with me. All that gun-talk had made my hip feel light without a piece on it. The security guard over at the construction site was still engrossed in his book and didn't look up as I passed by. I wanted to text Izzy to let her know that I was on my way but decided that taking my attention away from my surroundings wasn't a good idea. I took the route with the most shadows back to where I'd parked my car, hoping no one had messed with it while I was gone.

There was someone standing about ten feet from my rear bumper, wearing jeans and a heavy canvas jacket. I couldn't make out his face but something in his stance told me he was young. I took my hands out of my pockets, pepper spray in my left fist. "Evening," I said.

"Hey, can I get a ride back to town?" He took a step towards me. He had a thick accent; I recognized it as Russian. "My motorcycle broke down."

I found the trigger button with my thumb. "I don't think so," I said. The hairs on the back of my neck stood up.

"I think so," he said. He took another step forward. I raised the can of spray.

"This doesn't have to get ugly," I said. "Just turn around and -"

I didn't get any warning. My vision went dark and close as a bag went over my head from behind.

Eric Plume

Chapter 11

My body froze as my world went from tension to violence. It happens.

Someone got hold of me from behind; a bear-hug, sloppy but hard enough to make me lose the pepper spray. He tried to pick me up. That shook the cobwebs out of my mind as survival instinct re-asserted itself, adrenaline shooting through my veins like electric current. I arched my body to make some space and rammed an elbow backwards as hard as I could.

I'm five-five and I don't work out much, but no one has ever accused me of being a waif. I felt a jolt as my elbow struck home, heard a grunt, and the arms loosened. I reached backwards, felt denim and a zipper under my fingers and squeezed. Hard, with a twist. The grunt became a scream and the arms holding me went away. I reached for the hood.

A bomb went off behind my eyes as a club struck me in the back of the head. I fell down hard enough that my hands and knees gave skin to the pavement. A hand grabbed my ankle and I threw a kick that way with my other leg, spitting half-formed curses; it connected and there was a confusion of swearing, then someone kicked me in the ribs and I lost all the air in my chest. I stayed down. My body didn't give me a choice.

Snick.

Few sounds are as distinctive as the sound of a push-button knife. I tried to localize it, but hands lifted me up and threw me backwards. My back hit a wall and *boom* went my head as my neck snapped back. *Boom, boom,* two bright orange flashes as someone backhanded me.

"That's enough." The voice was male, and sounded bored.

"Bitch got me in the balls!" Another voice, thick with an East Europe accent and angry. hands pulled the ties on the bag tighter and I choked. Pains rattled around in my body like change in a shaken cup.

"Then be more careful next time," said Bored.

Hands grabbed the lapels of my coat and bounced me off the wall again. It hurt.

"Enough, I said." Bored again.

"*Idi na khuy.*" Angry said in a petulant tone.

"What was that?"

Silence followed. My head was hot inside the hood, dizzy and loose on my shoulders. Two sets of hands restrained me in a position that was less than comfortable. My heart pounded and it was work to get a breath.

"You're Amber Eckart," Bored said. He worried me more than the other two. Angry would talk all day long about what he would do to me, but Bored would leave me bleeding out on the bricks and not think twice about it.

"Yeah," I rasped. "If you'd like to make an appointment, my office hours -" The rest came out in a gust of air as one of my handlers gave my right arm a sharp wrench.

"That wasn't a question," he said. "Now shut up and pay attention."

A sharp, cold point appeared at the hollow of my throat. "You're poking around something that doesn't concern you," he said.

"Is this where you tell me, 'get lost or you have an accident'?"

"No, this is where you tell me who's holding your leash," Bored said.

"Can't do that," I said, "But I can scream."

A punch smashed into my ribs. I took an utterly gratuitous amount of pain served with a side order of nausea. I coughed and did my best not to puke.

"You sure?" Bored said.

I didn't have the breath to respond.

"Fuck her up," another of my assailants said. He had an accent and he also sounded angry. "Gimme the knife, I'll make this bitch talk."

"Ms. Eckart, there's no need for this." Bored ignored the suggestion about the knife, or at the least didn't take it which suited me fine. "Just give us your employer and we'll be on our way." His voice had a weird ring to it, a generic Southern jerkwater drawl that came off as fake along with something else which didn't.

"No," I said.

"Why?"

"I tell you, you kill me."

"Hmm." There was a ratcheting click, metal on metal; the sound of him closing his knife.

"Last chance, Ms. Eckart...who you working for?"

"The Easter Bunny," I said.

"Guess I gotta beat the shit out of you now," he said. I caught the other accent in his voice; East coast, New York.

"It's that tough-guy thing," I muttered.

"I'll lay off your face," he said, "you're a girl."

"And they say chivalry is dead," I managed to say, right before a fist crashed into my stomach.

I hadn't been in a fight since high school; getting beaten up was much worse than I remembered. He had fists like hammers and he worked them up and down my body, *boom boom boom,* like a boxer might work a heavy bag. The punches caught me from the bottom of my breasts to just below my navel; the low blows lifted my feet off the ground. The second punch made me puke into the bag and I gagged on it, tried breathe, tried to scream.

He left my face alone. That surprised me.

When the men holding me let me go the ground just came up to greet me with the loving gentleness that only wet pavement can have. It was the effort of ages to put air into my lungs.

A hand grabbed my hair through the hood and pulled my head off the pavement. "I hope you know we're serious," Bored said. "Don't go to the cops. Don't go on looking. Just go away. We won't tell you again."

He dropped me. My head hit the concrete. It would've hurt far worse on a different day.

It took me three tries to get the bag off my head; by

the time I did there was no one around. I lay there on the pavement while the world did revolutions around me. I watched the rain hit the puddle next to my cheek and thought about not throwing up. It didn't do any good. I rolled over and pushed myself onto all fours and heaved into the puddle. I had nothing left to bring up and it hurt, but at least I didn't have to wear it. Cold greasy sweat broke out all over my skin. I tried to find my feet, but they weren't where I'd left them; I fell down again and had to crawl to my car. I fumbled with my keys and unlocked the door and pushed myself inside, anything to get out of the rain. I shuddered with cold and pain, the smell of street scum and vomit heavy in my nose.

Somehow I drove home.

I didn't remember doing it, or even deciding to; I blinked and I was in my apartment parking lot wiping my mouth.

"Bad Amber," I muttered.

I got out of the car, trying to walk straight, really trying, but the world kept spinning and tilting; the only thing I could manage was to weave like a drunk, one foot in front of the other. The cold felt good on my face and the rain did its best to make me clean. I think Bob Dylan might have said that. Then again, maybe he didn't.

I tried to unlock my door, but my car key did not also unlock my apartment. "Stupid, stupid," I said. I laughed, and that hurt.

The door opened and I fell inside. That hurt too, but less because someone caught me.

"What the fuck!" The voice echoed like the singing on an old rock album.

"I got beat up," I said. "Don't feel so good..."

"Jesus." Drake helped me towards the couch.

"Yeah," I said, "I had a rough day on the job."

"Okay, you stay here," said Drake. "I'll call the cops."

Fear crawled out of the confusion in my head. "No. No cops. The men said no cops."

"What men?"

I blinked at him. There were two Drakes in my vision and that wasn't right. "There's dirty money and Russians, and a little old lady...I need my phone." I reached into my pocket but it was sewn shut. When had I done that? *Had* I done that?

"Damn," I said. "I need to talk to Izzy. Someone's about to be hurt." I blinked, tried to focus. Thoughts ran round and round in my head and it was hard to grab them for sentences. "They're *serious*, Drake," I said. "They said so before they beat me, and I didn't listen."

Drake got closer and looked at me. "Amber, you *aren't making any sense.*"

I started to tell him that I was fine, really truly okay, but he put his hands on my arms and that sent me back, back to the beating, and I whimpered and pushed at the hands, tried to get them off, get them *off.* But then the world disappeared in a swirl of red sparkles and the blood pounded in my head, *boom boom boom*, and I decided it was okay to check out for a few minutes.

Chapter 12

I didn't go all the way out; everything was just far away, as if my body and my mind were at each end of a long tether and I was a distant observer, floating. I watched Drake strip off my wet clothes and wrap himself and me into a blanket, which made sense because my body shook with cold and shock. The warmth of his body brought me back to mine. I blinked and the world around me was more or less normal. I sat up with my head between my knees, my old fleece blanket wrapped around me.

I took a breath. It hurt. "Okay," I said. "Okay."

"Can you hear me?" Drake's voice no longer echoed.

"Yeah." I looked down. "I'm like naked and stuff."

"You were shocky," he said, "and your clothes were soaked."

I nodded. Big mistake. The world wobbled and sprouted weird trails of light. I fought the temptation to close my eyes and instead focused on a burn in my carpet. One of my ex-boyfriends had done that with a joint. We'd fought about it. I stared at the spot until I could see straight.

"Amber, you need a hospital," said Drake.

I reached up and touched my head. He was right. A

hot lump the size of my thumb had swelled up on the back of my skull. "Ow," I said. I touched a spot under my right breast and my chest twitched. "Ow, again."

"Like I said." He crouched to my left, wearing jeans and no shirt. "Cops, hospital. We need them."

"No," I said, "and here's why." I told him what the bad guys had told me.

"So? What these assholes did is called assault, and I'm pretty sure it's still against the law."

"Drake," I said, "when in your troubles did calling the cops ever help you any?"

He blinked. "Well never, but what does -"

"I might be dealing with the same kind of people." I took a deep breath. The nausea had receded and the pain had followed suit, but I still felt awful.

He looked at me. "This has to do with your job?"

"Yep."

"So what did you do to get this shit dropped on you?"

"My guess would be I found out something someone doesn't want me to know."

"What was that?"

"Wish I knew." I pointed at my purse. "Hand me that, please."

My purse was muddy but still intact; I thanked God and the Brenthaven Company's lifetime guarantee before digging in it and coming up with a five dollar bill. I handed the money to Drake.

"Okay," I said. "I'm hiring you as a consultant. Now I can talk to you." He took the bill. "First I need to call Izzy."

"She called here, "said Drake. "I told her I hadn't seen you, and she said her and Julian were going to come here."

"I thought I told you not to pick up the phone."

Drake shrugged. "She sounded scared and I figured it might be important."

"I guess it was," I said.

After that I told him everything I knew. It didn't take long, because I didn't know all that much. Drake fetched me an ice pack and a glass of water while we talked and they helped as much as they could; by the time I was done explaining my situation I merely felt elderly as opposed to three quarters absent.

"Miserable sons of bitches," Drake muttered. "What do you need me to do?"

I smiled at him. "Glad I took you in," I said.

"Glad to be here."

I took a sip of water. My mouth tasted like a bathroom floor. "I need a shower and new clothes," I said. "Go into my office and pack up my laptop."

"We aren't staying here?"

"You Googled me and found my address, right?"

"Yeah," he said.

I stood. The world wobbled but I could handle it. My feet were unsteady but I could walk.

"You just answered your own question."

I went and found the bathroom. After shutting the door I dropped the blanket and surveyed the damage.

The mirror gave eloquent testimony to why Drake was so worried. The aging process being what it is, I wasn't fond of my naked reflection on the best of days. In addition to bulges and sags I now had purple-black bruises all over my stomach and ribs. An angry red mark stippled with violet marched from my ear to my jawline. My lip was split and there were raw patches on my palms and both my knees. I had bits of puke in my hair and down the corners of my chin. Where my flesh wasn't dirty or bruised it had a grayish pallor to it, like sooty Styrofoam.

"Yuck," I said at my reflection. At least there wasn't much swelling; with some makeup I could hide the bruises.

I ran the shower as hot as I could stand it and scrubbed away the vomit and the sweat. I turned the water to cold and ducked my head under the spray; it worked for hangovers and it didn't do a bad job on the aftermath of a beating either. After drying off I pulled on jeans and a black turtleneck. I dug out my old Flight Decks and laced them up, on the theory that steel-toed boots might come in handy. My hair was a wreck, so I raked it into a loose ponytail. The brush scraped across the lump on my head and I swore about it.

When I stepped back out Drake had my laptop bag ready. "Okay, what now?"

I sat down at the kitchen table. "In the hall closet there's a box on the top shelf marked 'documents'," I said. "Get it for me."

"What's in there?"

I sipped some water. "Insurance policy," I said. He fetched me the box. I opened it, heart pounding.

My pistol was a Heckler & Koch P7, compact and

southpaw-friendly. Mine had served its time with the West German police before my uncle had bought it; he'd given it to me after he'd heard about my career choice, but it had mainly been because the gun's oddball ergonomics hadn't agreed with him. Other than a weird purple tinge to the finish it had held up well for being over twenty years old. I broke it down and oiled it with a strange sense of foreboding. I'd never needed to carry a gun before.

I loaded my three magazines with eight 9mm cartridges, the expensive kind with a dish in the tip wide enough to mix a drink in. On impact they'd blow a hole in a human the size of a tennis ball, or so the trade publications said. I'd never had occasion to find out and hoped I could keep it that way.

Drake watched me put the rest of the gun together and load a magazine. "You think that's a good idea?"

I squeezed the grip and the slide went forward, chambering a round. "Yes, unfortunately." I popped the magazine out, pressed a final round into it and slid it back in. "I've never had to pull this on anyone, but I've never had anyone beat me up on the job either." The pistol went into a waistband holster on my left hip, the two spare magazines into a pouch on my right.

There was a knock at the door. Drake started for it but I held up a hand. "I'll get that," I said. I drew my pistol again.

"Your friends," he said.

"Maybe. Maybe not."

I got up and kept my gun aimed at the floor, trigger finger along the slide; pointing a firearm at the unknown is a bad habit to get into. A quick peek through the peephole revealed my two employees, both bundled up against weather and looking nervous. I opened the door.

Izzy's eyes went as wide as saucers when she saw my face and the gun in my hand. "Holy crap, boss."

"I know, I look horrible and shit just got real." I gave the parking lot behind them a scan. No vehicles I did not recognize. "Get inside," I said. They did. I locked the door behind them.

 We all sat down at the kitchen table. I dearly wanted some coffee and some Advil but my stomach could barely handle water.

Julian eyed the bruises on my face. "What happened?"

I was pretty sure my grin came out crooked. "An occupational hazard I've yet to warn you about."

"Shouldn't you be in the hospital?"

Drake snorted. "Apparently she thinks she's Spenser with tits."

"No," I said, "I think I'm Amber with problems."

Drake flinched. "Sorry."

I smiled. "Guys, getting the cops involved right now is pointless...what would I go to them *with*? No one saw what happened, and I didn't get a good look at any of the people who did this." I patted my hip. "Also I'm the only one here with a gun and the license to carry it."

Julian spoke. "What does that have to do with anything?"

"They might come after you next," I replied, "and these are the sort of people who won't stop unless you make them stop." I looked around the room. "Anyone still want me stuck in a hospital bed?"

No one spoke. I took it as a cue.

"I'm not trying to be Supergirl," I said. "I'm just trying to figure out what the hell is going on." I sipped some more water. It tasted like chemicals, the way everything does when your stomach is empty. "So, case stuff."

"Case stuff?" Izzy looked surprised.

"I just got the shit kicked out of me," I said, "and I would really, really like to know why."

"Okay," she said. "I broke Hastings' number. It's a go-phone."

"So that's a dead end," I said.

"Looks that way," she said.

I sighed. "Guy walks in with a fancy suit and a business card and I just buy it." I rubbed my temples with my fingertips. "From now on, we check out our clients....even when they're lawyers from a firm we know."

"So how do we find this Hastings guy?" Izzy took off her glasses, cleaning them with her t-shirt. "Everything we know about him is fake."

Julian looked up. "No, it isn't."

Everyone glanced at him. "What do you mean?"

He stopped chewing his lip. "I mean, the number...he's expecting us to call, right? And he doesn't know anything has happened. He doesn't know we know. We just like...call him and ask him to come to the office."

"I'd kiss you," I said, "but that would be wrong."

He grinned. "The answer isn't always complicated, boss."

"Glad you pay attention." I believe I've mentioned that there is nothing wrong with Julian's brain. "Okay, so we can call our friend Hastings any time we want. We'll have to decide when." I paused as a thought struck me. "Izzy, Google the name 'Andrew Stark'. You're looking for a private investigator."

She nodded and cracked her laptop. After a bit of key-tapping she leaned back from the screen. "I found a news article. Andrew Stark has been missing for about five months now. Why'd you have me look?"

I closed my eyes. "Because the same guy was looking into what we're looking into, about five months back." A charming man with a nice smile floated out of my memory banks; I did my best to ignore him. So, from the looks I saw around the table, did everyone else.

"Here's the deal," I said. "We're caught in the middle of something people are willing to kill to keep quiet. We need to find out what that is, and stay breathing in the process." I looked over at Izzy. She had gone pale. "Get us a reservation at the nearest hotel. Two rooms. I'll pay cash. We have to assume the bad guys know where we live." I stood up. "The rest of you, help me pack what I need. Drake, get Zork into his carrier."

Drake looked up. "You're taking the cat?"

"Damn right, I'm taking the cat. I'm not leaving him here to get gutted for some kind of messed-up message."

"The hotel won't like that," Julian said.

"That's unfortunate," I said.

We split up and went to packing. I packed clothes and the rest of my defensive gear; two cans of pepper spray, Flex-Cuffs, an expandable baton and a four-inch Benchmade folding knife. Julian got the other can of pepper spray. I didn't give Izzy a weapon because she wouldn't use one. I handed Drake the knife.

"No need," he said. He dug in the pocket of his jacket and came up with a small handgun. I recognized it as one of those California pocket pistols popular thirty years ago. In Drake's big hands it looked somewhat ridiculous, but a .22 or .25 could kill people just as dead as my own 9mm would if the user put the bullet in the right place.

"You've had that the whole time?"

"I bought it after that rent-a-cop shot me," he said.

"It have a provenance I should know about?"

He shrugged. "I used it to cap off some rounds at two assholes trying to rape a runaway," he said. "That count?"

"Only if you hit them," I said. I went and found my pea coat. It was stained with puke and scummy water and the left sleeve had a tear in it from elbow to shoulder. I swore and emptied its pockets, transferring the stuff to my trench coat. I looked at the gag-gift fedora and smiled.

"Hell with it," I muttered, plunking it on my head. "It's raining anyway."

Once the car was loaded I drove to the hotel Izzy had found. She'd chosen well; it was one of those non-chain places where you can drive right up to the front door. I signed the paperwork and paid cash, slipping the clerk an extra twenty to skip some of the more invasive identity procedures. By the time we got everything inside and the rooms locked I was nearly asleep on my feet.

I'd put Izzy and Julian in one room, Drake and I in the other. It wasn't until I'd hung up my coat and looked around that I realized the room had only one bed. Drake looked at me. I looked at him.

"Izzy must have assumed," I said.

"I can sleep on the floor," he said.

"You can," I replied, "but you aren't going to."

"You sure?"

"You've done enough sleeping on the ground," I

said. "There's more than enough room for both of us."

I grabbed my bag and went to get ready for bed, changing into a set of sweats and a long sleeved t-shirt. By the time I got back out Drake had the sheets arranged and was under them. I set my pistol and spare magazines on the nightstand where I could reach them and crawled in beside him, too tired to feel any awkwardness about splitting a bed with a man. Indeed I was glad he was there; in the quiet darkness of the hotel room my mind was full of angry voices and my bruises twinged in time to ugly memories edged in red. I found myself sliding closer to Drake, shivering under the blankets in a way which had nothing to do with being cold.

He didn't say anything. He just wrapped an arm over me, careful not to bump any of my bruises, and pulled me all the way close. He held me until I stopped shaking and fell asleep.

Chapter 13

I woke up the next morning feeling like a failed suicide. My first considered action was to groan and stick my head underneath the pillow.

"Morning," I heard Drake say.

I muttered an inarticulate string of syllables in response, but managed to peel myself out of the bed's warm embrace after a few tries. I smelled coffee. It was a good motivator.

Drake was sitting at the little table all hotels seem to have. There was a paper bag with coffee and what appeared to be cheese-stuffed croissants. I sat down and sipped at my coffee, careful to take small bites of the pastry; I was hungry enough to feel spaced and dizzy but I didn't want breakfast to come right back out. As was his custom Zork wandered in around my chair legs looking for crumbs. The move to the hotel room hadn't fazed him much. I wondered sometimes if anything except vet visits ever would.

Drake warmed his hands with his coffee mug. "So what happens now?"

"We go to the office and set a trap for Hastings." I sipped some coffee. "Also, I've got a list of phone calls to make and leads to chase down."

"Is this how your job usually is?"

I laughed. It was brittle. "Hell no. I've never had a case get this pear-shaped before."

"Comforting," he said.

I set my coffee aside. "If you want to go, you can go," I said. "So far no one knows you're involved. I wouldn't take it personally."

"I'm not going anywhere," he said.

For some reason my face grew warm. "Sense of justice?"

"Call it a displaced need for balls-kicking," he said.

"That's as good a reason as any," I said.

I finished breakfast and readied myself for the day, doing my best to hide the bruises on my face with cosmetics; I looked like the bad end of a failed marriage but it could not be helped. We rallied the troops and headed for the office. I made sure to take Zork with us; there was no telling what might happen if we left him at the hotel room.

When we got there the door was locked and the security system armed, but I still went in first with my gun in my hand. I checked every room, every closet, even poked my head into the room we stored case files in. No one jumped out at me. I came back to the front door.

"It's clear," I told them. They all hustled inside.

Drake looked around the office. "What should I do?"

I shrugged. "You any good with computers?"

"I know my way around online," he said.

"Good. See if Izzy needs a hand." I handed him my stack of notes from yesterday's investigating, as well as a thumb drive. "All my notes and the pictures I took. Izzy's got a bunch of information on the development trying to bulldoze Kitsmiller's home. You two get to see where this all fits in." He nodded and disappeared into my office.

Julian looked lost. I went over to his desk. "I want you to try and reach a lawyer named Maria Rosales," I said. "She works for BC & C, and she was apparently handling Kitsmiller's case. See if you can find out how Hastings ended up with the files."

"What should I tell her?"

"As little as you can," I said. "I don't think BC & C would get involved in corporate espionage but we don't know that for sure."

"That's going to be tricky," he said.

"Pretend she's a hot young thing and you're trying to talk her out of her underwear," I said.

He laughed. The laughter was strained; the tension of last night was plain on his face.

"We'll get through this," I said. "We always do."

With that I let my employees carry out their orders and sat in the conference room for a good think. Sitting didn't work so I stood up and paced instead.

There were a good many angles on my case and almost none of them lined up. Big developments squeezing the little homeowner were hardly an earth-shattering development, but why was the bank involved in it? Our preliminary research had shown two discordant facts: Fact One, there was not much connection between First American and the development group Ironhorse had put together. Fact Two, the banks - and the realtors - had sold the properties to the development at or below market value...which ran counter to any business sense I'd developed. If you have a hot property and know it, you mark it up to hell and gone. Ironhorse's development was hardly a secret; articles about it were all over the Internet. So why would a bank pass up a chance to make more money?

And then there was the matter of the gangsters who had beaten me up. From Kitsmiller's testimony regarding her harassment it was quite likely the same group that bothered her had bothered me. Sure, a gang enforcing the will of the rich and powerful was a common enough staple in fiction...but this was reality, and the reality was that such behavior was too easily stopped by law enforcement. So why were Russian gang kids involved in matters? It made very little sense.

I sighed, realizing I was just delaying the inevitable necessity of confronting my fake client. I was scared and didn't want to admit it. I pulled out my pistol, checked the magazine and put it back; I knew damn well the thing was loaded, but checking reminded my fears that I had it. "You're armed now," I said to myself. "You're armed and you're aware. So get on with what needs doing, or admit defeat and call the cops."

I rounded up the troops and brought them back into the conference room for planning. I'd never been good at admitting defeat.

"Okay," I said, "here's how we're going to play this. I'll call Hastings and tell him I've got a witness, someone who wants to give a statement and that it'd be easier if he were here. Then we start asking him what's really going on."

Julian raised a hand. "Question...how do we get him to talk?"

I shrugged. "We handcuff the bastard to a chair until he does," I said.

Julian winced. "Is that legal?"

"About as legal as pretending to be a lawyer," I said.

I saw Drake grin, but he didn't say anything.

"We have every reason to believe that Hastings is up to something illegal...my guess is some form of corporate espionage, but who knows?" I took off my coat. "If he doesn't talk to us, we call the police and let them handle it."

Julian looked confused. "Boss, I thought you said -"

"-that getting the cops involved wasn't an option?" I sighed. "Julian, you do realize that if Hastings *is* up to something illegal we don't get to keep the money he gave us, right?"

"...oh."

"Thus why I want to at least try to get answers before I go playing the good citizen," I said. "Being law-abiding is great and all, but we need to get paid."

Izzy spoke up. "I think we need to be careful, boss. I did some more poking around about that Stark guy."

"And?"

"And there's next to nothing," she said. "I found one news article and a couple of blogs on it...apparently he was last seen in West Seattle, but there was no mention of the development or of mortgage fraud."

"Interesting," I said.

That statement sobered everyone. I picked up my phone and punched in Hastings' number. I heard three rings before a familiar male voice answered.

"Hastings," he said.

"It's Amber Eckart. I've got a witness with some pertinent information...an employee at the bank who's having second thoughts."

"That's great news," he said. "Get a statement from him and send it along."

"Not that simple," I said. "He wants to be assured that he'll be protected from his former employers. Apparently they aren't nice people."

There was a short silence."What do you need me to do?"

"Come down to my office and reassure him," I said.

Another, longer pause. I was starting to think he wasn't going to buy it when I heard him say,"That's fine. I'll be by in an hour."

"I'll keep him here." We exchanged polite goodbyes and I hung up.

"He buy it?" Izzy, from the doorway.

"He did," I said.

Izzy hugged herself and looked at the floor. I was reminded of how young she was, and how vulnerable. "Boss," she said in a small voice, "what happens if he...you know, gets violent?"

"I get violent back," I said. I stood and walked over to her. "Izzy, if anyone wants to hurt you they have to talk to me first, okay?"

She shrugged. "You let people hurt *you*," she said.

I patted the butt of my gun. "Momentary lapse. It won't happen again."

"I hope not," she said.

We got ready for Hastings. I gave Drake the knife and the Flex-cuffs. Julian got a cell phone and orders to split if he heard gunfire, calling the cops on his way out the door. Guns made Seattle PD react in a big awful hurry. I hoped things wouldn't get to that point but there was no telling what might happen.

Amazing how many minutes can be in an hour when one is waiting. I drummed my finger on my desk and tried to look nonchalant. After all, the troops were watching. My phone buzzed. I picked it up. Izzy.

Whered you meet Drake? He's cute. :3

We're just friends, I texted back. **I knew Drake in college. We studied together.**

Oh. Okay, cool. >:)

I smiled. **One more thing. The surveillance system running?**

Yeah want me to disable it?

I smiled. **No I want you to set it to record.**

KK

With that we waited, Drake and me in the conference room, Izzy in the office, and Julian out front, all of us ready to pretend everything was business as usual. Five minutes before the hour I heard the front door open and Hastings' friendly baritone. I took my gun out of its holster and put it in my lap.

The conference door opened and Hastings walked in. He had on the same suit as the first time we met, but a different tie. He saw Drake and nodded. "This who you wanted me to see?"

I swung the H & K up and pointed it at him. "No, this is."

He didn't freeze the way normal people did when confronted with a gun; instead his body adopted the terse fluidity common to the well-trained. His feet went apart, his head dipped and his right hand went for his waistline all at the same instant, two fingers moving his jacket out of the way. If I hadn't had my gun out he might've made it. I squeezed the grip on my pistol; there was a *click* as the striker cocked. Hayes' hand froze in mid-action.

"I guess you can make a good decision when you try," I said.

The door behind him swung shut. He didn't take his eyes off my gun. "What the hell are you doing?"

"Finding answers," I said. "Both hands up against the wall. Now."

"Are you out of your goddamned mind?" he said, but he did as he was told. I nodded to Drake and he patted him down, pausing at his waistband.

"Well, look what we have here," Drake said.

Drake pulled a clip-on holster off Hastings' belt and put it on my conference table. I glanced at it; a third generation Glock compact in quality leather. A magazine pouch and a BlackBerry were soon set next to it.

Drake claimed his wallet and stepped back, flipping through the various cards. "No carry permit," he said. That was worth a raised eyebrow; criminals did not as a rule bother with quality gun leather. Law abiding citizens got carry permits.

"Cuff him," I said.

Drake pushed him into a chair; Hastings wasn't a creampuff but Drake had four inches and twenty pounds on him. A moment with a pair of Flex-Cuffs later and Hastings was my prisoner. "What the hell is this about?" His voice came out with anger in it, but the anger didn't convince.

"That's a very good question, Mister Hastings...what *is* this about?" I stood up and walked towards him, keeping my pistol out. "Neither the Bar Association or the firm of Burton, Cameron and Clive have any clue who you are," I said. "The money you paid me with came from a bank in the Caymans. Then last night some very nasty men cornered me, threw me one hell of a beating. They wanted to know who I was working for."

I sat on the edge of the table. "And hey, guess what...so do I."

Out of nowhere his face broke into a smile. "You would have been wasted on the Lynden police, Ms. Eckart."

His words hit me right in the pit of the stomach, just like the punches last night. I wanted to take my pistol and break his face with it. My hand went tight around the grips. I settled for holstering it instead, though with more force that was necessary.

"Listen here, asshole," I snapped, "I almost got killed last night, so I'm not in the mood for footsie. Either you tell me what this is about or I call the police and you can explain it to them." I held up my phone. "This smells like corporate espionage, and I'm thinking I want out of it." I punched buttons on my phone as Izzy and Julian came into the room.

"I wouldn't do that," Hastings said with a tight smile.

"You'd have to give me a compelling reason," I replied.

He glanced at Drake. "Your searches need work," he said. He looked back at me. "Left breast pocket."

I looked at him. "What's in there?"

He shrugged. "A reason."

I closed with him and stuck my hand in his jacket. My fingers found a square of smooth leather too small to be a wallet. I knew what it was by the feel. I pulled it out and flipped it open, tossing it on the table for everyone to see.

It was a badge.

Not just any badge, though; a gold shield,

emblazoned with the symbol and credit of the Department of Justice. Next to it was a photo and signature which stated that the bearer was an agent of the Federal Bureau of Investigation. There was a pregnant, awful silence.

"Fuck me gently with a chainsaw," I muttered.

Everyone started talking at once.

Eric Plume

Chapter 14

I let the babble happen around me while my brain shifted from first to third and mashed on the gas, staring at the badge and trying to assemble the facts I knew regarding it. It didn't take long to do. I tuned back into the conversation around me and the situation up into a solution I could use.

"-have to let him go," Julian was saying as I tuned back in, "or we go to jail."

"Hell with that," Drake said. "That badge probably isn't real."

Hastings showed teeth when he smiled. "Keep on believing that. I hear Marion's nice this time of year."

Drake didn't smile back. "So's the bottom of Elliot bay."

"Yes, threaten me. That's a great idea."

Izzy gave Drake a worried look. "Come on, let's not make this worse."

Hastings puffed up. "You people have any idea of the trouble you're in right now? I can have you all in cuffs -"

"No," I said, "I don't think so." I didn't try to talk

over anyone. I just started in and didn't stop. It was a good trick to get people to listen and it worked.

"If this was a *real* FBI operation," I said, "we'd *already* be in cuffs because there would be someone watching out for you, in case this went bad. That's how this sort of operation works, isn't it Agent..." I picked up the badge and gave it a look. HAYES, JOHNATHAN W it said. Cute. "Agent Hayes? You have all that manpower from the Seattle office...tell me, where is it? Where are all the big nasty men with the machine guns?" I made a show of looking around.

Hayes didn't respond. I kept talking.

"They aren't here because you're operating outside your jurisdiction, aren't you? I mean, what could you possibly need a shoestring investigation firm like us for...unless you're trying to do something that you aren't supposed to do, of course."

His face darkened with anger. "You stuck a gun in my face and strapped me to a chair. That's six kinds of illegal, you know. Stripping your license will be child's play."

"Bullshit," I said. "For one, you can't strip my license...all you could do is file a complaint with the state board of licensing. They'd review it, and then they'd interview me. That's the point where I'd have a chance to tell *my* half of the story. I'd certainly be sure to include the part about how you, a federal agent, came to me and lied your ass off."

"Is that supposed to be a threat?"

"No, it's due process." Despite the gravity of the situation I found myself taking a certain poisonous thrill out of our conversation. "I've got admissible proof that you gave me false credentials and paid me out of what are quite likely to be illegal funds. Then you showed up at my office wearing a gun – and I, fearing that something illegal was afoot, restrained you."

Everyone else had stayed silent, watching me. Drake's expression was unreadable. Izzy and Julian's were twin reflections of astonishment.

Hayes sputtered. "That isn't how a court would see it."

"It's fifty-fifty at best," I said, "and you know it. Besides...you really want the FBI Internal Affairs department sniffing around whatever crack-ass operation you're running?"

I sighed. "You've been watching too many movies, Hayes...or you hoped I had, I'm not sure which. You should've known better – since you pulled my file, didn't you? That's how you knew about my Lynden background, right?" I leaned forward. "Tell me...what federal crime was I under suspicion of committing?"

"Recent developments in DC," Hayes said, "have made getting personal information easier for people in my profession."

"I'm well aware of the Patriot Act, Agent Hayes...but my question still stands."

His face turned red and he looked at the floor.

"You submitted a false report," I said.

He didn't say anything. I took two steps across the room, got his chin in my hands and made him look at me.

"This cowboy-cop shit might fly in Hollywood, but we're in the really-real world. You know, where little people like me have rights. As someone who knows I have six generations of law enforcement in my family tree, you should've assumed I'd be aware of that. But you didn't. That's why you're the one tied to a chair and I'm the one telling you how badly you fucked up."

I let go of his face. "Now, will you stop trying to scare me and tell me what is really going on before I call Seattle PD and have *them* deal with you?" I took a step back. "Because something tells me, Agent Hayes, that they know who are you are and they don't like you."

He deflated. "First, untie me."

"You aren't in a position to negotiate," I said. I picked up the badge and tossed it to Izzy. She caught it by reflex. "Find out if this guy really is who that says he is."

She nodded and scurried off towards her computer. I leaned against the table and watched as Hayes' face ran through anger, shame, and finally acceptance.

"Definitely wasted on Lynden," he said.

I ignored him. I'd already made one slip and that was two too many. "Talk," I said. "What is this all about?"

"Exactly what I told you it was," Hayes said. "If you've been poking around enough to suffer a beating, you've found that out already."

"There are some shady shenanigans afoot, I won't deny that." I paused as a thought struck me. "You used Kitsmiller on purpose, didn't you?"

"I don't know what you're talking about." He shifted in his seat. Drake had made the cuffs too tight, but I really didn't care too much about that.

"Bullshit."

"I didn't use her," he said.

"Bullshit again," I shot back. "Hayes, you ran down the list of people affected and picked the most pathetic case you could find...knowing that I, being the person with all that public service in my blood, wouldn't be able to walk away."

He didn't respond. He didn't have to. His answer came from how he didn't meet my eyes.

Julian looked at him with an expression of contrived solemnity. He raised one eyebrow and said, in a dead-on George Takei impression, "You, sir, are a douchebag."

I didn't giggle. Tough gumshoes don't giggle. It's bad for the image. I wanted to, though.

"Look," Hayes said, "this fraud is *really happening.* I didn't make all that up, did I?"

"No," I said, "you didn't. So why in the name of fuck are you getting me involved?"

He shook his head. "Because the Seattle police are in on it somehow." He shifted his arms again and glared at Drake. Drake smiled at him. He turned back to me. "You were smart not to go to the cops about your assault, Eckart. They wouldn't have helped you. Oh, they'd have filed a report and made all the right noises...just like they did with

Kitsmiller. In the meantime, the same nasty men you met would give you a more permanent version of what you got last night...And Seattle PD would do piss-all about it."

I nodded. "Like they did with Andrew Stark," I said. "Tell me, what line did you feed him?"

Hayes winced. "None," he said. "Stark was working for me directly when he disappeared. I made the mistake of sharing the operation with the city police...you know, like I'm supposed to do?"

"Okay, so if SPD is bent why not take the fact to your superiors?"

He shrugged as much as the cuffs would allow him to. "There's what you know and there's what you can prove."

"So you cooked up a story and dropped my firm in a blender," I said.

"I tried to warn you," he said. "If you want to walk away you can. Keep the money. Just cut me loose and we'll both forget about it."

My eyes narrowed. "Hayes," I snarled, "you feed me one more line of crap and so help me I'll clean your teeth with my boot. I've already become a known quantity to whatever group is running this scheme...tell me, you really think they'd leave me alone even if I did walk away?"

"All right," he said. "You want a deal? Here's a deal. Someone is kicking people out of their homes, buying off the police and burying people who get in their way. I know what's happening but not who's doing it or how. You find out what I want to know." His stare was hot.

"That's a bit outside the scope of our normal work," I said.

"Name your price," he said.

"That's more like it."

I tapped my finger against my chin and thought about it for long enough that people in the room started to fidget. "Okay. Here's what I want." I ticked off each point on my fingertips.

"One. I want an expense account and I want it to be large. I won't have time to fill out paperwork and I doubt you'd need it in any case. This will get pricey. I hope you realize that."

He shrugged. "Easy enough."

"Two. I've got a government-backed loan I took out to keep my firm running and a set of student loans I'm in danger of defaulting on. I want those paid in full. I want tax paperwork, the whole nine yards."

He flinched, but I didn't stop there.

"Three, I want a contract. You'll sign it, and so will I. We'll make copies, and Izzy here will notarize each. My copy will be in a secure location you don't get to know about. You fuck with me on this in any way and I'll mail that contract to your superior, once Izzy finds out who it is...and she will. What I'll be doing is legal on my end, just not on yours."

His smile was wry. "Anything else?"

"I think that'll do it."

Izzy came back into the office. "He checks out," she said. "Unless the real FBI Agent Hayes has an evil twin or something."

"That's possible, considering the situation," I said.

"I hope you're quite finished," Hayes said. "Now, what makes you think I'm going to accede to those kinds of demands? Add it all up and you're asking for a little over a hundred ten thousand."

I smiled. "Because if you don't, I'll make sure the whole world knows about Andrew Stark."

I watched as Hayes' jaw dropped open.

"Riddle me this, Secret Agent Man...Was it legal for you to put a private citizen at risk like that? Was it ethical? Would the FBI like that you did it to become public knowledge?" His face had gone from red to white. "Or, how about the fact that you've been pulling files on citizens without any reason whatsoever...even stuff you shouldn't have access to, like my fucking financial records? Or are you going to try and tell me that hundred and ten-k amount you just named was a lucky guess?"

"I...you can't *do* that."

I laughed. "Hayes, this is the Internet age. I can do it in fifteen minutes with *this*." I held up my phone.

"Bullshit," he said.

I spoke to my assistant but stared straight at the man tied to my chair. "Izzy, how public could we make what we're talking about here?"

Izzy snorted. "Are you kidding? It'd be on CNN in four hours." Her smile was a delicious slice of mischief. "Government dick-fuckery is trending right now."

Hayes recovered his poise. "I don't believe you," he said.

"That's unfortunate," I said.

A long silence followed. I stared at Hayes. He stared at me. The only sound was that of a computer's cooling fan, louder than a jet engine in the stillness as the room held its breath. Finally Hayes slowly shook his head. "You," he said in a tone somewhere between wonder and irritation, "are one cast-iron piece of bitch meat."

"I take it you agree to my terms."

"Yes...but you'd better deliver."

I smiled. "I always deliver, Agent Hayes."

Hayes shifted against the cuffs again. "Now, you want to let me out of these damn things or are you waiting for them to give me gangrene?"

"One sign of trouble and I'll have Drake mummify you in speed tape." I turned to Drake and tossed him my folding knife. "Cut him loose."

Drake flicked open the knife and slit the cuffs, leaving the knife open just long enough for Hayes to get a good look at it before ostentatiously closing it and clipping it to his belt. Hayes stood up and flexed his hands. He and Drake traded alpha-male power glances. I let it happen.

"Now we draw up that contract," I said.

And we did. It took a good deal less time than I thought, but then again it was, on the surface, a fairly standard contract. It just covered some fairly non-standard circumstances. I made him sign it first. He picked up the pen and paused.

"I thought you wanted the expense account," he said.

"I'll give you an hour," I said. "If you don't show up, I'll shred the contract and call Seattle PD. I'm sure they'd have a fun time with a cowboy like you."

"Yes, because you've never bent the rules in your profession," he said as he signed his name. "As evidenced by this contract."

I picked up the pen and put my name on the dotted line. "I'm a businesswoman. You're a policeman. There's a difference, and you damn well ought to know it."

He shrugged. "Go ahead and get self-righteous if it makes you feel better," he said, folding up the contract neat as you please. "This -" he held up the contract, "- puts you just as much in the shadows as you feel I am."

I didn't like it, but he was right. I swallowed my next barb. We completed the business with the contract and Hayes made as if to go. "One more thing," I said. He turned around.

"Another request?"

"Just simple curiosity really...how did you get Kitsmiller's file from the lawyers?"

He shrugged. "I walked in, checked it out and left.

For a large law firm, Burton's security is terrible."

"So you stole it."

"I needed it."

I thought about ribbing him on that but left it alone. After all, he was right; I was walking in the shadows now, and self-righteousness wouldn't serve me. He tapped the contract to his brow in mock salute and collected his coat. "I'll be back in an hour," he said as he walked out the door. Drake closed it behind him and locked it. I turned back to Izzy.

"Did we get all that?"

She grinned. "Clear as a bell, boss."

Julian looked at me. "You were recording him?"

"The whole time," I said.

"But...isn't it illegal to record people without their knowledge?"

I shook my head and pointed behind him, at the sign which read *THESE PREMISES UNDER AUDIO AND VISUAL SURVEILLANCE.* I had stuck the sign to our inter-office bulletin board amidst all our licenses and papers we were required to display.

"There's no reasonable right to privacy in a place of business," I said, "and Hayes was notified of the recording by that sign. The fact that Mister Federal Agent didn't pay attention to his surroundings is his problem, not mine."

"But...Isn't that sign a little hard to see?."

"The law is like the Purity Test, Julian...All technicalities count." I gave him my sweetest eyelash-bat.

"Remind me never to play poker with you," Drake said with a grin.

Julian's eyes were the size of boiled eggs. "Holy crap. Where do you come up with this stuff, boss?"

"I come up with it as I'm laying it out," I said. "Julian, sometimes to win you just have to talk faster than the other person can think."

It was Izzy's turn to chew her lip. "So what now?"

"Now," I said as I went to the door, "We have our own little talk."

Chapter 15

I stepped outside and dug out the cigarettes I'd bought to befriend Tiera. I lit one and watched the clouds scud across the sky in a lazy swirl. Burnt tobacco tasted a good deal less terrible now that my life was on the line. I'd never noticed that before, but then again I'd never lit up right after a life-threatening situation either. The last of the cigarette turned to ash and smoke while I put my thoughts in order. When it was all the way gone I flicked the filter into a puddle and headed back inside.

Everyone was waiting in the conference room when I got back; three sets of eyes followed me with three sets of emotions as I walked in and set down my coat. I gave them each a look in turn, trying to gauge them. A good leader knows his troops, my uncle always used to say.

Julian had the nervous excitment of a young idealist. Izzy was scared. Drake, I couldn't read, but I could tell he wasn't afraid. That made sense; after all, what did he have to lose?

"Okay," I said, "now you all have a decision to make."

"I think you kinda made it already," Julian said.

"For myself, certainly," I said. "Now its your turn."

"Huh?"

I smiled. "Guys, this is way too serious for executive privilege. I'm your employer, not your military commander. I can't order you to risk your lives for me."

Izzy blinked. "Boss, what are you saying?"

"I'm saying that if anyone here wants to walk away, they can." Julian went to speak. I raised my hand. "Before any of you say anything, I want you to know two simple facts." I stood up. "One, I really mean it about leaving. Izzy, Julian, you both have some vacation time coming. If you want to take it now, take it now. I won't be insulted. If anything, I'll be relieved I'm not risking your lives."

Silence. I continued.

"Two, this situation is dangerous. Real, no-shit dangerous...and once you come across the line, the only way out is through. I can't say it any clearer than that."

"Why don't you leave, boss?" Julian's voice was quiet.

"Because I can't," I said. "The bad guys know my face and they know I know things they don't want me to. I walk away now and either a gang kid puts a bullet in my back or some rich asshole takes my life apart one lawsuit at a time."

I saw Drake flinch.

"I'm thirty-three, single and poor," I said. "I've got a useless art degree and every red cent I could chase down tied up right here. I'm not about to walk away from seven years hard work just because me staying is inconvenient to somebody." A tide of emotion swelled against my ribs like heartburn. "This business is my life. Right or wrong, I'll fight for it."

Drake's face had a set to it one usually saw in preachers, the kind who really believe. "Then I'm still not going anywhere."

"Hell yeah, boss," Julian said. "Count me in."

Izzy looked at Julian. "This isn't a movie, man. Look what happened to that Stark guy."

"I can handle it," Julian said.

Izzy looked up at me. "Boss, you don't have to do this. Let's just go to the cops."

Julian snorted. "You heard that Hayes guy...the cops are in on it."

"We don't *know* that," Izzy said. "He's probably lying...he's done it a bunch already."

All three of them started to talk at once and I let them argue it out. It did not take long for people to start repeating themselves; after all, it was a binary solution and there is only so long that such situations can be debated.

"Guys, I've made my choice. You need to make yours. If you want to go, I'm okay with that. If you want to stay, great...but you need to be one hundred percent about it. I'll need to be able to depend on you, even when things get scary." I gave Julian a hard look. "And they will."

Julian nodded. "I'm still in."

Drake spoke next. "Me too."

Izzy stared at the tabletop for a long moment. Finally she sighed. "If you're staying, boss, so am I."

"You sure?"

She looked up at me, eyes shining. "You know I don't have anywhere else to go either."

I tried not to wince. It was true, she didn't. But one reality about objective fact is how there's no sense in regretting its existence. I nodded, getting a warm sensation in the pit of my stomach. These were my people, and they were proving it in the clinch. "Okay then. Time to go to work."

"Izzy, two things...one, get Drake some paperwork and list him as a proper employee." I smiled at Drake. "I hope we can discuss pay later."

He spread his hands. "Look, I'm not expecting you to give me a job."

"Drake, there are some serious rules about this kind of work. If you are going to help, you need to be on my payroll." I gave each of them a look in turn. "One thing to be clear on, guys, we play this by the rules whenever possible. I don't want to end up in jail any more than I want to end up in the ground."

Drake nodded. "I won't turn down some work," he said.

"Julian, get Drake a new employee pamphlet and get him all in our system. Drake, fill out the forms Izzy gives you." They both nodded and headed back out to Julian's desk.

I turned back to Izzy. "Before everything went to shit, you said you'd found out information on the big man behind the development. I guess I need that now."

Izzy cracked open her laptop. "The guy's name is Govrolev...Anatoliy Il'ych Govrolev. He came over to the States in 1993, worked for a few construction companies as a laborer and foreman before starting his own business in '96."

"That'd be Ironhorse?"

"Yeah."

I took a look over Izzy's shoulder at a picture of Govrolev himself. He was in his middle fifties, built like a bricklayer but with the dignified good looks some older men are lucky enough to ease into. His broad face had a gentle cast to it at odds with his bulk; he didn't look like a gangster, but successful gangsters seldom did.

"The company struggled for a while, then went public in 2004. The stock offering went better than expected and they were able to expand their operations. I also found some articles describing them having to fend off lawsuits. So maybe they are dirty after all."

"I doubt it." I started pacing again. I wanted a cigarette but resolved then and there not to start smoking in the office. "Remember, Izzy...*We've* been sued a couple of times too. Anyone who's been in business longer than a couple of years probably has a few lawsuits in their history."

"So it doesn't mean anything?"

"Not by itself it doesn't. How did the suits play out?" Pace, pace.

Izzy scanned her screen for a moment or two. "All over the map."

"Show me," I said. She spun her laptop around and I started reading though the articles.

There is an art to picking facts out of a pile of irrelevancies; I won't say I've mastered it but its a skill any investigator must possess. I skimmed through all the journalism and saw the pattern; anytime Ironhorse was obviously to blame, they settled out of court quite quickly and the settlement amounts were generous. However, in cases where it was more of an open question where to put the fault, Ironhorse fought to the bitter end - including one case that cost them more in legal fees than the settlement was worth. Govrolev himself was quoted in the final article. I read it. *"Reputation is worth more than money,"* He had said. *" If my company has erred, I will pay. But I will not admit fault where there is none."* I pondered that.

"Govrolev's a fighter," I said. "He knows when to stand and when to back down."

"How do you figure?" Izzy cleaned her glasses on a tissue.

"Because I feel the same way," I said.

Drake and Julian came back into the conference room. "I got him all squared away," Julian said.

"Welcome aboard," I said, and Drake smiled at me.

I brought them all up to speed; it did not take long, but that was because there wasn't much to share.

"So what about the kids that beat you up," Drake said. "You think they work for this Govrolev character?"

"That'd be the obvious answer," I said.

"But you don't think so?" Julian said.

I shrugged. "I don't know enough to decide one way or the other." I turned to Izzy. "You know more about Russian gangs than the rest of us. Any notions?"

Izzy was quiet for a moment and I knew why. Her knowledge about Russian criminals came from being raised around them; she didn't like talking about it and I didn't blame her. "Well," she said, "a businessman using *gopniki* to get things done would be pretty normal in Russia, but not here."

Drake blinked. "*Gopniki?*"

"Gangstas," Izzy said, "only Russian."

"Got it," he said.

"Anyhow," I said, "you don't think it's likely?"

"For one of the mob guys, it wouldn't be, not here," Izzy said. "But you don't have to be in a mafia to do bad things, right?"

"No you don't," I said. "I guess we need more information. Let's table that for the moment.

Anything else?"

Izzy snapped her fingers. "Jeez. All this other stuff...I forgot something I was gonna tell you." She started frantically moving her mouse around. "Remember how you told me to look into that Hansen guy?"

It took me a minute to remember his name. "Oh right...the loan officer on Kitsmiller's foreclosure. Weston's, too."

Izzy smiled like a cat in cream. "Nope, Hansen the senior regional manager who handled all the foreclosures."

I blinked. "What do you mean, 'all'?"

"Every single foreclosed property Ironhorse bought went through his department. And, get this...remember how there were a bunch of houses First American didn't hold the mortgages on?"

I nodded.

Izzy's grin got wider. "Hansen authorized the purchase of them," she said. "Paid more than they were worth too, in a couple of cases."

Drake leaned back. "Son of a bitch," he said.

"Yeah," I said. "Hansen gets the mortgages under First American's control, then jiggers the paperwork so that the bank can foreclose...and Ironhorse swoops in and buys the property." I squeezed Izzy's shoulder. "Good work, girl."

She blushed. "I couldn't sleep."

"There's just one problem here," I said. "The bank didn't mark up the properties at all. According to what you found, Izzy, the bank lost money on some of the deals."

"About half of them, yeah," she said.

"Why would they do that?" Julian said.

"Good question," I said.

"Whether or not the bank profited," Drake said, "I know for a fact that sort of shit's illegal."

"Oh it is," I said. "But it'll be hard as hell to prove." I started pacing back and forth, resisting the urge to light up another cigarette. "Land development deals are Byzantine...sure we can see they're *doing* this, but who exactly is responsible? How do we bring them into court? We go after Hansen directly, he'll pick a subordinate and drop the blame on their head. Same thing with this Govrolev guy.

"There's a reason the Mafia got into construction over in New York, why half the Miami skyline was built by the coke trade," I said. "A company can hide all the lawbreaking it wants to in a deal this size. Just figuring out who owns what would take an army of accountants big enough to take over China."

"So other than starting a land war in Asia," Drake said with a grin, "what do we do?"

"Complexity cuts both ways," I said. "Somewhere in this mess someone's bound to have gotten careless."

Izzy cracked her knuckles. "So we keep digging?"

"Yeah," I said. "And Izzy...you know how I'm always reminding you to keep your computer work within the law?"

"Yeah?"

"Well, I'm not saying it now."

Izzy's eyes gleamed. "Message received, boss."

There was a knock at the door. I went and answered it to find Hayes waiting on the stoop. "You're early," I said.

"Better than late," he said. He handed me an unmarked envelope. I opened it to find a credit card. DAVIS-CALLION CORPORATION was printed in raised capitals below the number. I glanced at Hayes.

"How much do I get?"

He shrugged. "You couldn't max it out if you tried."

"My tax dollars," I said, though I was pretty sure the money came from some other source; tax dollars left paper trails and I was sure the owners of this account didn't want that. Touching the card gave me an unpleasant tingling feeling; I was definitely outside the law now, no question about it.

"You have slightly less than two weeks," he said. "I'll leave you to your work."

With that he walked away and was gone like he'd never been there at all.

Chapter 16

We spent the rest of the day organizing what we had and filling in what we didn't, as much as we could from the safety of the office. Soon I'd have to go out and actually pound pavement, but with goons gunning for us I didn't want to risk it until I had something definite to hunt for. In this business it's considered poor form to let the pavement pound you back.

The development deal proved every bit as complicated as I had predicted, and even bigger than I'd feared; three major banks, twenty-six investment firms and over one hundred sub-contractors were involved. Ironhorse was acting as both broker and general contractor, coordinating the lesser contractors and providing the general labor for all the steel fabrication. The company stood to make out like a bandit on the deal, and so did the investors.

"Seven hundred fifty million dollars," I said. "That's what's changing hands here. Add up all the stock options and rent and it could be double that over a few years."

Drake whistled. "No wonder people are getting killed over this."

Izzy gave me a worried look. "Gee, boss...are you *sure* we can't just walk?"

"You want them to get away with this stuff?" Julian's voice was scornful.

"I want to keep living," Izzy shot back.

I closed my eyes and leaned back. Putting in a full day's work hadn't gone well with a beating. "We always deliver," I said. "Besides, would you guys rather tangle with the FBI?"

No one had anything to say to that. I sighed. "Okay, I'm done playing Supergirl for one day. Tomorrow, Drake and I will go stake out Hansen's house...it's up in Hunt's Point, so I'll have to do some work for a cover story."

I turned to Izzy. "I want to know if Hansen and Govrolev have any connection at all...financial, personal, social, anything. If they were ever in the same room at the same time I want to know where and why. Also, if we get any good pictures on the stakeout I'll want you to analyze them."

"You got it," she said.

Julian looked at me. "What do I do?"

"You," I said, "get to help with the stakeout. I'll need someone who can go mobile in case Hansen leaves the house, and you're it."

He grinned. "Awesome."

We spent the last half hour loading everything related to the case into the trunk of my car before we left; a bit of a tight fit with my cat and all our stuff but it couldn't be helped. I made sure Izzy and Julian grabbed the spare sets of clothes they kept at the office for emergencies; at some point I'd make sure to get them some other stuff but right now survival and safe haven were the primary imperatives.

I let Drake drive us, ostensibly so I could watch out for tails but really because my motor skills weren't up to controlling a car. As we approached our hotel I saw a van parked across the street, between two streetlights. "Keep driving," I told Drake.

He did as he was told. "What's going on?"

I watched through the mirror. The van did not follow. "They've got the hotel staked out," I said.

Drake swore. Izzy stared out the window with an empty expression. "Jesus," Julian muttered.

"Head towards Sea-Tac," I told Drake. I took out my iPhone and the credit card Hayes had given me, using the browser to get the number for the Doubletree Hotel. "Julian," I said as I worked my fingers across the little screen, "take your piercings out and pull your hair back. I need you to look respectable."

He blinked. "Why?"

"Because when we get where we're going you'll need to look like a high-powered executive assistant," I replied, punching in the number the browser told me to.

It was the work of a few moments to get last-minute registration at the Doubletree, for four very tired Davis-Callion Corporation salespeople. I told Drake to park the car at the Denny's across the street and gave Julian his instructions as I wriggled out of my trench coat. "Put this on and button it all the way up," I said. "Give them the card and the name on it, tell them you need four keys. If they ask where the rest of us are, tell them we're across the street having dinner. Text me when you have the keys, and be sure to ask for a parking pass."

Drake looked at me. "Why'd you give him your coat?"

"High-powered executive assistants don't wear skinny jeans and Atreyu t-shirts," I said.

Julian slipped into my coat and headed for the crosswalk. I grabbed one of the cigarettes out of the center console and lit it.

"Why'd you send him?" Drake watched him dart

across the street, borrowed coat flapping in the rainy breeze.

I shrugged. "You look like a cage fighter, Izzy hates talking to strangers and my face is ground hamburger," I replied. "Julian's the least memorable of us, and he's the one the bad guys are least likely to know about."

"...and none of them will know about the company name," Izzy said. "They won't have a clue where we are."

"Not to mention they won't dare try something at a nice hotel right near the airport even if they *could* find us," I replied.

My phone buzzed. **Got the keys, we're in Wing 3. This hotel is HUGE O.o**

OMW, I sent back.

It took some careful maneuvering to get us, Zork, and all our stuff up into our rooms without attracting any attention. I'd selected the Doubletree on purpose; it was the only hotel I could think of large enough to have multiple entrances. I didn't want the front desk seeing us toting a suspiciously cat-carrier-shaped box, from which could be heard the occasional meow.

I got Izzy and Julian settled; they both had the

nervous excitement of young people in danger.

"You guys get hungry, hit room service," I told them. "Don't worry about the bill. Just remember, we've got an early morning tomorrow...Hansen might be an early riser so I want to be in position before he wakes up."

Julian nodded. "What should I wear?"

"Warm, comfortable clothes," I said. "You'll be doing a lot of sitting. We'll talk about it more in the morning."

Drake had been nice enough to get my stuff and my cat stowed away in the other room by the time I got in there. I hung out the DO NOT DISTURB sign and made arrangements for a 4:30 am wakeup call.

And then there was nothing left to do.

I sat on the corner of the bed, wrapping my arms around my aching ribs as the gravity of my situation caught up with me. Andy Stark's face made a hazy memory in the back of my mind, but it was there and it didn't go away.

Drake came out of the bathroom and saw me sitting there. "You okay?"

"Nope," I said in a small voice.

He sat down next to me. "Can I do anything?"

"Pour me a drink, please." It was work to talk.

He walked over to the minibar. "What's your pleasure?"

"The strongest thing in there," I said.

He came back with something brown in a water glass. I took three quick swallows and closed my eyes as the liquor burn expanded in my stomach like a firebomb. When I opened them I realized the glass in my hand was empty. It's a bad sign, drinking 151 rum neat and not caring.

I could see worry on Drake's face. "Feel better?"

"Not really," I said, as a brittle giggle threatened to worm its way out of my chest. I forced it down. Drake was one of the troops now, and he was watching. "I'll make it."

"Can I do anything else?" I could see he was still worried.

"Not unless you can magic away this awful pain in my neck," I said.

"Want a back rub?"

I set my glass down. "Is this a trick question?"

I took my coat off and sat in front of one of the armchairs. Drake sat behind me. "Oh the hell with it," I said, pulling off my shirt. "You've already seen most of me."

"I was distracted by how you were in shock," he replied.

He went to work on my back; it hurt in that special way that a good massage tends to, which was massively preferable to the throbbing ache I'd been dealing with. My face grew warm and my fingertips tingled and for a bit I let myself forget about what was going on. For the first time in two days there was a part of me that didn't hurt. It was glorious and I enjoyed it.

"Hnnng," I said. Between the double shot of rum and the massage it was all the conversation I was capable of.

"Cross your arms in front of your chest," he murmured. I did so. I felt my bra come undone and I gasped without meaning to.

"You okay?"

I took another breath. "Yeah. It's just...been a while since anyone but me did that."

"Oh." He went to work on the knot that had been hiding under the straps. "You want me to stop?"

"Not even vaguely." I leaned into what he was doing. The top of my head tingled along with my fingertips. "I had no idea I was this good a friend to you back in the day," I said.

"If you want to know the truth," said Drake, "back then I had a massive crush on you."

I glanced over my shoulder. "No shit?"

He had a faint grin on his face. "So hard to believe? You were a college girl. You talked to me. I was seventeen and a complete nerd. Those things do not go together." He worked on my neck and I lowered my head to make it easier. "Besides, you didn't try to take advantage of me like the other girls did."

"Come on," I mumbled. "I shamelessly leaned on you for study help."

"You did your share," he said.

"I wasn't cute enough to get away with not doing it."

The pressure on my neck eased; his fingertips brushed along my shoulder blades. "Plenty cute enough for me," he said.

All of a sudden bruised ribs weren't the only reason it was hard to breathe. "A-are you hitting on me now?"

"Yeah," he murmured, caressing the skin just below my hairline, "I guess I am."

"Just checking," I whispered. We stayed like that for several long moments, him with his hand on the soft flesh of my neck and me just breathing, wondering what I should do next. The warmth in the pit of my stomach took on a different meaning. He made no advance beyond a gentle caress which raised goosebumps along my arms. It was clear that whatever happened next was my call to make.

"Oh, screw it," I whispered.

"What do you me-"

I turned around, cupped Drake's face in my hands and pressed my mouth to his. Our kiss started fragile and clumsy, but when he kissed me back a hot jot flashed through me, a sharp hungry pressure I'd all but forgotten existed. I pushed myself against him as his hands snaked into my hair, heedless of how my bra fell away. I bit his lip and pulled him towards me.

We didn't make it to the bed.

I was battered and out of practice and neither of us knew anything about the other but it didn't matter; I lost myself in the moment anyway. Afterward we wrapped arms and locked hands, my only concern the warmth of his body. We were both quiet for a long time.

"I guess...I'm okay with being hit on," I murmured into his shoulder.

He traced a fingertip along my spine. "I believe you," he said.

"Did that just happen?"

He smiled. I liked seeing it. "Christ, I hope so."

For some reason Andy Stark's face came back to me just then, and right behind it a cold hard dose of reality. I'd wagered four lives for a hundred thousand dollars, against people who in all likelihood had killed another person who'd made a similar bet. Four lives, including the one in my arms...and all of them could die if I made a single mistake. I shuddered.

"Are you okay?"

"No," I said.

"What do you need?"

It took two tries to speak.

"Permission to act like a silly girl."

"Granted," he said.

I didn't cry; what lumbered out of my back brain was an emotion way too big for tears and sobs. I just buried my face in his shoulder and shook like a leaf in a windstorm. He held me while I let it out, the two days of wet red terror I'd kept shoving aside and not looking at. *One, two, three, four*, I said to myself as I pushed the awful ugliness back down deep, down where it had to stay. For better or for worse, I didn't have time for it.

I had too much to do.

"Okay," I said, "better now." I loosened my grip on him and he did the same. He brushed a stray strand of hair out of my eyes.

"You're one gutsy woman," he said. "Anyone ever tell you that?"

"Sometimes." My voice shook. "Never after I've just wigged out in front of them."

"If I were in your shoes, I'm pretty sure I'd still be freaked."

The carpet wasn't the most comfortable place to lie. I sat up and so did he. Before he could have a good look at me, I wrapped my arms around my knees to hide myself. I couldn't remember the last time I'd been naked around a man and I was all too aware of how ugly my bruises were, how spongy my midsection was, how much of a number gravity had done on my figure.

"This was probably not a good idea," I said.

"I'd disagree," he replied.

"You're biased."

He grinned. "So are you."

I smiled back at him. I couldn't help it. He looked even better without clothes than I'd imagined. He sidled over and kissed me; he meant it to be brief, but his mouth was sweet and I kissed him back longer than he anticipated. By the time I broke it off his eyes had a molten quality to them.

I stood up. "Discuss this later?"

"Sure." He glanced at the two beds. "Where am I sleeping?"

I bent down, took his hands and pulled him upright. "With me," I said, "if you want to."

"Damn well bet I do," he said.

His hands across my hips and pulled me close. I still wasn't a waif, but Drake hoisted me into his arms without a strain and carried me to the bed.

Eric Plume

Chapter 17

Four thirty in the morning came around way too early. It always does.

I woke up to the warm weight of a man pressed against my back. It took me a minute to remember who it was and how he'd ended up in bed with me. I stayed still and thought about what had happened the previous night for several minutes. Drake, half-asleep, made an inarticulate sound and wrapped an arm across my chest. I found myself smiling. I couldn't bring myself to regret what I'd done, even though a part of me tried to.

I slipped out of bed as carefully as I could and went through my morning routine; by the time I wanted breakfast Drake had sat up and was blinking the sleep out of his eyes. I found it hard not to watch him.

"Morning," I said.

He nodded and gave me a tired smile. The following silence was as obvious as silence could be. I walked over, sat down on the corner of the bed and planted a kiss on his cheek. He blinked in surprise.

"I don't have time for one of those morning-after talks," I said. "Can you live with that?"

"How about this," he said. "You wanted it, I wanted it, we did it and we'll figure out what it means when people aren't trying to kill us."

I giggled like the last ten years hadn't happened. "Fair enough."

"One question," he said. "Will we need the extra bed tonight?"

"We'll cross that bridge when we come to it," I said.

"Okay. Breakfast?"

"God, yes."

We called for room service; I said to hell with being good and ordered the bacon, sausage, and pancakes I wanted. A day of not eating much had left my body craving calories. While I munched I sent Drake to fetch Julian and I examined Hansen's neighborhood via Google Maps.

Hunts Point was one of the richest neighborhoods in Seattle, a long thin spike of land with houses up and down both sides. Hansen's place was on a small offshoot to the east of the point proper; I made notes and copied addresses and figured out a surveillance plan.

Drake came back in with Julian in tow. He had on jeans, heavy boots and his Kevlar riding jacket. His hair was tied back and he had ditched most of his piercings. I nodded my approval. "Okay guys, here's the plan."

Drake and Julian crowded around my laptop screen. "Hansen lives here, up in Hunts Point. Now, there's only one road into and out of his neighborhood...which means, Julian, that you'll take position here." I pointed at the screen. "That's a city park...why am I putting you there?"

"It's a public place where anyone can hang out for hours and not make people nervous," Julian replied.

"Yeah," I said. "You'll stay there. Your job is to follow Hansen if he decides to leave his house today. Drake and I won't be able to manage it because of where we'll be set up."

Julian stuck his hands in his pockets. "So I just park and wait?"

"Until I tell you to move. Keep your phone handy, I'll call if I want a car tailed. I'll give you the make, color and model, after that it's your show. If you think you should get pictures, get them, but don't lose the quarry and for God's sake *don't get made*." I paused. "These people are serious, Julian."

He nodded. "I know. I won't let you down, boss."

"Good. The stakes are pretty high here."

"I get made, they might beat me up?"

"No," I said. "You get made, they kill you."

"Oh."

Drake leaned down and snagged the second-to-last piece of my bacon. He would've grabbed both but I snatched the other before he could snatch it. "Where will we be set up?"

I pointed at a patch of woods east of Hansen's home. "Here," I said. "There's a park we can leave my car at, and then it's a long hike to get where we're going. I'd park closer but there's nowhere to do it and anyway, the bad guys know what kind of car I drive. Don't want to risk them becoming suspicious."

Drake nodded as I pointed out our route. "Long hike," he said.

"Good thing you're in shape," I said.

"Good thing," he said.

I stood up. "I need to get dressed, and then we need to go to the office and collect Julian's bike and the surveillance gear, plus a few things we need for our disguise." I grinned at Drake.

After I was dressed Drake and Julian and I found our way down to the car. It was right where I left it. I gave the undercarriage a cursory glance and checked both bumpers. No dynamite or tech with flashing lights was apparent. Neither were any suspicious-looking vehicles when I looked around. Drake watched my behavior. I shrugged.

"Just because you're paranoid doesn't mean someone isn't following you," I said.

"In this case someone is," he said.

"Indeed."

Ordinarily getting from Sea Tac to Kent involved dealing with a fair measure of traffic; however, making that drive at around five in the morning meant that everyone who would normally be an annoyance was in bed. I kept yawning and ended up hitting a coffee stand for a triple-shot mocha. By the time we reached my office the coffee had kicked in and I felt a good deal better about being awake.

I made sure to check the office; the security system was still armed but it was old and probably wouldn't cause an experienced cracksman to even break stride. Nothing appeared out of place or missing, and again no one jumped out at me. It paid to be careful, however.

We loaded up the car with two cameras, two sets of marine-grade 7 x 50 binoculars and my in-the-field laptop. Drake grunted when he picked it up. "What the heck is this thing?"

"Field laptop," I said. "Water and impact proof."

"It's monstrous," he said.

"So was the price tag," I said.

Julian got a compact set of binoculars and my spare camera; it wasn't as high-res as the Canon DSLR I selected but it was much less obtrusive.

"Keep your cell phone on and handy," I said. "By my calculations you'll have less than five minutes warning before a car gets to your stakeout spot, so stay alert."

He looked up from giving his bike a once-over. "I got it, boss."

"Now, tell me the rules of tailing."

He settled his helmet on his head. "Always keep a car between me and him, don't get in front of him, change my appearance if I can, communicate wherever possible...and expect bad driving from the subject." He pulled on his gloves. "Don't let him get close enough to confront me, and document everything I can."

"Spoken like a true prodigy," I said. "Remember...if the choice is losing the subject or risking getting made, fucking well lose him. Like I said last night, these people won't hesitate to hurt you."

He flipped the visor down; it made him faceless and a good deal less young-looking. "I got this, boss."

He fired up his bike and took off. I felt a sick flutter in the pit of my stomach. The reality was that I had to use Julian this way, but my protective instincts didn't like it one bit. I could only hope he would remember his lessons.

"I sure hope you do," I said softly.

With that I went inside and dug through the back closet for all the parts to one of my favorite outdoor disguises; a Navajo-pattered sweater and Gore-Tex poncho, along with some thick waterproof boots and a set of dangly wind-chime earrings left over from college. In the back I found a waterproof parka for Drake, as well as a tie-dye bandanna, reversible to a dark bluish gray. I pulled two Audubon field guides out of the closet and handed him one.

"Bird watchers?"

"Yep. Rich hippie bird watchers." I was in the process of putting my hair in Pocahontas braids. "It's a good reason to go tromping around in the woods carrying lots of cameras and binoculars and such." I tied off the second braid end. He shrugged out of his worn out coat and swapped it for the parka I handed him.

"What happens if someone sees us and wants us to

leave?"

I shrugged. "We go, politely and with many apologies," I said. "We aren't police, and I don't want to have to show my license to a rent-a-cop. They sometimes abuse their authority."

Drake's fingers brushed his shirt where the bullet scar was. "I'm aware," he said. Suddenly he grinned. "Y'know, you ought to wear your hair like that more often."

I looked up from checking the batteries on all my devices. "Why's that?"

His grin got wider. "It's cute."

"We're on the job now, buster." I tried to be stern, I really did.

"It's still cute."

I put a multicolored stocking cap on over the braids. "You do remember that I'm wearing a gun, right?"

"You win, Pippi Longstocking."

I laughed. We got the last of the stuff into the car and headed for Hunts Point - or rather, Fairweather Nature Preserve, which was the closest public parking area I had been able to find. One of the challenges of fixed surveillance work is finding a place to park the car; people get suspicious of strange vehicles that sit for hours at the curb with people inside, doubly so when they point cameras out the window. The big firms used vans with fake company logos on the side. Being stuck with my ratty little Golf, I had to make creative use of Google Maps and occasionally take the risk of being rousted.

The park was just opening when we pulled in; there was a park ranger doing rounds and I walked up to him, all smiles and giggles, informing him of our quest for pretty bird-things and asking if it would be all right if we left the car in the lot all day. I made sure to twine the end of my braid around my finger and look vacant. The routine worked better than it usually did; I had the ranger eating out of my proverbial hand by the second sentence. It helped that he was over forty, built like a gumdrop and sporting something of a deficiency in hygiene. By the time I said my goodbyes I could have gotten his wallet with a polite request.

Drake was waiting by the corner where I'd told him to go, backpack full of camera gear braced against his knee. "No towing?"

"No towing," I said. "And you might be right about the hairstyle thing." I glanced back at the ranger, watching me and trying not to. "What's the appeal...schoolgirls?"

He donned the backpack. "Handlebars," he said.

I did not reply, being busy asking my face to stop flushing quite so bright.

It was a fair hike to get from the park to Hansen's backyard; the trail paralleled the 520 highway for most of the way and I made sure to stay in-character the entire time, pointing out birds and pretending to snap pictures. Drake played off the cue pretty well. I was happy to see it. I kept an eye on my phone's GPS so that we did not overshoot. There was a low fence separating the trail from the woods; no sign warned against trespassing but a fence was a fence and the meaning is generally universal.

"Here's where we start breaking rules," I said. "You watch for cars and people." When there were none I vaulted over the fence. Drake did likewise, careful not to jar the cameras.

Dawn was more or less upon us by the time we'd found our way to Hansen's backyard; I hadn't seen any signs but I figured getting noticed here would not be good. Should be just beyond those trees," I said, pointing. "Let's start being careful."

Drake nodded. We both stayed behind cover as we approached.

Hansen's house turned out to be a gorgeous split-level timber frame with more glass than an office building; the house did not have a view of the water but that hadn't stopped the architect from wanting the owner to get as much of what was there as possible. The trees pressed close to the house, an advantage for us and a disadvantage for anyone trying to see out.

"Damn," Drake said, making it a five-syllable word. "Nice digs."

"Wonder how much something like that runs for," I said.

"If you have to ask..."

We did a slow half-circuit of the property. I settled on a spot off to one side, where we could see the driveway and into both the living room and the kitchen. We would have to keep shifting our position to avoid glare but those were the breaks. "Let's get set up," I said.

We dug out my Canon 30mp DSLR and tripod, a shotgun microphone and a set of marine 7 x50s that came with a stand; all things a bird-watcher could conceivably possess, all vital for my trade too. I unfolded the laptop, fired it up and started searching for wi-fi signals. There was plenty of 4G cell coverage to work with, but I'd found it always paid to check for free stuff. In this case I found it.

"Irony of ironies," I said, "Hansen doesn't secure his

wi-fi."

Drake laughed. "Awesome."

It was the work of a few seconds to get my computer buzzing along on Hansen's borrowed signal. I got the camera hooked up to the laptop and pinged Izzy. **Testing, Testing** I typed.

Seconds later I got a response. **Word up boss gimme a pic**

I zeroed in on Hansen's driveway and snapped a test shot. **You get that?**

Yep. Wow, nice cars.

OK it works gonna put it to sleep for the moment. Stay on the line.

KK boss, I got back before I closed the laptop lid. The other camera I left standalone, along with the shotgun microphone. I had plenty of battery life for a full day of staking out but there was no sense in wasting it. With the setup complete, I texted Julian. **You in position?**

yep already bored christ how do you stand it??

I smiled. **Welcome to the glamorous world of fieldwork.** I set my phone aside and gave the driveway a scan through the binoculars; a Cadillac sport-utility, a Mercedes sedan and two European sports cars I did not recognize were parked there. "Izzy's right about the rides," I said. "For all we know he's out driving a fifth."

Drake motioned for me to move aside. "He isn't," he said after peering into the binoculars. "Mercedes is his day-to-day car."

"How can you tell?"

Drake looked back. "There's mud in the wheel wells. Car washes miss that sometimes."

I looked. Drake was right. "And how do you know that?"

He shrugged. "I worked for one for a while."

"Points for you, if he's home," I said. "Start checking windows."

Drake pointed. "We don't have to."

I swung the binoculars over to the wide deck. A blond man of medium height was just closing the sliding glass door, a steaming mug of something in his hand.

"Hello, pigeon," I said.

Eric Plume

Chapter 18

Even through the binoculars Bradley James Hansen looked to be quite the specimen; his Facebook profile put him at forty-one but had I not known that I would have guessed thirty, maybe less. Thick, center-parted hair brushed his collar, just shaggy enough to suggest 'sexy young rock star' without running afoul of corporate policy. Bright green eyes, a high-tech tan and a Bowflex body rounded out the look.

"I want to punch him in the face," Drake muttered.

I looked up from texting a picture of Hansen to Julian. "Why?"

"His face," Drake said. "It's too perfect." He had the Canon's viewfinder to his eye and was snapping pictures. "Would you go out with a guy like that?"

"No idea," I said. "No guy like that has ever looked twice at me."

We watched as Hansen sipped his hot whatever and gazed out at the view. From the open door I heard the phone ring. He hurried back in to catch it; the sound cut off as the door slid shut behind him. I cursed. "Should've known all that glass was too good to be true."

Whatever the windows were made out of, it completely defeated my shotgun mike. Not that anything I recorded with it would be admissible evidence but I was hoping we could find a clue; something that would lead us *to* admissible evidence. I could see him on the phone, pacing back and forth, but I couldn't hear anything.

Wash, rinse, repeat, wait. The joy of a long stakeout.

Drake proved to be a good stakeout partner; he made just enough conversation to keep things from getting boring without being a distraction about it, and he didn't take his eye off the target the way some people did. I had done long stakeouts before, but seldom with a partner because neither Julian nor Izzy was suited to the work; Julian lacked the attention span and Izzy lacked the stamina. Drake it appeared had both. Maybe hiring him wasn't such a bad notion. That is, if I could stop myself from sleeping with him again.

For want of anything better to do I gave Hansen's living room a scan, paying attention to decor and literature. It is possible to learn a great deal about someone by the way they keep their home. Hansen's was obviously coordinated to impress a guest, but there were personal touches. His collection of crime fiction was much more extensive than mine; collector's edition hardcovers from

Hammett, Chandler, Ross MacDonald and Robert Parker lined the shelves. I drooled a little inside and found it harder to hate the guy. I also noticed the vintage movie poster hanging framed over the fireplace; *Scarface,* the one with Al Pacino divided into black and white.

I took a break to find a bush, so I could get rid of a distraction caused by too much coffee. "He doing anything?" I kept my voice down.

"Nope." A pause. "Sorry, this must be embarrassing."

I smiled. "Are you kidding? This is hardly the most adventurous place I've ever peed." I pulled up my jeans and crawled back to our redoubt.

He looked at me. "Morbid curiosity compels me."

"Let me put it to you this way," I said, watching Hansen putter about his office through the binoculars. "You're on a twelve-hour stakeout, you're stuck in a car, and you have to go. Something needs to give, and it's your dignity."

He thought a moment. "Wow," he said.

"Yeah." I grinned. "I'll just say you don't need external plumbing to write your name in the snow, either."

He didn't have much to say to that and I didn't

blame him.

A little before eleven a car pulled into Hansen's driveway; another fancy sport-utility, packed to the gills with people. I got the camera up and the laptop ready before they started exiting; as they did I snapped photos of each one, along with a shot of the license plate. I knew I had seen at least two of them somewhere before but I wasn't sure exactly where. **Profile the people and the plates** I typed to Izzy, looking back at the action before she could respond.

All of them were male, dressed in casual clothes that nonetheless looked expensive; the sort of things rich office workers wore on their day off. Hansen came out of the house to greet them with a big, friendly smile. I watched a lot of handshaking and shoulder-slapping; through the shotgun mike I got a bunch of first names and I frantically typed each down along with a distinguishing feature while Drake snapped more photos. "Wonder what's going on," Drake said as they went back into the house.

"No idea," I said. "Maybe they're just here to watch a football game."

"Maybe," Drake said.

"Yeah," I said, "I don't believe it either."

Once again I had to curse Hansen's expensive glass as the group settled into the couches in his front room and began talking animatedly. Hansen played host, getting beers and snacks for his guests. I could tell from the expressions I saw that this was not precisely a social call. One of them, a lanky man of balding middle age, brought a piece of paper out of a briefcase at his feet and passed it to Hansen. From the angle I could see there was a picture on it but nothing else. Hansen gave the piece of paper a look and his face grew a shade paler beneath his tan.

"Brad-boy looks nervous," Drake said. "Give a lot to know what's getting talked about in there."

I watched as the taller man walked up and said something to Hansen, tapping the paper in time with his words. "Some sort of bad news," I said.

"Think it has to do with you?"

"That's a reasonable guess," I said.

The computer pinged softly. "Watch them," I said as I returned my attention to the screen. There was a long post from Izzy.

Okay I started checking names and faces. The driver of the car is Stephen Klausman...he runs Bright Promise Property, a big management firm in town. The darker dude is Andreas Kotok; he's on the Seattle zoning board. The tall skinny guy is Matthew Libby, a big stockbroker in town. He works for the same firm Hansen's daddy used to.

The short guy with the bald spot is Ryan Holmes. He's the realtor who sold most of the properties to Ironhorse. I haven't run the rest of the guys yet...but boss, ALL of them are connected to the development deal in some way. Usually through stock investments in companies that are involved....like Ironhorse.

"Jesus," I muttered. **Good work girl keep at it.**

"What's up?" Drake had the camera to his eye and was snapping pictures.

"The plot just thickened," I said. I gave him a rundown of what Izzy had learned.

"Looks like we picked a good day to come out here," he said, "Instead of staking out that Govrolev guy."

"I figured it would be," I said. "I poked a stick in the hornet's nest two nights ago, and I figured if Hansen was our guy, the weekend was when he'd meet up with his buddies to discuss it. I'm just glad we didn't miss anything." I smiled. "Besides, there isn't any proof yet that Govrolev's up to anything, whereas Hansen's the one doing all the shenanigans with the mortgages."

"There's still the matter of the gang kids," he said.

"There is that," I said, "but there's no proof Govrolev's involved there."

"Just a hell of a coincidence," Drake said.

"Not enough," I said.

The meeting kept going on; the rain started to come down hard but I made no move to pack up. The men inside started passing a tablet computer around, pointing at something on the screen and nodding to each other. I couldn't see what was on it and I still couldn't hear what they were talking about. "Goddamn those windows," I muttered. "Goddamn them to hell."

"Try and get closer?"

I shook my head. "Wouldn't make a difference except in our likelihood of getting seen."

So we sat in the rain and watched Hansen play host. It was obvious from watching that he was the leader-figure of the group in his den; he circulated from person to person, shaking hands, conversing, obviously cajoling and reassuring the various men about something. When he got up in front of them to speak, his manner was effusive, excitable; I watched the other men leaning forward to follow his words.

Eventually I saw him disappear back into another part of the house for a few minutes; when he returned he had an envelope in his hand, the sort of thing one might send a letter in. I zoomed my binoculars in as far as they would go just in time to watch him take a jump drive out of the envelope and insert it into his laptop. The other men crowded around the screen to see; an accident of angles meant that the back of the laptop was to us.

Drake cursed. "This is like watching porn with all the good bits removed," he said.

"There are good bits in porn?"

Drake's words caught up to him and he blushed. "Well...sometimes," he said.

"Don't sweat it, on both counts. For one thing, this sort of crap is normal when doing a stakeout...you always feel like the best stuff happens out of sight. The only thing we can do is watch and wait and count our blessings that we're getting as much as we are."

"Okay. And the other thing?"

I kept my eye buried in the camera. "I've been known to watch a dirty movie or two."

The tall man - Libby the stockbroker, according to Izzy - opened his briefcase again and brought out a sheaf of papers. I tried to get a look at them but again the angles defeated me. Hansen looked them over and made some entries on his computer. "Records," I said. "The flash drive is where he keeps his records."

"Wish we could get it," Drake said.

"Not possible," I said.

"Wait till he's asleep, then break in and take it?"

I sighed. "Even less possible," I said. "For one thing, I don't know how. For another, Hansen's security system is probably smarter than we are. For a third...B & E is a felony. I get caught doing it and I'm done for."

"Ah. It isn't like the pulp novels?"

I smiled. "Bingo."

My phone buzzed; Julian. **Boss I'm getting soaked is anything happening up there??**

Patience, Grasshopper, I texted back. **Didn't I tell you the bike was a poor choice for Seattle?**

Chicks dig bikes.

Then suffer I guess. It's not easy being as pretty as you, didn't your mother tell you that?

Inside it looked like the meeting was breaking up. Hansen did a reverse of his greeting ritual as the men all got their coats and headed for the car, though he did not follow them outside. I dialed Julian voice.

"Okay, get ready," I said. "There's a Cadillac Escalade that's about to come down the drive...emerald green." I rattled off the license plate.

"Awesome, I'll be on it." His voice sounded a little hoarse, but I could hear the nervous excitement in it.

"Wait," Drake said. "Look."

I glanced through my binoculars at Hansen; he was setting out two place settings at his table. And a candlestick.

"Dinner for two," Drake murmured. "Candlelit."

"Yeah," I said.

"Talk to me, boss," Julian said.

I watched the Escalade back up and knew I had to make a split-second decision. So much of this kind of work depended on following one's hunches...or more correctly, knowing which hunches to follow.

"Belay that," I said to Julian. "Stand fast."

I heard Julian sigh. "Okay," he said.

I signed off with him and looked at Drake. "Good catch," I said.

"Think it's worth it not to follow the carload of yuppies?"

"Yeah," I said. "We know their names and faces. Izzy can find out where they live without Julian having to take a risk tailing them. Besides, they're done for the day I'd guess...they're going to go have a couple of martinis or whatever and head home. I want to know who's coming to dinner."

Full dark came on while we watched Hansen putter about his kitchen; all the makings of an intimate dinner for two took shape. A bottle of Veuve Cliquot in a silver bucket of ice. A single candle. What appeared to be some sort of pasta dish. Drake snorted laughter.

"Yeah I know," I said. "He's probably trying to be original."

"Wonder what sort of girl Brad's into," Drake said.

Full dark came on and with it more rain. I was glad for the poncho but my shoes and head were completely soaked. Drake's jeans were black with rain. I winced; it had been a while since I had done a woods stakeout and some aspects I'd forgotten, like just how wet the day-long Washington rain could make a person. A pair of headlights came up the drive. The headlights belonged to a late-model gray BMW, lovingly maintained. Three figures got out; one was a tall woman in an evening dress.

"There's your answer," I said.

Eric Plume

Chapter 19

The woman had the sort of polished beauty to her that always made me feel dumpy and inadequate whenever I saw it. Slim, long-legged and full-breasted with glossy chin length hair and a complexion that could have given fresh paint lessons in perfection, she walked with the kind of come-hither stride that had always been beyond my ability. Her dress was a slinky black confection of sheer silk only a woman with an ideal body would do anything other than dream about. The side slit flared in the evening breeze, revealing bare smooth legs and black patent stilettos laced to her knee.

One man was a nasty piece of work in his middle forties with a stooped way of walking. The stubble on his face matched the stubble on his head, as if he had just run a set of clippers over his entire skull. His eyes were close-set and small, his nose bent in the middle from having been broken and not properly reset. He had on dark slacks, shiny dress shoes, a leather jacket and a red silk shirt open at the collar. When he hitched up his pants I saw the flash of gold at his neck and wrist.

The other was a boy barely out of his teens, wearing a hooded sweatshirt and track pants. He kept his hands in his pockets and hung back.

"Damn," Drake said, drawing the word out for emphasis. I throttled an irrational surge of jealousy and didn't say anything. "Hello high-class hooker," he said after a second. I felt a little better about things then.

"How'd you guess?"

Drake grinned. "She's wearing the dress and the heels and that's it. Call girls often skip the undies so that clients don't pocket them."

I cranked the zoom on my field glasses and gave the woman's swaying hips another glance. He was right. There was no panty line breaking the silk of her dress and the material was far too thin to hide it.

"Points given for noticing, deducted for looking," I said, but I grinned when I did so. I hadn't known the bit about prostitutes and underwear.

Brad came out onto the porch to greet them despite the rain. The woman he hugged and went in to kiss her; she offered him her cheek with indifferent grace. The man he shook hands with, exchanged some words. I reached for the shotgun mike but the sound of the rain drowned out their voices. "Dammit," I muttered. All I was able to get was the ugly man's accent; it was Russian. "Well that's something," I said.

Hansen talked with the older man while his date - if

that's what she was - folded her arms against the cold and looked miserable. The teenager ignored everyone and was ignored in turn. The ugly man nodded and turned back towards his car, teenager in tow. I reached for my phone. "Julian's gonna follow this one," I said.

But my cold-numbed fingers picked that moment to go on strike. My phone slipped out of my hand and tumbled under the log we were using as cover. I let fly with some of my more creative cussing as tight quarters, darkness and our intricate little nest of surveillance gear all conspired to get in my way. By the time I got my phone up and ready the BMW was already down the street. There was no way Julian would get to it in time.

"Goddamn it," I hissed.

"Sorry," Drake said.

"Not your fault," I said, trying to get a choke valve on my temper. "Also not a catastrophe. Someone's going to have to come pick her up eventually."

"What happens if she's spending the night?"

"Then we all get to be very, very miserable," I said. I flexed my numb hand and swore again, resisting the urge to drive it into the log by way of punishment. "Back to business," I muttered.

Hansen and his date went back inside. He poured two glasses of champagne and smiled a lot while he bounced words off of her. That was the best way to describe it; she didn't react except to give the occasional half-smile that didn't come within a mile of her eyes. She didn't look like someone on a date, but rather someone on the job; about the way I looked when I was serving papers. "I think you're right about the hooker thing," I said.

Drake adjusted the camera, trying to keep it out of the rain. "Think that ugly little guy is her pimp?"

"I think there's a lot going on here that we don't know yet," I said.

In the kitchen Hansen toyed with her hair. She smiled at him. Her eyes were blue, as blank and clear as a winter sky. While they flirted I got the pictures of the BMW, the ugly guy and the hooker off to Izzy. The power was running low on the laptop and I put it into sleep mode, not wanting to waste it. My stomach growled and I did my best to ignore it. Instead I turned to Drake.

"You holding up okay?"

Drake smiled back at me. "This isn't the first time I've spent a cold hungry night."

"I guess not," I said.

"Hey look, things are getting interesting."

I put my binoculars to my eyes. Drake leveled the camera.

There was an embrace, followed by a long, slow kiss, one I watched her move to his left ear. She slipped her dress off her shoulders and it pooled around her feet just like clothing always does in the movies. Drake's call had been right. Underneath she was bare flesh and black boots and nothing else. Her body language was considerably more relaxed as she toyed with him.

"Maybe your job doesn't suck after all," Drake said.

"There is the occasional benefit," I said.

What followed was an adroit display of sexual hydraulics. I could tell Drake was made uncomfortable by having to observe it - probably because he liked seeing it but didn't want to. Between wild parties in college and my current occupation I'd lost my ability to care about such matters. Instead, I found myself distantly critiquing her performance. She approached the task before her with the detached proficiency of a world-class surgeon.

"I guess you could call that art," Drake said.

"Nope," I said. "Science. And she's a hooker, no

doubt about it."

"How'd you know?"

"She put a condom on him," I said. "No girlfriend would do that."

The scene in the kitchen did not take long to finish up. Hansen had the glazed gratitude men often got at such times painted all over his face. After a bit of caressing they walked over to the table to eat. Hansen remembered to button his pants. The girl didn't trouble to put her dress back on. By the halogen bulbs in Hansen's kitchen her flesh was firm and smooth, figure as sleek and functional as the fuselage of a fighter jet.

"Think she's going to spend the night?"

I kept watching while they ate dinner. "Not a chance," I said. "Hookers fuck their clients, they don't sleep next to them. She'll do what she's being paid to do and then someone will come collect her."

"Sleazy business," Drake said.

"Why? Hansen isn't married. She's obviously of age."

"It's illegal," Drake said.

"So was smoking that joint in the WWU library but you and I did it anyway," I said.

"*Touche,*" he said. "Can we go home now?"

"Not yet. I want to see what happens after Hansen falls asleep."

"What makes you think he's going to?"

I grinned. "That bit in the kitchen was just a warm-up....and if what we saw is any indication he'll be ready to pass out after she's done with him. I want to see what she does then."

He stuck his hands in his pockets. "You have a weird job."

"Don't I just."

The two of them finished dinner and disappeared upstairs, her holding both his hands and leading him on with a smile much like the one Eve might've given Adam before handing him the apple.

It took longer than I had expected before I saw a flicker of movement at the staircase. Sure enough, the girl came slipping down the stairs alone. She still had on her boots. Judging by how intricate the laces were I guessed she hadn't taken them off.

She didn't bother with the come-hither walk as she picked up her dress and slipped into it. Next she dug into her purse and came out with a pair of black gloves. Hansen's coat was draped across the back of one of the chairs. She picked it up riffled the pockets, pulled out his cell phone and did something to it that involved comparing it to her own. An accident of angles meant that her back was to us. Drake snapped off some pictures. "What's she up to?"

"If she'd turn around we'd know," I said. She didn't.

The girl put everything in his pockets back the way she had found it, except a handful of rumpled bills. Those went into her purse. She then checked out around the phone, snapping pictures of the messages tacked to the board with her cell.

"She's a honey-trap," I said. "Someone's paying her to spy on Hansen."

"She's robbing him too."

"I think she considers it a tip."

What followed was a quick and quite thorough tossing of Hansen's house, done with the brisk surety of someone who knew their way around. She even produced a key and got into his desk and riffled his files, going through them much too quick to be even reading the titles.

"She's looking for something specific," I said. "She knows what it is and where she's likely to find it."

"Yeah," Drake said. "But who for?"

"That is the question," I said.

"Her pimp, maybe?"

I kept watching. "We'll know soon enough."

Five minutes later the girl re-appeared in the kitchen, holding something. I cranked at my binoculars and got a look at it just as she put it in her purse. It was Hansen's thumb drive.

"The files," I said. "Hansen's business files. She's got them." I got my phone up and speed-dialed Julian.

"Hi boss," he said. He sounded tired.

"Just wanted to make sure you're awake," I said.

"Do I get to do something soon?"

I watched the girl step out onto the porch and flip open a cell phone. She pressed it to her ear. I motioned for Drake to try the shotgun mike.

"Yeah," I said to Julian. "Listen...pretty soon you are going to need to follow someone. Be extra fucking careful okay?"

"I know," he said. "What's the car look like?"

"I'll let you know as soon as I do," I said. "Stay on the line."

I plugged the spare earpiece into the shotgun mike and listened. The rain noise came through like someone rolling cellophane around in their fist, but I could still make out the cadence of her words. Like the ugly little man, she had a thick East Europe accent. The tone of her voice went from disinterested to annoyed before she snapped the phone shut with more force than was necessary, spitting out several curses and glancing around. I flinched by reflex.

"What, you think she got told we're here?"

"No, I just moved when I shouldn't have."

Drake squinted at her through the binoculars. "I wonder what's she's pissed about."

"Maybe her ride's late," I said.

The hooker hunched up in Hansen's doorway and folded her arms against the cold. In about fifteen minutes I heard the distinctive sound of a Detroit V-8 engine, the throaty rumble muscle cars make. A set of headlights resolved into a black Camaro, the old good one every teenaged boy worth his hormones lusts after.

"Damn," I muttered, pressing my phone to my face. "Okay, Julian...you'll be following a black 1969 Camaro, lots of chrome, with a blower on the hood." I tried to get the license plate but the rain and dark defeated me. "You'll have to make do without the plates," I said.

"I got it," he said. I heard the sound of his bike start up.

"Good luck," I said, and signed off. I didn't tell him to be careful again. Either he would or he wouldn't be.

The driver got out. He had on a dark blue windbreaker and black pants, his close-cropped hair a vague shade of dark blond. In the backwash of the headlights I could see where a bald spot had almost formed.

She walked towards the driver with the sort of body language people normally demonstrated around angry snakes and live explosives. I could see her mouth moving, but between the wind and her accent I could not make out what she was saying. I cursed softly and tried fiddling with the controls. "This damn thing was a waste of -"

I froze as I heard the driver's voice. I knew it. Lazy, cold and disinterested, with a fake jerkwater drawl covering a genuine New York clip.

"His photo," I said. "Get it. Get all that you can."

"Why?" Drake was already snapping pictures as fast as the camera would go.

"That's the guy who beat me up," I said.

Eric Plume

Chapter 20

I watched the call girl get into the Camaro with an obvious sense of hesitancy, but mostly I focused on trying to get a good look at the driver's face. The backwash of the lights made it difficult. He didn't look all that dangerous; maybe a touch over six feet with a slim build. I remembered how much his punches hurt and wondered where all the power had come from.

"You sure that's him?" Drake had the camera up and was snapping away.

"I'm sure," I said softly.

"I can't get a good angle on him," he said.

"Do your best," I said, trying to get a good view of his face. I couldn't; between the rain and the weird shadows from several lights I couldn't get a good angle.

He gave the area a brief scan, not gazing in our direction but instead turning around to look down the street. For an instant, a white logo on the back of his jacket flared like a neon sign. I caught letters, but it was gone again before I could read it. I bit back a creative chain of curses as he got into the Camaro and started it up.

"Maybe we'll get the plates when he backs out," Drake said.

We didn't. The shadows got in the way. It happens. "I need a night scope," I muttered as I watched the tail-lights disappear up the street.

"Come on," I said, let's get out of here. It's a long hike back to the car."

"I heard that," he said, gratitude plain in his tone.

It was indeed a long hike back, made longer by stiff muscles and cold fingers. My car was right where I left it; we got in and cranked every heating device we could to its topmost capacity. The heat was the only thing that worked properly in my aging chariot, and right then I thanked Volkswagen AG for the fact. I resisted the urge to call Julian; he was on his bike and couldn't afford to be distracted from his first tail job with a phone call.

We were mostly silent on the way back to the hotel, Drake being tired and I being deep in thought. Specifically, I was wondering what the connection was between the call girl, the leg-breaker and the bank manager.

"One of these things is not like the other," I hummed under my breath, "one of these things just doesn't belong..."

Drake looked over at me. "How's that?"

I stripped off my gloves to give my fingers better access to the heat. "I want to know what a white-bread yuppie like Brad Hansen is doing with these people," I said. "I saw the background Izzy put together...that guy's got everything going for him. He could be running that bank in another five years. So why is he risking it hanging around with criminal types?"

Drake shrugged. "Money?"

"This guy's loaded, Drake. His dad's a big-time stock trader...he's got an inheritance coming that'd make your eyeballs fall out. Combine that with the money his own investments have made and he's sitting pretty for life."

"True," Drake said, "but he won't have earned it so it won't really count to him."

"What do you mean?"

Drake thought for several long seconds before answering. "I met guys like Brad Hansen, both in grad school and in the ad business. Rich, smart, good-looking...you know, the guys who have just about everything in their corner. And you know what? They were the most competitive...they always had to be first at everything." He paused. "Me, I was just glad to be there. But these guys, they had to come in first or they weren't happy."

I checked my phone for the fifth time. Nothing from Julian. "So he's the stud-duck quarterback type, all grown up?"

"Sort of." Drake thought some more. "You said his dad's in stocks...so tell me, why isn't he in stocks himself? It'd be easier, and he'd be helping to run the show by now, right?"

I went over it for a few minutes. "But that wasn't enough of a challenge," I said.

"Right. Except Hansen's been blocked off over at the bank, and he's unhappy about it."

I went to reply, but the driver of a big semi forgot to check his mirrors; I leaned on the horn and took my foot off the gas, dropping back enough to avoid being flattened. "Asshole," I muttered. "Anyhow, explain...'Blocked off?' Blocked how?"

Drake toyed with the end of one of his dreadlocks for a second before answering. "I saw it happen a couple of times when I worked in advertising. Some young hotshot with all the right moves would show up, climb the ladder really fast for a couple of months, and then end up stuck in a place where they'd get regular raises but no more promotions."

I risked taking my eyes off the traffic to glance at

Drake. "Why do that? Sorry, I've never worked corporate."

"Because there's only so much room at the top, and it's full up already," Drake said softly. "Someone making it means somebody else has to step aside. And the people who sit at the top aren't the sort to do that without a fight."

I returned my attention to the road. "So Hansen's too ambitious, the people at the top stuck him in a filing cabinet, and he's looking for a way to keep climbing?"

Drake nodded. "That's my guess," he said.

I checked my phone again. Still no word from Julian.

"Kid's going to be all right," Drake said.

"I know."

"He'll call when he gets a chance," he said.

"I know that too."

"So put the phone down and concentrate on the road," Drake said.

"Can't," I said. "Worried."

"What's the deal with Lynden?"

The question threw me. "What do you mean?"

"You know what I mean. Back when we caught Hayes, he said something about you being wasted on Lynden. You looked like you were going to shoot him for bringing it up."

I sighed. "It's a long story," I said.

"So talk, or drive," Drake said. "Either way, trust the kid. He isn't stupid."

I managed a tired smile. "All right, you win." I stuck my phone in my pocket and left it there. I did, however, pull one of the cigarettes out of the center console and light it. Drake didn't comment.

It was quite late when we got back to the hotel and Julian still hadn't called; I plugged in my phone and tried not to stare at it. For want of something to do I started organizing the massive pile of pictures we had collected while Drake headed for the shower to defrost. My own clothes were all but soaked through, so I took a moment to strip them off and slide into one of the hotel bathrobes. Zork watched me from his new favorite perch, the pillow on the bed Drake had yet to use.

First I downloaded all the photos from the memory sticks we'd filled up and began organizing them; some people dumped photos that did not turn out, but I never did. I can buy all the hard drive space I need but I've yet to see a store that sells clues. I flipped through the stack until I got to the shots of my mystery man.

Drake came out of the shower with a towel wrapped around his waist, drying his dreadlocks with a second one. I said to hell with girlish prudery and spent a second eating the eye-candy. He grinned and blushed, but it came off as appreciative rather than embarrassed.

"Did we get the plates?"

"Doubt it, and that's not what I'm looking for." I kept clicking the slide-show button until I got to what I wanted. I found it. "Yes!"

Drake leaned over my shoulder. "The logo on his jacket?"

I nodded. "It's not a logo. That's a tavern jacket...an old one. Which means he either goes to that bar a lot or he works there." We had finally gotten lucky with the pictures; the white lettering stood out on the satin perfectly. I patted Drake on the arm. "Perfect timing with the camera by the way."

"You think someone at the bar can identify him?"

I grinned. "Likely, they already have and don't know it. Watch and learn."

I Googled "GRIDIRON BAR SEATTLE WA" and got a few hits. One was a website that was amateurishly done; the black décor and rectilinear framing looked like a relic from the Web of my high school years. I flipped through it for a while but the site hadn't been updated in five months. I abandoned it and tried their Facebook page, noting down their physical address before I left.

The updates here were more recent; I "liked" the bar with my throwaway account and scrolled through the pictures. There were plenty, as there always were; pretty college-age waitresses, leathery bar veterans, heavyset sports fans in denim and plaid. I was always distantly amazed at how many urban cowboys a city like Seattle could support. "Come on," I muttered, waving my cursor over the faces in the images, "I know you're in here..."

He was. I picked him out by him being the only man over thirty not sporting a beer gut. He was standing almost out of frame, wearing black jeans and a polo shirt with "SECURITY" emblazoned on the front. He wasn't smiling. "Charles Kasey" sprang into being next to my cursor when I moved it over his face.

"Tag," I said, "you're it."

"I'll be damned," Drake said.

"Criminals use Facebook. And like the rest of us they can't figure out the privacy settings either." I clicked over to his page.

"No way he's that stupid."

I gave Kasey's page a quick scan. No posts, no picture, no address. "He wasn't," I said. "Someone where he works probably made this account just so she could tag him in pictures. He's never used it. I doubt he even knows it exists."

"How do you figure?"

I smiled. "Because airhead college waitress-types do stuff like that. I caught a cheating husband this way once...found a tagged pic of him slurping Jell-O out of some girl's cleavage in a strip bar over in Spokane." I chuckled at the memory. "Fifteen minutes work, and I made five hundred dollars."

I studied the face in the picture. The camera was low-quality, probably a cell phone, and the lighting was bad. Charles Kasey didn't look dangerous or threatening at all; just another working-class white guy about my age, maybe a little older. I studied where he stood and how; he wasn't looking at the camera, and his back was to the wall in the darkest corner of the room. I brought up one of my stakeout photos and studied his stance there.

"I'll be damned," I muttered.

Drake looked at the picture. "Problem?"

"Yeah," I said. "This guy's good." I pointed at the pictures, putting the batch on slide show. "See how he stands...he's staying either in the backwash of the lights or in the shadows between them. Someone could have been three feet from him and not gotten a picture."

"Where do you learn to do that?"

I shrugged. "You don't need to learn it anywhere. You just have to be smart, keep an eye on your surroundings and know how cameras work."

"He doesn't look like much," Drake said, studying the picture over my shoulder.

"I think that's the idea," I said. "You beat people up for a living, it's good to blend in."

"I could probably take him if I had to," Drake said.

"Don't depend on it."

I opened up some new tabs and brought up the collection of data brokers I had access to, punching in the name "Charles Kasey". I got surprisingly few hits back; a few old addresses in Atlanta and Chicago, one from an apartment building in Bothell that a side search told me had since been torn down. No registered firearms. No criminal record. The only thing I found was a security license. The lack of information was chilling all by itself. I'd always known that there was an armed professional class of men in America who if they filed with the IRS would've put "criminal" as their occupation, but I'd never had dealings with one. From what I read about Kasey, that had just changed.

"Oh well," I said. "I know what he looks like, where he works and a name he goes by. That's a good start."

My phone buzzed. I dove out of my chair in an unladylike scramble, grabbing for my phone. The text was from Julian.

Finished the tail no one saw me have I got news for you I'll give you the scoop when I get back be there soon, I read on the screen. Drake looked over my shoulder.

"Score one for the kid," he said.

I turned around and hugged him, feeling a big knot of tension drain out of my stomach. "He's okay," I said.

"He is."

"Thank fucking God," I murmured into his chest. We stayed like that for a long moment.

"Y'know," Drake said, "you might want to make yourself decent before he gets here."

I looked down. My robe had come most of the way open. "Oops," I said.

Drake looked down at my exposed front. "No need to apologize," he said. "I don't mind at all."

I blushed and grabbed sweats and a t-shirt. I didn't feel like getting dressed again but neither did I feel like flashing my impressionable young assistant. I had finished getting dressed and was nervously sipping on some Gray Goose and tonic from the minibar when there was a knock at the door. I answered it.

Julian stepped in, soaking wet and disheveled but with a grin that nearly split his face in two. I hugged him, damp leather and all. "Damned glad to see you," I said.

He blushed. "I got it, boss. You aren't gonna believe what I saw."

"Lay it on me," I said. "As many details as you can remember."

He unzipped his jacket and started pacing; if he had any more nervous energy he probably would have exploded. "Okay, so I tail the Camaro all the way to Capitol Hill, right? It wasn't easy, there was lots of traffic on the 520 and this one asshole truck driver wouldn't stop trying to run me off the road..." He kept going on about the tailing, words bubbling out of him like carbonation, and I let him ramble. I remembered how excitable my first bit of real PI work had made me. Eventually he got back on topic.

"...so they pull up at this restaurant on Cap Hill - Sebastian's - and the girl gets out. I was going to keep following the Camaro but someone pulled out in front of me and I would have had to gun it to get around them. You said not to risk getting made so I backed off."

I grinned. "Right decision."

"So I park across the street from the restaurant and find a spot to wait so I can see who the girl's meeting." He pulled out his camera and unfolded it, clicking through images. Finally he held one up. "That guy look familiar?" I glanced at the screen. On it was a broad-beamed man in his mid-fifties wearing a business suit. Even on the small screen I recognized him.

"Oh holy crap," I breathed. It was Govrolev. The fatherly Slavic face was unmistakable.

"Yeah," Julian said. "So anyway, they get a table and talk for an hour or so, get a couple cocktails, whatever." Julian flipped through a couple more images. "Then the girl digs around in her purse and they stand up and shake hands." He showed me the picture. "Look at her right hand," he said.

I did. It was closed into a fist. In the next shot she shook hands with Govrolev. In the third picture, her hand was open and empty. Almost out of frame was Govrolev's right hand; he was sticking it into the pocket of his suit.

Julian's eyes glowed with excitement. "She passed something to him boss, I know she did."

"The files," Drake said.

"Yeah," I said. "Only thing small enough to fit in her hand." I looked at the pictures again. The sequence Julian had shot left it clear as day.

"Son of a bitch," Drake said.

"Plot thickens," I said.

Julian looked between us. "You know what it was?"

I looked at Julian. "Yeah I do," I said. "We watched her take it from Hansen's place. We watched Hansen use it for something and go to great lengths to hide it again. I don't know what it is exactly, but I know it's important...and because you decided to stick with the girl instead of being dumb and ballsy, you may have just cracked this case wide open." I reached out with both hands, cupped his face between my palms and kissed him loudly on the forehead.

"So...I'm cool?"

"You," I said, "are one steely-eyed Sam Spade motherfucker."

Julian blushed scarlet.

Eric Plume

Chapter 21

The next morning I assembled everyone for a session of plotting.

The previous evening had been a little awkward at first; there was the small matter of sleeping arrangements but that had ended up working out...well. I was pleasantly relaxed upon waking, and wondered idly if some of my constant low-level stress over the last five years had been due to a bad sexual diet. I tried to keep the smile off my face as Izzy and Julian filed in, thinking how much Candi would have fun with my predicament.

I waited while Izzy helped Julian set up the Skype extension for our office line. Current events were certainly extraordinary but I still had a business to run. I hoped no walk-ins showed up at our office, but that could not be helped. The table was crowded with breakfast and technology and printed paper; I made a mental note to have Izzy collect anything we did not need and set it aside for shredding.

"Okay," I said as soon as I had everyone's attention, "last night we learned a hell of a lot. Also, I want to know about a few things I haven't had a chance to ask about." I turned to Julian. "Were you ever able to get hold of the lawyer - Rosales?"

"Nope," Julian said, "but I reached her secretary. Apparently Rosales was working the case and then fell ill suddenly."

"How convenient for our friend Hayes," I said.

"That guy's a dick and a half," Izzy said.

"No arguments." I paced back and forth. "Izzy, where do you stand?"

She pushed her glasses up on her nose. "Well, I went back and compared the realtor names to some of the photos you took at Hansen's place."

"And?"

"And either they were there, or the realtors you found down at the development work for guys who were there."

"Explains why they wouldn't talk to me," I said. "Also explains why I got jumped outside of Kitsmiller's."

Julian spoke up. "You think they ratted you out?"

"Who else could have known to?"

Drake flipped through the stack of printed photos Izzy had brought with her. "Stockbrokers, realtors, bankers, the zoning commissioner… Christ, everything they need."

"Except a contractor," I said. Everyone looked up. "Which brings me to our second find, courtesy of the Young Detective over here." I smiled at Julian and he beamed. "Govrolev has Hansen's hooker in his pocket...and he's apparently paying her to spy on her customer. So why is he doing that?"

"Also," Drake said, "if what we saw yesterday was a meeting for a conspiracy why wasn't this Govrolev character there?"

"Good point," I said.

Julian left off chewing his lip. "Well," he said, "everybody can't know everybody, right? Otherwise it's too easy to get busted."

I felt a stirring of pride but I made sure it didn't show on my face. "Explain," I said.

He grinned. "Come on, boss. Aren't you always saying it isn't like the movies? In the movies all the bad guys always talk to each other, know everything about what's going on...but in the real world that gets people put in jail. Maybe Govrolev wasn't there because the other guys couldn't risk being seen with him. Remember, all the thugs and stuff showed up after the rich guys had left."

"Way to be genre savvy," I said.

Drake toyed with one of his dreadlocks. "So who is

running the gang kids?"

"My guess is Mister Pimp," I said, shuffling through the printed pictures until I found one of him. "This guy. See how he's got a shady-looking teenaged boy with him."

Izzy leaned forward. "Let me see that," she said.

I handed her the picture. She scrutinized the printout, gave up on it and pulled up the raw image on her laptop. I saw her zooming in close, on the man's forehead. "This guy's mobbed," she said, "or was."

I walked over. "How do you know?"

She pointed at the screen. "See the scar tissue on his forehead? That's where a tattoo was removed. Could mean any one of a few things."

"Which are?"

"Most likely that either the guy was expecting a life sentence, or he was somebody's bitch."

I gave the picture another look. The scar tissue was blurry, but easy to see once Izzy had pointed it out. "Since he's walking around breathing free air I'd guess the latter."

"Yeah," Izzy said. "And since he got the tattoo removed he's probably trying to stay away from his former friends."

"I want to know who he is," I said. "I also want to know if Govrolev ever did time back in Russia."

Izzy grinned. "I figured you'd ask. Govrolev spent 1984 to 1990 at the Bolshoy Dom in Saint Petersburg. Theft and sale of State property, six counts."

I blinked. "Will I be hearing from Interpol next?"

"You said to take the gloves off, boss."

I took a deep breath. "So I did," I said.

"Here's the thing though...the Bolshoy Dom isn't a place they let people out of. And the records of him being there weren't easy to get."

Julian cocked his head. "So, why'd they let him out?"

"Same reason they let people out over here," I said. "He probably gave the authorities something they wanted, and in exchange they shortened his sentence and cleaned up his records. Probably encouraged him to leave the country too."

Izzy whistled softly. "If he ratted on the *Bratva* he wouldn't have needed any encouragement to get the hell out of Russia."

I nodded. "Which brings us back to the question of

why he'd be getting into crime over here."

"Old habits," Drake said.

"Could be," I said. "We still don't know enough. All the facts we have could be used to either convict Govrolev or exonerate him. I'm not convinced either way."

Drake looked at me. "Why do you care?"

"Our friend the FBI agent," I said, "has shown a marked lack of concern for collateral damage. Sorry if I don't want to send an innocent man to jail."

The phone rang and Julian slipped the headset on, dropping into the smooth charm of his phone voice. After a brief exchange he looked up. "Boss, it's a Mister Burton for you."

I crossed the room and took the headset. A deep male voice rang in my ears. "Amber Eckart?"

"This is she," I said.

"Carter Burton, of Burton, Cameron, and Clive. I think the two of us need to talk, and soon."

I got a small twinge of adrenaline at the tone in his voice. "Might I ask why?"

"With all due respect, Ms. Eckart, I believe you know why." There was a pause. "I will be at a Mrs. Cordelia Kitsmiller's residence in about two hours. I would appreciate it if you would join me there."

"I don't suppose you would take a rain check," I said.

"I'll hand it back with a subpoena attached," he said.

"I'll be there," I said.

"I look forward to it." The line went dead. I let out a long breath and set the headset aside, letting my brain shift gears once again.

"Julian, go back to your room and pack up the file on Kitsmiller that we got from Hayes. Make sure we have copies of everything important and make sure everything is in order. Izzy, go through the surveillance footage of Hayes in our office and get me the part where he admits to stealing files. And hurry, both of you."

Drake watched my two assistants hurry out of the room. "Problem?"

"Do we get anything else?" I sighed. "That was Kitsmiller's attorney. He doesn't sound happy, and if he knows what I think he knows I don't blame him at all." I unzipped my bag and rooted out my good clothes; a dove-gray suit, cream cotton blouse and sensible heels. For accessories I went with a belt holster and magazine pouch; function before fashion, that's me. I laid everything out on the bed and made sure there were no wrinkles.

"You're coming with me," I said. "Can you make yourself look presentable, yet dangerous?"

He blinked. "Maybe. Why?"

I smiled at him. "Because you get to play my rough-hewn bodyguard. Again, we want to look like a larger firm than we are."

He appeared confused. I elaborated.

"Drake, most PI firms can't afford to detail more than one investigator per contract. Either the client won't pay for it or the firm can't spare the manpower. So, if we show up with three investigators, one of whom seems to only be there for protection..."

He nodded. "We look like one bad-ass team," he said.

"Exactly. Someone Burton will figure he can't lean on."

"Who else are you planning on bringing?"

"Izzy." I dug out my pistol and made sure it was loaded. I knew it would be, but one always checked. "I might need her to dazzle Burton with some tech-talk."

My two assistants came back in each bearing gifts. I

told Izzy what I needed her to do. She did not look happy about it. "Boss," she said, "I don't do fieldwork."

"You do today," I replied. "I might need you to blindside Burton with techno-babble. We need to appear competent and professional. You talk tech better than any of us."

She nodded. "Okay."

"Go get a shower, make yourself as presentable as you can. Wear the good clothes we grabbed from the office. I've got to do likewise."

Julian spoke up. "What do I do?"

"Go to the office and check the mail," I said. "If the check from Andersen Law isn't in our mailbox, call that slimy SOB and don't rest until you find out why."

"Wow," he said. "I'd forgotten about that."

"I'm sure he wishes I would too," I said. "Off with you."

Drake and I headed to the shower. There wasn't time for both of us to get separate turns so we crowded in together. I was distantly amazed by how quickly I'd become comfortable with sharing intimate moments with him, but that was a matter for a later date. "So, this lawyer's going to want to know who was running around pretending to be part of his firm, but you don't want to spill the truth because...why?" He sounded confused.

"Hayes can't pay me if the FBI fires him," I said, ducking my head under the spray.

"So what are you going to do?"

"I'm going to grab this unfortunate situation and take it three times around the dance floor," I said. "Wish me luck."

He grinned and came closer. "I think I can do a little better than that."

"What do you -" I found myself cut off by a kiss. "Oh," I said, thinking that he had meant something else but not knowing what that might be...and then a furious few minutes happened where I didn't do much thinking at all.

Then, clean and groomed and freshly made up - with a flush to my cheeks which had nothing to do with my cosmetics kit - I collected my tech assistant and my pistol and went to try and outfox the senior partner from the most potent law firm in the Greater Seattle Area.

Who says I don't get to have any fun?

Chapter 22

On the drive over I went over what I expected everyone else to do, which was basically to speak only when spoken to and to act as professional as possible. I took it as a point of high irony that a meeting with a lawyer was making me more nervous than a meeting with a professional leg-breaker. I supposed it made sense; after all, the leg-breaker could only beat me up.

"Do you know this guy?" Izzy was at her lower lip with her teeth. She looked uncomfortable in the business clothes she had on, and I didn't blame her. The world of fashion has never been kind to the plus-sized.

I nodded. "I met Carter Burton once. He looks harmless - don't be fooled. The guy makes sharks look positively cuddly."

"So he's an asshole?"

I smiled. "He's an excellent attorney, and a brilliant legal technician."

Drake glanced at me from the back seat. "And you're going to try to out-talk him," he said.

"Yep."

Izzy nodded. "And we're here...why?"

"To make me look cool," I said. "Oh, I have no illusions that Burton's going to fall for it. What he will do is respect the fact that I thought to do it."

Drake laughed and Izzy gave me her 'are you kidding' look over the top of her glasses. "Boss, that's bonkers."

"No, Izzy...that's corporate politics. We're playing with the big boys now, we need to play like the big boys play. Looking cool is what the big boys do."

No one had an answer to that so I returned to the act of driving, running through the list of deals I'd struck so far and the ones I could afford to make in the future. Things had grown so complicated that I was having difficulty remembering whose side I was on. I drove with a mechanical sort of habit, sorting through the applicable rules, both written and unwritten. There were plenty to choose from.

Outside my car rain threatened to start falling at any moment, a threat I had no problem believing the weather would carry out. The trees were still but the air was crisp and cold. I kept the heater on and the radio off all the way to Kitsmiller's house.

There was another car parked in the driveway as we pulled up; a dark gray BMW, the sport-utility variant that manages to be spacious and sleek at the same time. The bodywork gleamed with a results of a fresh detail job. I eased my battered little Golf in next to it with as much space between the vehicles as the driveway permitted. "No one even breathe on that car," I muttered.

"Because it's nice?" Drake looked like he wanted to key it on general principle.

"Because it belongs to a lawyer," I said, giving my face a glance in the rear view mirror. The bruises still showed but only a little. Otherwise I looked as slick as my budget and the time frame allowed for. I settled my face into a mask of friendly professionalism before sliding out of the car.

Kitsmiller was there to greet us at the door; I introduced my two associates, who were both wise enough to don their best behavior. We shucked our coats and our shoes and put them where Kitsmiller told us to.

Waiting in the living room was Carter Burton, the attorney. His comb-over looked sparser and his waist looked wider than the last time I'd seen him, but otherwise he was still the same; a roly-poly man with a round face, a flat nose and the eyes of a stone professional. His smile was a warm courtesy and his glance a calculation. I crossed the room to shake his hand.

"Amber Eckart," I said. "It's a pleasure to see you

again, Mister Burton."

"You as well," he replied.

"This is Erzsébet Dzerzhinska, my research assistant, and Jim Nelson, one of my security specialists." I prided myself on not tripping over Izzy's given name, sure I'd got it wrong but equally sure that Burton wouldn't know it. Drake glanced at me sidelong when I introduced him but had the wit to roll with it.

He sized up my two associates with a detached glance before returning his gaze to me. "Business must be good," he said.

"At the moment," I said.

"I am to understand that a certain individual came into your office claiming to be an employee of my firm," he said. "I'm sure I don't have to explain why this concerns me."

"Of course." I took a seat. "The name he gave me was John Hastings. He had a business card from your firm and claimed he wanted me to look into a piece of foreclosure fraud."

"I am aware of that," he said. "What I want to know is where I can find him."

"I've no idea," I said.

"Well then I would like you to tell me everything you know about him," Burton said.

"Caucasian," I said. "Six feet, maybe one-seventy. Brown hair, blue eyes, fit build. Baritone voice, no visible scars or distinguishing marks. No older than forty-five. Wore a gray suit, navy tie, and he smiled a good deal."

"I have all that already," he said. "What I want is his real identity."

Act one, scene two; I made myself wince. "That I can't do, Mister Burton."

"Excuse me?"

"Client privilege." I put on a look of strained apology.

"Ms. Eckart, you know perfectly well that client privilege does not apply here."

"I have since been employed by a different client, Mister Burton...your interests and theirs intertwine, and I'm sure you can appreciate the difficulty this puts me in."

I had to give Burton credit; he didn't waste time with angry bluster. He simply sat back and gave me a long, measuring look. "I see," he murmured, in a tone that said he didn't and very much wanted to. "In that case, I'm sure you can appreciate the fact that, when and if this matter comes to trial, I will be sending you a subpoena."

"I don't think you want to do that," I said.

"And why would that be?"

"Reasons," I said.

"This is all very suspicious," he said.

"It is that," I said.

"I'm trying to prevent my client's house from being bulldozed out from underneath her and repair the credibility of my firm."

"In a way, so am I."

I could tell I was wearing on his patience. "Ms. Eckart, is there a point to this conversation?"

I glanced at Kitsmiller very briefly, gambling that Burton would see it. "I'm going to make a phone call," I said. "Excuse me for a moment." Favoring Burton with a significant glance and pulling out my phone I stepped outside. One handed I texted to Izzy **U and Drake stay inside.**

K I got in return.

I dug in my pockets for my cigarettes and lit one. Ordinarily smoking betrayed nervousness and therefore wasn't a good idea, but in this case appearing nervous worked to my advantage. By the time half my cigarette was gone the door opened and Burton stepped out. He had taken the time to wrap himself in a heavy Burberry overcoat; I wished I'd thought to do the same.

"If this is going to be more fencing," he said, "I don't have the time for it."

"It isn't," I said.

"I mean it about the subpoena," he said.

"I did too." I flicked ash off the tip of my smoke. "Look, if you put me on the stand I will be forced by the law and the ethics of my profession to tell everything I know - whether or not it benefits the person who subpoenaed me."

"I'm aware of that," he said.

"This includes the fact that someone was able to simply walk into your filing room and walk back out with one of your cases, no hassles."

Burton blinked. "I don't believe you," he said.

I pulled out my phone, clicked over to my email, and hit PLAY on the sound clip Izzy had sent me; the one where Hayes described the ease of his theft. "I've also got the file," I said, "because he gave it to me."

"That's receiving stolen property," Burton said. I could see a flush creeping up his fleshy neck, but his voice was dead calm. "And you're an accessory."

Despite the cold a drop of sweat ran down between my breasts. "I'm aware of that. But I would ask you what the public revelation that your firm's filing room is less than secure would do to your reputation."

Burton was quiet a moment. I knew he didn't like the idea of me saying that in a courtroom, and he knew that I would have to if he put me on the stand. "Are you trying to blackmail me, Ms. Eckart?"

"No, I'm about to try and bribe you."

I took a drag on my cigarette. "I'll return the file to you, and I'll get you the man who took them, and I'll get you proof that Mrs. Kitsmiller isn't the only victim here. How's a class-action lawsuit going after First American bank strike you on the profit scale?"

Burton stroked the line between his first and second chin with a finger. "I see. And in exchange for all of this...?"

"You let me give these things to you at times and places of my choosing, and we do it off the record," I said.

"So in exchange I have to trust you," he said.

"That's about right."

"I'll confess to having no idea what kind of game you're playing," he said softly.

"You aren't alone there," I said.

"I don't have to explain to you what will happen if you try to back-door me on this," he said.

"You'll take my business apart one lawsuit at a time?"

His shark's grin finally came out to play. I took that as an affirmative.

"I'll have to consider this," he said.

"Just as long as you consider it in private," I said.

He nodded.

A noise came from up the street; motorbikes, the Japanese kind, heading my way at a good clip. The skin on the back of my neck turned to ice as I watched eight single headlights make the turn onto Kitsmiller's street.

"Mister Burton," I said, "Get back inside."

He blinked. "Why?"

I loosened my handgun in its holster. "Things aren't done getting interesting yet."

He saw the bikes and didn't bother asking any more questions. We got the door shut just as eight rice rockets pulled up outside; some just had a rider, others carried a passenger. I did a fast head count and came up with a baker's dozen. At least that many curse words ran through my brain as I closed the door behind me.

"What's going on?" It was Izzy, sounding nervous.

"Uninvited guests," I said, making sure to keep my voice calm and level. "Izzy, take Kitsmiller and Burton upstairs and lock yourself in somewhere with a window. Get on the phone with the police and report a home invasion in progress." I looked over at Drake. "Watch the back door. Don't let anyone come in."

"What do I do if they try?" His voice was tight with tension.

"Shoot them until they stop," I said.

I picked up Kitsmiller's cigar box, the one with the Smith & Wesson in it, and handed it to her. "You remember what I told you," I said. She nodded.

"Boss," Izzy said softly, "what are you going to do?"

I pulled out my pistol and my flashlight, turning the light on and checking the beam. It was a little weak but it would have to do. I also took the time to grab my coat and hat; no sense in being uncomfortable while risking my life.

"I'm going to go have a chat with some folk," I said. Then I opened the door and stepped out onto the porch.

Eric Plume

Chapter 23

There was a brief instant where I felt like a true bad-ass stepping out onto that porch; in my trench coat and fedora, pistol in hand like the gunfighters of old, taking a walk into the rain to confront the doers of evil. Then I caught a look at the odds and realized my piece didn't have enough bullets in it for all the bad guys. That sort of magic has a habit of dissolving in the face of reality.

I was a tired thirty-three year old doing a dumb thing. I took a deep breath and got on with it.

The bikers had pulled up in a rough half-circle. The riders were the sort that frightened decent folk; old enough to cause harm, mean enough to do it and young enough not to fret the consequences. Most sported brand-new sports clothes, the expensive kind, and halfhearted goatees. I could see lumps and bulges in their clothing that could only have come from weapons.

At the sight of me they all stopped moving. Blank eyes fixed on me. I ignored the stares and made myself not zero in on any one of them. "Evening," I called out, loud enough to be heard.

No one spoke. I saw a hand move for a jacket pocket. My piece was already in my hand; I brought it to low ready, flashlight coming up likewise into what police called the Harries technique.

The would-be pistolero froze mid-draw. Thirteen young male faces transformed into identical expressions of shock.

"Don't," I snapped. My heart was a big bass drum inside my ribs.

One of them said something I didn't catch. I saw bravado edging back into their expressions and knew I'd better think of something quick. "The cops are already on their way," I said.

The biggest among them, a fox-faced specimen with a shaved head and an ugly smile, took a couple of steps towards me. "I ain't 'fraid of no bitch," he said. He took another step forward, hand coming up with something in it; not a gun but worrisome nonetheless. I squeezed the grip and felt the gun cock.

"Cool," I said. "That means you die first if the balloon goes up." He stopped moving, face going blank with surprise.

"Then the guy next to you," I continued. "After that, the one in the red hoodie. I hate hoodies."

Each one flinched as I singled them out; I knew they would. A mob is only as brave as the weakest member and their resolve cracked under the weight of individual fear. There was a moment where time seemed to stop, where the world narrowed to the gun in my hand and the crowd of boys in front of me. I didn't want to shoot them. I made my eyes say that I would.

"Everyone show me your hands, now." I put as much ice and rock into my voice as I knew how to.

Some of them started raising their hands, others started backing away. I shifted aim to one of the quickest backers and he froze where he stood. The rest got the picture and started putting their hands on top of their heads. The blood ran hot and fierce in my veins and some dark part of me clamored to shoot some of them anyway, just for daring to come here, for daring to fuck with me. I didn't listen but I wanted to and that scared me worse than dying.

Sirens started whooping in the distance, lots of them, and the angry gang fractured into scared teenaged individuals. Two took off down the road and I let them, three more dived between the houses and I let them go too. Six SPD black-and-whites screamed into the cul-de-sac as more patrolmen came running on foot from three different directions; there was a confusion of police jargon and barked commands as cops corralled the kids and put them in cuffs.

A big patrolman with a flashlight and a drawn service piece approached me. "Easy," he said in a gentle voice. "Just stand easy."

I wondered why he was telling me that until I realized my pistol was still in my hand; I stuck it back in my holster. It took me three tries to get it in. My hands didn't want to work right and then the strength went out of my legs, all at once. I mumbled something like "sorry I can't" at the cop before sitting on the steps and putting my head between my knees.

There was a blur where things happened and people said words I didn't respond to. I sat and counted cracks in Kitsmiller's front porch stair and tried not to throw up. It was loud and confused and I let it be that way because no one was bothering me. I felt like the time I'd tried mushrooms at seventeen; everything was scarier and blurrier and brighter than it should have been and all I wanted to do was sit and count cracks in the world.

"You okay?"

I jolted my head upright and saw someone leaning over me; my hand went for my pistol and didn't find it and that frightened me.

"Whoa, whoa," Drake said. "Relax, it's over, there are cops all over the place."

"My gun, where's my gun-"

"The cops have it," Drake said." You handed it to them."

"I did?"

"You did. All the gang bangers are in cuffs. It's over."

I took a deep breath and ran my hands through my hair. *It's over,* I told myself sternly. *Get a hold of yourself the troops are watching.* "Okay," I said. It didn't sound quite right so I said it again before getting to my feet. My legs were rubber and gooseflesh but after a second or two I figured them fit for standing.

I heard footsteps behind me and turned; it was Izzy, face locked in a mask of worry, eyes so wide the white showed all the way around. I did not have time to say anything before she seized me in a hug. I let her.

"It's okay," I said, "We're all okay now."

She said something in shaky Slovak, the words tumbling out of her mouth like dice. She was crying. I hugged her for a minute before gently prying myself loose and taking stock of my situation.

Around me a cold rain had begun to fall. There were squad cars and ambulances everywhere; their bright flashing lights made crazy patterns on the pavement and the air resounded with the sound of radios and men. I could see a pile of angular lumps on Kitsmiller's lawn, a patrolman standing over them with a notepad; weapons, taken from the gang who'd accosted me. A half-dozen pistols and twice as many knives. One of them had been packing a sawed-off shotgun. I swallowed and looked away.

A balding man about my height stood nearby wearing a gray suit, a frown half-hidden under a push-broom mustache. He had a notepad in his hands and a pencil which he tapped against the pad, impatience in his gaze. I was pretty sure I smiled at him.

"You ready to give a statement?" His voice was nasal and full of the same impatience.

I nodded. He asked me what happened and I told him. My words came out slow; one in front of the other, carefully placed like the steps of a drunk trying to act sober. I could tell this irritated him and I truly did not give a shit about it.

"...so, you just stepped out and faced down a dozen armed assailants?"

"Thirteen," I said.

He nodded. "You expect me to believe that?"

"Do a head-count."

"I did. They say they were minding their own business when you pulled a gun on them...threatened to kill three of them too, the way I hear it."

I laughed. He didn't.

"Look, Ms. Eckart...I've got thirteen witnesses that say one thing and I've got you saying another. No one in the house saw anything either."

"They have permits for that arsenal they were carrying? Is that shotgun barrel eighteen inches long like it's supposed to be?" I couldn't keep the contempt out of my voice. "Since when *can* you carry a shotgun around under your coat, anyway?"

"They'll do time for all that," The cop - Sanduski, his name was – said, "but in the meantime it's illegal to pull a piece on someone without cause."

I glanced over at the pile of weapons the cops were sweeping up. "Yeah, because I was totally out of line believing my life might have been at stake."

"You'd better drop the attitude," he growled, "or I'll book you for brandishing right here and now."

"Whatever gets you through the day."

His face turned red. "You think I won't do it?"

"I think you're about the fourteenth scariest person I've met this evening," I said. "Now, why don't you go find a doughnut and take a flying fuck at it so I can talk to a real cop, okay?"

The red in his face turned to white. He snarled something in Polish, and I thought he planned to hit me when someone barked "Sanduski that's enough!"

We both turned. Standing off to one side was a tow-headed slab of beef in a worn raincoat; he had a craggy face, a handlebar mustache and a glower that could have stopped a battle tank.

Sanduski started to bluster. The big detective silenced him with a look. "Take a walk, Sergeant," he rumbled.

I waited until Sanduski was out of earshot. "Is your department aware of the leash laws in this state?"

"Leash laws only apply to mammals," he said.

I grinned. "I'm Amber Eckart."

"I know." He showed me a badge. "Detective Lieutenant Mark Hammerman. I'm part of SPD's Gang Activity Task Force."

"Well, there's a gang force here that needs tasking," I said.

His smile was as fierce as his glare; in a chain mail

hauberk he would have looked right at home slaughtering Danes at Visby. "Do you think you could run through what happened here one more time?"

"I'll even do it with feeling," I said.

I went over it again; Hammerman listened and asked polite questions and took copious notes. At the end he asked me what I was doing at Kitsmiller's house; I showed him my PI license and invoked client privilege.

"Is Cordelia Kitsmiller your client?"

"I'm not at liberty to say," I said.

"Do you know a man named John Hayes?"

I hoped to hell that I managed not to twitch. "Excuse me?"

"Special Agent Jonathan William Hayes, Federal Bureau of Investigation," Hammerman said, watching me closely. "Do you know him?"

"In my profession I don't generally deal with the FBI," I said. "Should I know this guy?"

"Well, here's the funny thing," Hammerman said. "This Agent Hayes has been climbing up SPD's ass over some big fraud case he wants to run...problem is, he can't produce enough evidence to claim any sort of jurisdiction." He gave me another of his fierce little smiles. "Guy's a real pain in the ass."

"Can I ask what that has to do with what we're talking about here?"

"Kitsmiller's supposed to be one of the fraud victims," he said.

"I see." Again with the hoping there were no twitches; I was glad that Burton was here to keep Kitsmiller from blabbing everything to the cops. A drop of sweat ran down my neck as I mentally called Hayes every dirty name in the book.

"...And you don't know anything about this?"

I smiled at the big Viking in front of me. "Let me ask you a question, Lieutenant...how badly does your department want to avoid a sexual harassment complaint?"

He blinked. "What?"

"Sanduski leaned on me because you told him to," I said. "He's an attack dog and you told him to do what he did best...so you could show up and play reasonable father figure to his bark and bluster. Do I have that right?"

No response. That meant I did indeed have it right.

"Good cop, bad cop?" I shook my head. "I think I'm

insulted."

"You were in mild shock," he muttered. "It was a play."

"Better luck next time," I said. "But right now I want my gun back, I want my two friends released and I want to go home."

"Suppose I decide to bring you down for more questioning."

"Suppose I throw a big girly hissy-fit over the fact that one of your officers called me a cock-sucking whore when the reporters show up."

"Oh come on, he didn't -"

"Saying it in Polish," I said, "doesn't make it any less sexually harassing."

Hammerman tugged on one corner of his mustache while I silently blessed Izzy for teaching me to curse in other languages. Finally he turned to a nearby patrolman. "Get this lady her pistol," he said, "and let the other two go. We're done here."

The patrolman moved off, leaving me alone with Hammerman. He gave me a long silent look; the sort older men give out when their value judgment system ran through its metrics and bylaws. It was tough not to wilt under such a gaze but I managed. I'd learned how growing up; my father had been a master of that look.

"Okay, Ms. Eckart," he said. "I apologize for the bad behavior of my brother officer. If you'd like a written apology and some sort of punitive action to be taken, I'll see that done as well."

"An apology seems to have cured me of my hissy fit," I said. "I'll forget it happened. Especially when the reporters are around."

"Don't leave town, and answer the phone if I call," he said. "I will have further questions for you."

I put on my most respectful expression and threw in a sincere nod. There was nothing to be gained from antagonizing Hammerman further. He favored me with one last glance before ambling off, leaving me by myself for the first time in about two hours. I pulled out a cigarette, lighting it while I watched a score of police clean up an attempted home invasion.

"Lucky," I muttered to the night sky. "You got fucking lucky tonight."

Chapter 24

I finished my cigarette while waiting for the last of the adrenaline-induced silliness to wear off. I kicked myself for letting that cop Sanduski get me riled; he deserved to get cussed out for his bullshit but it never paid to antagonize the police and anyway, it was poor form to lose your temper on the job. Hammerman was more of a worry; not only was he a better class of cop and a sharper detective, he seemed to have suspicions already about my connection to Hayes. It was blind luck and a pinch of bluffing that had saved me from continued questioning, nothing more. I wondered what stray fact had made his antenna twitch like that.

Drake and Izzy came up to me as I finished the last drag; Drake looked tense and wired, whereas Izzy just looked shell-shocked. I patted her on the shoulder. Her smile was a faint thing, but it still showed up.

"Hanging in there, girl?"

"Yeah," Izzy said. "S-still a little shook up, y'know?"

"I know," I said.

Drake looked at me. "You face down all those dudes on your own?"

I nodded. "Mob mentality is simple to break when you know how it works."

"I guess that's why mobs aren't dangerous or anything," he said with a grin.

"I said simple, not easy." The rain had stiffened while I'd been smoking; I turned up the collar on my coat to keep out the cold.

"Definitely not playing poker against you," he said.

"I always preferred blackjack," I said.

"It shows."

Around us the cops were leaving, either fanning out to catch any stragglers from the posse that had assaulted me or to ferry those already caught for their date with a cell. There were two units parked in the cul-de-sac; I knew from experience they'd remain until morning. At least they had turned off their flashing lights; the moving shadows they threw off kept telling my hind brain that someone was trying to sneak up on me.

I saw Carter Burton picking his way across the street and walked to meet him halfway. His comb-over was askew and his face looked a little pale, but his eyes were still cool and calm. He favored me with a respectful nod.

"I have to thank you for what you did," he said.

"No you don't," I replied. "My people were inside too. You can call it professional courtesy if you like."

He nodded. "I won't forget it," he said.

"I know," I said.

I thought I saw a glimmer of humor in his eyes when he studied me, but that might have been a trick of the fading sunlight. He passed me a business card. "We have a deal," he said. "Stay in touch."

I took the card and tucked it in my purse, in the pocket I reserved for cards I actually wanted to keep. "I just might need to," I said.

His eyes gleamed when he smiled. "I thought so."

"How is Mrs. Kitsmiller?"

He tucked his overcoat tighter around his body. "Resting," he said. "The stress wasn't exactly good for her, but she's a tough little lady."

Izzy shivered and so did I. "I'll be in touch," I said, "but for right now I'm going to go find a place to pass out."

"Watch your back, Ms. Eckart."

"I plan to."

He turned around and headed towards his BMW.

We climbed into my gray Golf. I gave him plenty of space to pull out before doing the same thing. I waited for the squares of his tail-lights to recede completely into the distance before I started driving.

"Why the wait?" Drake asked.

"To make sure he's not following us," I said. "Also, watch behind us...make sure neither of those squad cars tries to tail us, now that I think on it."

"You think that Hammerman guy would try to tail you?"

"Wouldn't bet against it," I said as I put my car in gear. The clutch went through its normal litany of moaning and complaining; something in the bowels of my car was about to give out, something I needed to have looked at soon. Or maybe I'd just get a new car.

The streets were quiet as I threaded my way back to our hotel; Drake reported no sign of any tails but I kept my eyes checking the rear-view mirrors anyway out of habit. In them Izzy stared out the window with a fixed blankness that worried me. No one had much to say, and that was fine with me; my head was full of violence I was perfectly happy not to share.

My fingers tightened on the steering wheel as I recalled the hot feeling of adrenaline. It was somewhere between wrath and great sex you knew you shouldn't want, close to the one time I had tried cocaine but not quite as sinfully *good*. I tried to put the feeling out of my mind but it wouldn't go away.

I had wanted to kill those kids. Just to do it, just because.

"Hey," Drake said into my thoughts, "you okay?"

I nodded. I didn't trust myself to speak.

The hotel was dark and silent when we pulled up out front; I said to hell with it and gave them my keys for valet parking. The valet's professional courtesy was strained at the sight of my little posse and my beat-up ride, but he made a manful effort not to notice and I made a similar effort not to care. I was too tired anyway.

When we got up to the room I gave the minibar a glance but shook off the urge. One stiff drink and I might fall apart, and the troops were still watching. I settled for washing my face instead.

"Okay," Drake said as I finished drying off, "what's the thing?"

"What thing?"

He gave me a serious look. "The thing that's eating at you, that you didn't want to talk about in front of Izzy."

I shook my head. "I almost got killed tonight, Drake. It's bothering me some."

"And what else?"

"I can't do this right now," I said.

"Why not? You're heading for a crackup."

I took off my shoes and sat down. "No, I'm not."

"You sure?"

"I'm not," I said, "because I can't be."

He just stood there for a second, clearly at a loss. I dredged up whatever my brain could reasonably call a smile. "It's like this, Drake...I'm the boss. The boss always knows what to do, even when they don't. The boss is never afraid, even when they are. The boss is always in control, even when they aren't." I couldn't hold the smile. "Anything less isn't responsible leadership. Anything less could get my people hurt and I can't have that."

He walked over and crouched down next to my chair. "Careful with that," he said softly. "You get too wound, you start making mistakes."

I ran a hand over his dreadlocks. He smiled. "I know," I said.

"Please remember," he said.

"I will."

There was a knock at the door. I stood and pulled out my gun, keeping it behind my back as I went to the door and checked the peephole; it was Julian. I put my pistol back in its holster and opened the door.

"What's up?"

"It's Izzy," Julian said, sounding worried. "She's in the bathroom, and she won't come out. I think she's freaking."

I restrained a sigh. "Stay here. I'll go talk to her."

Julian and Izzy's room was considerably messier than mine; clothes covered a good part of the floor and the table was crammed with computer gear and empty soda cans. I wondered how two people could make such a mess in such a short time as I picked my way through the clutter and knocked on the bathroom door. No response.

"Izzy? It's me," I said.

After almost a minute I heard, "I-I'm okay." Her voice sounded raw even through the door.

"You sure? You want to talk?"

No response. I tried the door. It was unlocked; I slipped inside. Izzy was curled up against the far wall, arms around her knees. Her face was mottled red and white, skin damp with old tears while her eyes shone with new ones. I crossed the room and crouched down next to her.

"You sure don't look okay to me," I said.

She sniffed and wiped at her tears with more force than necessary. "I'll be fine," she muttered. "Sorry about this, boss."

I patted her on the knee. "Hey, things got scary tonight."

"Not for me," she said. "I just...I can't *deal* with this stuff, boss. I hate it...its stupid."

"No it isn't," I said softly. "I know why – you told me, remember?"

"Yeah," she said.

I gave her a hug. She clung to me and I let it happen. Izzy had come a long way from the twitchy recluse I'd hired a few years back...far enough that I sometimes forgot she still had demons in her closet.

We sat like that for a bit before I let her go. She blinked and wiped her face.

"I think...I think next time I'll bow out of the fieldwork, boss."

I nodded. "I'm sorry about taking you along. I

should've thought that through."

"Sorry I'm a wimp," she said.

"No need to apologize for something you aren't," I said. "Izzy, you've got your strengths and I have mine. Don't feel bad because violence bothers you...trust me, it's better than the other thing."

"Yeah. It's just..." she looked away. "I couldn't stand the thought of you getting hurt."

I blinked. "Why?"

"Without the firm, I'd...I'd have to go home." I felt her shudder.

"Izzy, that's not going to happen," I said. "We'll get through this. Now, I need you to work, okay?"

She nodded. "One question," she said.

"Shoot."

"Does Drake look as hot naked as I think he does?"

I snorted laughter. "Hotter," I said.

"Lucky," she murmured.

"I guess I am." I patted her on the knee. "Come on, let's get back on the case."

She pushed her glasses back up on her nose. "Yeah."

I let her wash her face and straighten up a bit before

we went back across the hall to my room. I found Drake showing Julian the finer points of holding his .22 automatic; Julian had the awkward interest of the gun-illiterate, but I figured there was no harm in him learning.

"Okay guys," I said, "here's what's next on the menu." I rummaged through the clothes I'd purchased and laying things out. "I need to know if there is any connection - at all - between Govrolev and Hansen. I also need to know who Mister Pimp is. If the information is online at all, find it."

"Just me?" Izzy said.

"All of you," I said, "Drake too. A lot of the looking is going to be straight up Google grinding and it'll go faster with all of you."

Izzy nodded. "Thanks."

Julian looked at me. "What are you going to do?"

I checked the action on my pistol. "I'm going to go get some other answers."

Drake looked at me. "How?"

"The old fashioned way," I said. "Ask somebody."

Chapter 25

The Gridiron Tavern was located on a side street off Aurora Avenue, where the hookers of Seattle had once congregated in droves. A host of new regulations made taking customers back to the cheap motels difficult. There were always still a few lonely holdouts plying their trade here and there, but nowhere near what it had once been. They hadn't disappeared, of course; they'd simply moved to another area. When the police left, they'd come back.

The rummage through my bag didn't yield much to work with; though I own a bunch of clothes purchased for the express purpose of changing my appearance, they were all safely back at my apartment, and I was not. I had debated running back there for something appropriate and decided against it. If the bad guys could stake out my hotel as quickly as they had, they could certainly stake out my apartment. I made do with a knee-length skirt, a pair of black patent heels and what I called my 'informant blouse'; a gray silk number that when paired with a lace push-up bra managed to transform my chest into something that was apparently hard for men to avoid staring at. I wore it when I needed to provoke a positive reaction from male interviewees, and it seemed appropriate for a single thirty-something female to wear to a bar. I went heavy on the makeup, both to conceal the bruises on my face and because I wanted to appear as someone in their thirties who wanted to look twenty-four. The end result hadn't looked all that great under the harsh florescent lighting in the hotel bathroom but would likely pass muster in the dimness of a bar. I left my hair down because I normally wore it up. I didn't look much different, but at least I didn't look like I had when Kasey beat me up. That was something.

Drake had wanted to come with me; fortunately I managed to convince him to stay behind, on the premise that someone ought to watch Izzy and Julian while I was away. He hadn't liked it but in the end he had bowed to the logic.

I pulled into the lot at half past eight, found a spot with a burnt-out streetlight above it and parked there. Other than a few cars and one cold-looking girl in ripped jeans, the only people in sight were the smokers out front of the bar. I brought my binoculars up and gave the bouncer a scan; not my guy. Which was all to the good; from my memory of bar schedules, ten o'clock would be shift change.

I hefted my H & K and debated for a second; carrying handguns into bars is illegal in

Washington, and losing my CPL would be just as permanent a problem as getting killed, if less serious. I decided to depend on pepper spray and staying public for my safety, however reluctantly. The gun went under the seat.

A quick dash across the street caused a drunken whistle from one of the smokers. I ignored it completely; experience had taught me that the sort of man who catcalls at strange women views any reaction from her short of a kick in the groin as a come-on.

The Gridiron turned out to be a dive in the great American tradition, a cheap bar patiently grown from the preserved tissues of that one Patrick Swayze movie. The influence showed. Greasy roots-rock swaggered out of sub-par speakers. Leather-faced cougars armored in cosmetics glittered and posed beneath flickering neon, their eyes as blank and brittle as marble glass. Blustery college boys swilled beer and fondled tramp-stamped coeds in tight pants and halter tops. Hard-core regulars drank their way through another wobble in their personal burnout cycle. Long spirals of unfocused conversation crashed into each other, each contributing to the noise they wanted to be heard over. The place reeked of beer and body fluids and Lysol. There was little danger, just glazed-over lust and curdled hope and artless frustration. I wanted to walk out before I'd come through the door.

I pushed my way through the cloud of smoke and beer-breath infecting the entryway. The bouncer, a tall specimen with the boulder-shaped muscles of a bodybuilder, let me through with a nod and a glance at my chest. I didn't object to the ogling; I'd worn the blouse for a reason.

I staked out a corner booth and made a show of checking my makeup in my compact mirror, keeping an expression of wary interest on my face; just another thirty-something, looking for love. A waitress in her forties with fissured skin and stiff blond hair asked me for a drink order. No way would I trust the wine in a place like this, so I ordered Smirnoff and tonic. She brought it quick enough that I told her to keep the change. A sip told me I'd made a mistake. The vodka tasted like the back wall of a medicine cabinet. Wolfschmidt's maybe, or Monarch. I hid my grimace.

After an hour and three propositions Kasey still hadn't showed. I made myself finish my drink and sure enough Blondie appeared and asked if I wanted another.

"Is Chuck coming in tonight?" I set my face into what I figured was an expression of bashful hope.

The waitress hesitated. "We can't discuss schedules," she said in a gummy voice. "Sorry."

I dropped a twenty on the table. "Another one please," I said, "and keep the change." The twenty vanished. "You know, I really was hoping to see him."

She shrugged. "He comes in at ten. I didn't tell you."

She moved off to fill my order, coming back a good deal quicker than the last time. When I sipped, the sour taste was gone. Amazing how much courtesy the right dead President can provide.

The crowd got thicker and louder; by three-quarters past nine I'd started to wonder how anyone could delude themselves into thinking romance happened in such a place. From watching the various pair-offs I could see from my booth, I was pretty sure the delusions of those involved had grown quite frayed. I nursed my second vodka and tried to stay inconspicuous; a couple of drunks wandered up anyway and I gave them the brush-off. Fortunately they were the harmless kind that went away when a woman got frigid. I was about to text Drake with an update when a shadow fell across my table. I looked up to brush off the next drunk.

Chuck Kasey looked down at me, face set in an expression of faint amusement. "Evening, Miss.

Mind if I sit down?"

I tried not to flinch at the sound of his voice. "If I do," I said, "you aren't going to care."

He smiled and slid into the booth. "Heard you wanted to talk to me."

"Wanted is the wrong word," I said.

"And yet you haven't told me to fuck off," he said.

"No, I haven't."

Up close he was as average as he had looked through my binoculars; a bit fitter than I had first thought but otherwise just a face in a crowd. He had the close-cropped cut most men settle on when their hair starts to part ways with their scalp. Pale eyes set in a long face with a Northwest complexion. He didn't look like a thug. He looked like anyone who might show up at my high school reunion.

My waitress placed a Rolling Rock in front of him without being asked. He tipped the bottle at her with a smile before taking a sip and looking back at me. "So how'd you find me?"

"I looked."

He sipped some beer. "You know, I didn't like roughing you up."

"I bet you say that to all the girls you almost put in

the hospital," I said.

He studied my face for a moment. I could feel his gaze examining my bruises. "My apologies about the other two. I didn't want them there."

I laughed without humor. "Whatever," I said. "I'm more curious about the why behind the bullshit you pulled."

He blinked. "Bullshit?"

"Cornering the PI and throwing them a beating, hoping they'll back off? Come on, everyone knows that never works." I stirred my drink with the little plastic sword in it.

"I was looking for the name of your employer," he said.

"And you thought I'd cave under some punches," I said.

He shrugged. "I underestimated you. It won't happen again."

Since I was taking such an awful risk simply sitting this close to him I gave him a closer look. The evidence of his trade was there, just not obvious. His nose had been broken numerous times. There were tiny white scars on the backs of his hands and fingers, fainter ones around his eyes. His knuckles were swollen and his skin had the gritty look of someone used to having it torn up. And his eyes never stopped taking in details.

"So," I said, "now you're here, and I'm here...what do we talk about?"

"I was hoping you'd know." He studied the bottle of beer in front of him. "Considering you came and found me and all."

"Didn't think I would?"

He smiled. Something about the way he did it made his teeth look like tombstones in a field. "Oh, I was pretty sure you would. I just figured you for the bullet-to-the-back sort."

"Don't know if I should be appreciative or insulted," I said.

"Settle for both," he replied.

I sipped some more vodka. "I don't suppose you'd tell me who paid to have my lights punched out."

"I don't suppose you'd climb under this here booth and polish my knob while I order another beer."

"From what I've seen, Hansen's pet hooker would be a better choice for that," I said.

For a moment he was silent. I could see the gears turning swiftly behind his eyes; whatever else he was, Charles Kasey did not appear to be stupid.

"What the hell are you down here for?"

I took another sip of my drink. "Why didn't you like roughing me up?"

Another shrug. "You didn't have it coming."

"Who does?"

"Plenty of people, and we both know it," he said. His voice hadn't changed at all, and neither had his smile. From a distance we looked like just another hookup in progress.

"Did Andy Stark have it coming?"

He shook his head. "That wasn't me, I'll have you know."

"You expect me to believe that?"

"I don't care either way," he said.

I set my drink aside and leaned in closer. "How did he die?"

"Why should I tell you?"

I made sure I looked him in the eye. "I'm asking nicely," I said.

He looked at me. I looked at him. His eyes were the color of pool water, a blue so pale it was almost clear.

People say that the eyes are the windows to the soul; it's true, but only when the person being viewed opens that window. Charles Kasey chose that moment to, and I knew what I saw behind the black humor and artful apathy; something old and ugly and very human. Something society has always been too frightened to examine but depends on just the same. I wanted to look away. I didn't.

"Stark was shot by a tweaker kid looking for fix money," Kasey said softly. "Same tweaker got himself stabbed buying that fix a day later."

"My," I said, "that's convenient."

"Not for either of them."

"Was the kid Russian?"

Kasey grinned. "Y'know, I do believe he was."

He paused as Blondie appeared with another beer for him, smiling at her as she put it down. She smiled back before leaving.

"So what happens now?"

"I ask you one more time to take a walk." His tone wasn't threatening; if anything I caught a note of pleading in it. He wanted me to say something. I had to figure out what it was.

"Maybe you should instead," I said.

"Not in my nature to quit," he said.

"Not in mine either," I said.

He leaned back, staring off into space. "Well, there it is."

"Let's play a game," I said. "Let's pretend someone *did* ask you to take me out of the picture...what would you do?"

"Ask for twenty five grand," he said. "Cash."

"That the going rate for a corpse these days?"

"So I hear," he said.

"Christ," I said, "I'd be worth more dead than alive."

"Most people are."

I took a sip of my drink and did my best not to think about the drop of sweat running down my spine. "Then I'd be dead and you'd be next."

"Maybe," he said.

"No maybe about it. You'd know too much."

He gave me his tombstone smile again. "In this game, we are both their creatures."

"Not a fan of that," I said.

"Neither am I."

I sat and added it all up, two by two; it didn't take long, and I did not like the result I got but then again I had not been expecting to. He watched me with the measured intensity of a scientist observing an experiment.

"I've gotta get to work," he said." You're a tough little lady, Ms. Eckart. You're tough and you're all right and I hope I don't have to see you again." He made as if to get up.

"Wait."

I waved to Blondie. Charles Kasey's eyes were still cold as stones, but I thought I detected a faint glimmer of hope. Hope, and an even fainter glimmer of respect.

"One more round," I said.

"Why?"

"I know what I want to talk about now," I said.

Chapter 26

I drove back to the hotel, checking my rear-view for tails the entire way. I didn't spot any and congratulated myself on avoiding the bad guys for one more night. A certain kind of excitement had set up shop in my back brain; the sort that's just to the left of fear, just to the right of adrenaline. It's the sort that will kill you on a long enough timeline but small doses of it feel almost like the first time you have sex. You have no idea why, but it's appealing and frightening and you want to keep doing it. It's the thing spies and criminals live on. By the time I was halfway back to the hotel I was pretty sure the feeling scared the hell out of me.

One of the nice things that had happened recently was the privatization of liquor in Washington; this meant that booze was available whenever grocery stores were open. I stopped at a QFC and picked up a fifth of Wild Turkey 101, paying with my magical expense account.

Drake was waiting for me when I got back. He yawned and stretched. "Everyone else is asleep," he said. "We found some stuff out." He passed me a printout I read it as I took off my pistol and set it on the nightstand.

I gave it a scan. "So Mister Pimp's name is actually Vadim Rodchenko...born in Kiev, family moved here in 1998."

"He had a fake identity," Drake said, "but it was thinner than a Guess model. It took Izzy less than an hour to poke a hole in it."

"That girl's a prodigy." I walked over to where the ice bucket was. Someone had been kind enough to fill it. I got a glass, filled it with ice and poured bourbon into all the spaces around the ice cubes, right up to the brim. *Sledgehammer* was what my college friends had called this sort of drink; I hadn't fixed one since before I'd learned better.

Drake watched me. "How'd it go?"

I took a long swallow of the bourbon. The ice in my glass had barely melted and I got the Turkey at full strength. It hit my mouth like a right hook.

"It went," I said.

"You okay?"

I gunned down another third of the drink. "No."

He walked over, sat beside me and put an arm around my shoulders. I was so wired that I jumped, but when he went to take his arm back I grabbed it and leaned against him instead.

"Want to talk?"

"No. Yes. I don't know. Not yet." I leaned forward, pulled the bottle and the other glass off the table and poured a second drink. Drake looked confused when I put it in the hand that wasn't holding me.

"Keep up," I said.

He took a gulp to match mine and coughed. "Jesus," he muttered, "this stuff tastes like paint remover."

"Means you need another one," I said.

We sat like that for a while; the only sound was the distant blare of traffic and the clink of ice from our glasses. The spring-steel tension in my back eased by the time my first drink was gone, replaced by warmth and the swell of nameless emotion. We moved from the bed to the table, the bottle between us along with the bucket of ice. There was an ashtray in one of the nightstand drawers and I went and got it, setting it next to the bottle. Then I dug out the cigarettes I and lit one. With the latticed shadows on the carpet and the curl of smoke in the air, I felt like Philip Marlowe. Only Marlowe always had a witty line to say and never looked like he was about to cry.

"I was sixteen," I said. "I was sixteen when I screwed up my life."

Drake stayed silent. I kept talking.

"My family has six generations of public servants in it, going back over a hundred years," I said. "My great-grandfather won a Silver Star at Argonne, then came home and chased bootleggers on the Hudson. His father fought the Chicago Fire. My grandfather was a county sheriff in Oregon. My father, thirty years with Seattle and Lynden as a police officer." I took another drink. "Three of my uncles have almost fifty years of FBI time between them. One of them got a Distinguished Flying Cross...rescue choppers, Vietnam. It goes on."

"And then there's you," Drake said.

I laughed. More of a snort, really. "I was an only child."

"And you wanted to live the ideal," Drake said.

"I wanted to be a cop," I said. "My dad was all for it. He'd known plenty of female officers in his time and figured they were just as good as any of the men. He backed me up against my mom when she didn't want me to do it. I studied about what I'd need to know. I was serious about it."

There was a lump in my chest, a pressure like acid reflux. I poured myself another drink just as ambitious as the last one and took a deep sip.

"But, you know, I was a teenager too. I tiptoed out of the house and went to parties. I had boyfriends that weren't good for me, that kind of thing. It's what you get into at that age...especially in a small town where there isn't much of anything to do." I stopped talking.

"So then what happened?"

"I applied to the Lynden City Police Department. And I was rejected."

Drake blinked. "Why?"

I took a big gulp from my drink. The walls were blurry and I couldn't feel the burn as the liquor slid down my throat. Part of me knew this wasn't a good sign and the rest of me didn't care at all. The lump of feelings now filled my whole chest.

"When you go to be a cop there's all sorts of questions you have to answer," I said. "My dad told me to be honest on all of them because they'd know if I lied and so I did. I told them everything. And when it got to questions about drugs I'd done, I answered those honestly too. Yes, I'd smoked pot. Yes, I'd drank alcohol. Yes, I'd tried mushrooms once."

The lump sprouted teeth and gnawed on my breastbone. I drank bourbon and smoked more of my cigarette.

"Apparently doing psychedelics of any kind makes you unfit to be an officer. One of those little bylines most people don't know about. They wouldn't take me, and that was that. They never would've known if I hadn't told them."

"Damn," Drake said.

"It took less than two days for it to be all over town. My father wouldn't talk to me. He wouldn't even look at me. So I left home."

"Where did you go?"

"As far away as I could get." I was surprised by how much venom was in my voice.

"You were living in Bellingham when I met you," he said. "That's about ten minutes from Lynden."

My laugh tasted like bile. "I didn't say I got very far."

Drake took a sip of his drink. "You ever patch things up with your dad?"

"No." I finished off my glass and poured another. There wasn't much ice left in the glass and I didn't add more.

"Maybe you will someday."

"I can't," I said.

"Why?"

I stared straight ahead. "He died three years ago."

There was a long silence.

"I'm scared, Drake. I'm scared because there was one thing I wanted to do with my life and I couldn't do it. All my family, all of them going back a hundred fucking years could do it and I couldn't. There's this big wall of medals and awards and photos in the house I grew up in and I'm never going to be on it and *that's all my fucking fault.* Do you know what that's like?"

"No," he said. "I don't."

Something about the way he said it made me look up.

"My mother put me up for adoption when I was born," he said. "I've never met her or my dad." He pinched the skin on his arm. "All I know for sure is that I'm not white. So no, I don't have any notion about what you're going through." He smiled. "Sorry."

I took a deep breath. "Jesus, I shouldn't have put this on you," I said.

"You didn't put anything on me," he said. He stood up and moved my glass out of my lap and put his arms around my shoulders. The room had started to spin and I could feel my stomach contracting around the whiskey.

"That big wall of medals your family earned," he said. "It's cool to be part of that, but it obliges you some...am I right?"

I nodded.

"You choose who you want to be in this life," he said. "All anything else can do is make suggestions."

I was torn between wanting to laugh and wanting to cry. "It's not that simple, Drake."

"It is," he said softly, "it just isn't that easy."

I felt a tear slide down my cheek and I wiped it away with far more force than I needed to. "Christ, I'm acting like a stupid twit." The words came out mushy and raw and I knew I'd had far too much to drink. Somewhere in there that had been a plan.

"No," he said, "you're scared and you want to talk. That's good. Maybe next time you won't feel the need to drink yourself sick before you do it."

"I'm not sick," I said. It took me three tries to say it.

"You will be," he said.

Fifteen long minutes later Drake was proven right, for all that I didn't admit it until it was almost too late; pride goeth before a fall. I careened into the bathroom when my guts went from discontent to open rebellion. He followed me and held my hair while I heaved bourbon and bile into the toilet.

"This is humbling," I muttered.

"Can't drink like you used to?"

"No," I said, "I just shouldn't."

Drake had to help me back out to the chair when I was done. I could smell bourbon fumes rising from the glass and it made my stomach curl into a ball. Drake capped the bottle and put it away. The room spun every time I closed my eyes, so I kept them open and focused on a discolored spot in the carpet. He rinsed the glass out and got me some water. I sipped at it.

"This was dumb," I said.

"So why'd you do it?"

"Wanted to talk. I'm bad at it."

"You're scared you'll screw things up again?"

I nodded.

"With other people's lives on the line this time?"

Nod, nod, nod.

He smiled at me. "I don't think you will. You've brought us all this far...and besides, you've always been smarter than you think you are."

He hugged me and I hugged him back. We sat like that for a time.

Drake brushed some hair off my forehead. "You ever talk about this with anyone?"

I shook my head.

"Why now?"

I sipped some water and listened to the traffic and smelled the cigarette smoke and watched the shadows on the floor. There was no poetry to it now, just irritating noise and a smell like used hamster bedding and a checkerboard shadow pattern on the carpet that didn't really mean anything. Finally I looked at him.

"I wanted someone to know," I said.

Chapter 27

Whatever trickster god responsible for dishing out hangovers left me alone the next morning; aside from a bit of stomach discomfort my misadventure with the whiskey the previous night didn't affect my functionality any. I was grateful because I still had work to do.

My first action was to pour the rest of the Wild Turkey down the sink. Drake watched me do it without comment. The next was to call my people in so we could plot our next move.

Julian spoke first. "I found something else out last night when I went to go visit Shelly," he said.

I cocked an eye at him. "You went on a date?"

"I've still got a life, boss. Besides, it ended up being a good idea." He unfolded a piece of paper and set it on the desk. "Shelly works for a catering company. She told me about this big party that's happening in a week...it's for a development group to celebrate their buildings being all environmentally friendly. Izzy ran a search this morning and found this ad." He grinned. "Recognize some of the names?"

I looked at the sheet. "I do," I said. "I'll assume you didn't tell your girl anything."

"Of course not, boss. She mentioned it and I just sort of kept her talking."

"Good boy." I smiled at him and he beamed. Izzy gave me an unreadable look but didn't say anything.

"So," I said after a moment, "I guess we need to be there. How do we get in the door?"

Izzy looked over at Julian. "Could your girlfriend get one of us in?"

Julian shook his head. "She's, like, low on the totem pole, y'know? I mean, I could ask, but -"

"Again with the not telling anyone," I said. "Besides, I'm guessing you don't want to put her in any danger."

"That'd be a good guess," Julian said.

"When is the party?"

Julian shrugged. "Friday evening, starts at six. We've got some time."

I thought for a moment. "There's always the classic approach," I said. "One of us gets dolled up and makes like we're supposed to be there. Straps on some recording gear, that whole gig."

Izzy nodded. "Also, I looked...the security on their website is horrible. I could get one of us on the guest list, no sweat."

I thought about the ramifications of that particular bit of computer crime and decided it was worth the risk. "Do it," I said to Izzy, "but don't get caught."

She made a face. "Boss, it's a hotel's IT department...They aren't gonna catch me. They could jump out a tenth-story window and not catch the ground."

I laughed. "Fair enough."

Julian spoke next. "How are you planning on getting in?"

"Having Izzy put me on the guest list and showing up," I said.

"No, what I meant was...well, this party's pretty upscale."

"I know, which means I'll need to look upscale," I said. "And I have a friend who can help me with that."

I pulled out my phone.

Candi's number rang five times before I heard a clumsy pick-up. "Yes?" Her voice was a little heavy on the breathing. I heard a crack, the sound of leather against flesh, followed by a guttural moan.

"I'm not interrupting anything, am I?"

"Nothing that cannot be interrupted, *cherie.*" she said. In the background I could hear at least two other voices; one male and soft, one female and full of giggles. "What do you need?"

"I need your expert opinion on fashion," I said. "Want to go on a shopping spree?"

In the background the female giggles turned into a gasp. "Give me an hour," she said. "I'll meet you at Pacific Place."

I smiled. "I'll give you two."

"*Bonne,*" she said and hung up.

I tucked my phone away and looked at Drake. "Come on," I said. "You'll need some fitting out too."

Going undercover as a private investigator is as much art as it is anything else; unlike a police officer, no one's generally backing you up and there is always the possibility that someone will violently object to the fact that you are where you've chosen to insinuate yourself. The fact that I usually don't have to perform surveillance on the sort of people who kill out of habit only partially makes up for this. And with the matter in front of me, they had already proven their desire – and ability – to do exactly that.

So I needed to spend a serious amount of Hayes'

money on a proper disguise. Spending serious money was something I hadn't done in a long time and I felt strange about it.

I set Izzy and Julian to figuring out recording gear; they were to text me what they needed if they found they needed something, but other than that to at least try and make do with what we'd already purchased. After all, there was using an expense account and then there was abusing it.

I met Candi at the Pacific Place Mall along with Drake; we beat her there, but only by a few minutes. She walked up resplendent in a cream silk peasant blouse, wine-colored skirt and Paris heels, an ankle-length black Burberry overcoat protecting her from the chill. She greeted me as she always did; I saw Drake notice.

"Morning, *cherie.*" She turned her gaze on my companion and her smile warmed several degrees.

"This is...my boyfriend," I said. "Drake, meet Candace Estermont."

They both looked at me. Candi raised an eyebrow. Drake's were busy trying to get lost in his dreadlocks. I didn't say anything further, so they turned back to each other and shook hands.

"So," Candi said, "you need to be fabulous?"

"I need to be fashionable and upscale," I said. "It's for a party."

"But you never go to parties."

"It's for work."

She nodded. "Anything I should know?"

"The less you do, the better," I said as we walked towards the entrance. Pacific Place is one of the most upscale malls in Seattle and the entryway showed the fact off.

She tapped one finger against her chin. "I will need to know more. Otherwise I cannot really help you."

I sighed. She was right. "The party is a bunch of high-class land developers and their financial backers doing a meet-and-greet at the Four Seasons. The invitation says black tie. I need to look like I belong there yet not attract any attention."

Candi nodded. "Your persona?"

I blinked at her. She smiled back.

"*Cherie*, if you are to look like you belong you will have to know what role you are to play."

Drake grinned. "She's got you there."

I tried not to look too flustered. "A wealthy investor," I said without too much hesitation.

"What is our budget for this endeavor?"

I held up the Davis-Callion credit card. "We buy what we need," I said.

Candi gave me a satisfied look. "Then let us get started."

With that, I followed Candi as she proceeded to turn Pacific Place upside down and shake until fashionable clothing for me fell out.

The first thing Candi handed me was a set of Spanx; I felt an embarrassed twinge at needing body-shaping underwear but cold facts managed to beat my ego into submission. Especially when I considered what I might look like without it as Candi began pulling gowns off racks and handing them to me. I took a glance at the price tag on the first gown and almost choked on my eyeballs. "This is seven thousand dollars, Candi."

"It is what you need," she said.

"The only time I've spent over five thousand dollars on anything, it ran on gasoline," I muttered, running the fabric of the dress through my fingers. It was silk, smooth and pliant as cool water. The finery felt intimidating; I wanted to put it down. Candi walked over and took the dress from me. "First," she said, "an exercise." She set the clothes back down and walked out of the store. Drake and I followed. I was confused and I could tell Drake wasn't far off.

"What's she doing?" Drake ran a hand over his dreadlocks.

"No idea," I said.

We walked into a perfume shop across the way from the dress store. I stood, feeling like half a teenager again while Candi chatted up the attendant. After twenty seconds of conversation Candi turned with a bottle of Chanel scent in her hands. "Buy it," she said.

Her voice rang with the cold indifference of an order; I found myself reaching for the credit card without meaning to. I watched as the attendant wrapped the bottle in paper and slid it into a box. She handed it to me with a professional smile. I hefted the bottle; it had rung up at more than my average budget for utility bills.

Candi led me out of the store; I followed, still holding the perfume bottle. She walked over towards a trash bin, turned and looked at me. "Now," she said, "throw it away."

"What?"

"You heard me."

The bottle felt heavy in my hands. "Look, Candi -"

"Do it."

My old friend struck the pose of a scholar. "To be truly wealthy," she intoned, "is to never have to remember to count. What you want, you buy. Money is a convenience, nothing more. If you are going to pull this off you must be able to display that...and others must believe it." Her eyes softened. "*Cherie,* you have never been rich in your entire life. I have. This is what it means." She pointed at the bottle of Chanel. "Throw it away."

I hefted the bottle once more before pitching it into the trash. It felt like someone punching me in the kidneys. I made myself not flinch, and I made sure not to look back at the trash can as we walked into the next store.

Drake did look back, but only once.

With Candi's help I bought a black Chanel gown, some nice stockings and a La Perla brassiere. The dress fit astonishingly well when I donned it in concert with the Spanx; the shaping underwear knocked an inch and four bulges off my midsection. A Prada purse and a pair of calf-destroying heels rounded out the look.

We sent Drake into the dressing room with a Hugo Boss tuxedo; I was wearing the heels and trying to figure out how to walk in them without dying when

Candi turned to me.

"Where did you meet the new man?"

"He's an old friend from college."

"Wait..." Candi's eyes scrunched up in concentration. "Not that skinny boy with the wild hair? I remember him."

"That's the one."

"He filled out," she said, eying the dressing room door.

"He did."

Drake stepped out of the dressing room adjusting the cuffs on his jacket and I had to blink twice; the tuxedo changed him from good-looking into astonishingly handsome.

Candi's eyes flicked from the tips of his shoes to the top of his head in one smooth, practiced motion. "It appears you figured out how to throw a net," she murmured to me. I tried not to blush as the tailor jotted down what alterations would be necessary.

We finished the shopping trip; I winced at the bill, but I tried to remind myself that it wasn't my money. Hayes would just have to deal with the expenses. I hoped to hell that I would get what I was hoping for out of the trip; proof of a wider conspiracy, and proof of whether or not Govrolev was involved. If I could prove get that, I had all the other information needed to bust them. Hayes would have to do some legwork of course, but I couldn't do his whole job for him.

Our group ended up at the food court. Drake excused himself to get some lunch; while he was gone Candi gave my face a critical glance. "The night of the party," she said, "come by my apartment. I'll do what I can to hide those bruises."

I winced. Apparently my cosmetic skills had not been up to the task. "They're that obvious?"

"I know bruises. Who hit you?"

My fingertips brushed the marks on my cheek. "Occupational hazard."

Candi looked worried. "You are into something dangerous this time." It wasn't a question.

I nodded. "Look, there's something I need you to do for me. I can't explain why and doing it might put you at some risk. You okay with that?"

She smiled at me. "You have to ask?"

"This is serious, Candi."

She reached out and touched my face, gently tracing the outline of the bruise. "I know," she said.

I reached into my purse and took out a sealed envelope; inside was the contract I'd signed with Hayes. "If I disappear," I said, "I want you to mail this. The address and postage are already on it. Do it from a post office and try not to let anyone see you do it."

She fingered the envelope. "This is addressed to the FBI."

I nodded. She looked at me with questions in her eyes and waited for me to explain. I didn't. After a time she put the envelope into her purse.

Drake came back with our food and we ate in silence. There was an awkward pall over the table; I did my best to ignore it. Eventually we walked to the front entrance to say our goodbyes; Candi and I made Drake carry the purchases. It was a thing.

Before we parted ways Candi caught me in a fierce hug, her lips brushing the skin just beneath my earlobe. "I will not need to mail this," she whispered, "because you are not allowed to disappear. Understand?"

"I do," I whispered back, giving her a kiss on the cheek.

"*Bonne chance,*" she said.

I grinned. *"Merci."*

It felt odd driving back to the hotel with almost fifteen thousand dollars' worth of designer clothes in my trunk but I found myself grinning anyway. Halfway back Drake turned to me.

"Boyfriend?'"

I shrugged. "It sounded more polite than fuck buddy," I said.

"From what I remember of Candace," he said, "she wouldn't have objected either way."

I shrugged. "Maybe I did."

"This feels suspiciously like dating."

I smiled at him. "It does at that."

When we got back to the hotel Izzy and Julian were waiting in my room around a table crowded with fresh electronics; two late-model iPhones, a Bluetooth headset and a pile of cable. Izzy grinned. "We've got you covered, boss."

"Lay it on me."

"We'll run this off a phone's video camera," she said, holding up one of the iPhones. "I'll sneak my way into the hotel's wi-fi and we'll stream the video to my laptop here. It'll take some fiddling but if I get the settings right you should have at least a couple hours of footage."

"More than enough," I said. "Where's it going to go?"

She shrugged. "We'll stick it in your purse and punch a hole for the camera lens."

I winced. "You mean the twelve hundred dollar Prada bag I just bought?"

"It's for a good cause, boss."

I briefly mourned the loss before acceding to Izzy's correctness. "I guess that's how it has to be. Sound?"

Her grin was that of a kid about to put their hand in the cookie jar. "We'll do that with one of my magic Bluetooth headsets. That'll have a bunch of hours of recording time and no one will ever know."

Drake walked over to the table. "Is this even legal?"

I shrugged. "Like most of what we've been doing, it's murky as hell," I said.

"So it's only illegal if we get caught," Drake said.

"Exactly."

Chapter 28

I had a couple of days off and that was plenty of time for me to get nervous.

I found myself getting up early to hit the hotel gym; having to wear Spanx to fit into a dress was apparently the straw that the broke my ego's back, because the more I thought about it the less I liked it. Some of the other women in the hotel gave me funny looks. It might have been the bruises all over me, most of which were in the process of turning an ugly yellow. I ignored them and concentrated on working up a good sweat on the treadmill.

I sent Julian over to the office to check the mail and the messages; in an irony to end all ironies there were several possible customers and even a check from the Andersen law firm. He deposited the check, took down the clients' needs and told them we were quite busy now but we would be happy to get to them in a week or so, we're just full at the moment, thank you and sorry for the inconvenience. Izzy spent the days compiling what we already knew and filling in whatever blank spots she could.

When I wasn't working out or on the phone I found myself in bed - or in the shower, or on the chair - with Drake, to the point where the irrational part of me started to regard my antics as just a bit unseemly. I hadn't had this much sex since college and it was both glorious and awkward. It wasn't the fireworks; it was how all the exchanges between us were so damn *comfortable.* It bore thinking about...later. As far as I could tell Drake didn't mind the lack of a Serious Conversation and I would have thanked him profusely for that, if I had wanted to even mention it.

Hayes called me on the second day. I had just finished a hard twenty minutes on the treadmill and had to take a moment to catch my breath before answering. "Eckart," I said.

"I just checked the statement on your card," he said. "I can get behind the hotel...but the rest looks like a damn shopping spree."

"There's a fancy party I need to case," I said. "I warned you this would get expensive, didn't I?"

"Thirteen thousand dollars for clothes?"

I could tell he wasn't really irritated; he was just pushing to see if I'd apologize or stand behind what I'd done. I stepped out into the hall so I could talk more freely. "Hayes, this kind of stakeout costs what it costs. Besides, it was your lousy operational security that almost got all of us arrested the other night." I filled him in about the incident in front of

Kitsmiller's house.

"Damn," he muttered. "Russian gang kids?"

"Probably," I said. "Anyhow, there's a cop sniffing around your little game. His name's Hammerman. I think you pissed him off somewhere in there."

There was a short silence. "Hammerman's a good cop," he said. "He's absolutely relentless and pretty damn sharp. Sometimes I wish he wasn't on the other side of the fence from me."

"Maybe you shouldn't have hacked him off," I said.

"And that big cash advance you took out?"

"Operational expenses," I said. "Look, you'll have what you're paying for by the end of the week."

"I'd better," he said.

"Hayes, don't bother threatening me. We both know the last thing you want is for me to end up inside a courtroom."

"Accidents can happen, Eckart. Just remember that."

A sort of cold heat passed over my skin. "You think I'm not smart enough to put a dead man switch on the career-seeking drama missile I've got dialed in on you? That's so cute I could fold it up and wear it in my hair."

He did not have anything to say to that; the silence on the line stretched out like a corpse on the end of a noose. Sometimes a lack of communication is scarier than the loudest threat. Eventually I spoke.

"Vise," I said. "Your balls are still in one. I'll do what I said I was going to do...now, back off and let me work."

There was a measure of respect in his voice when he finally answered. "I'm looking forward to your report, Eckart." He hung up before I could respond.

"Asshole," I muttered at my phone without thinking. There was something about Hayes that just set me off a little even though I wished it wouldn't. I found the changing room and hit the showers to cool off.

When I got back up to the room Drake had his tuxedo all laid out; the party was scheduled for later that night. I had an appointment with Candi to get my makeup and hair done but there was still some time before that...time enough, as I said before, to get nervous. The phone call from Hayes had not helped that. It was easier to be tough when someone is there to see it.

"I wasn't aware you knew how to wear a tux," I said as I walked in.

Drake looked up and grinned. "I went to a couple of

black-tie parties back when I worked at the ad firm. You'd better know how to look good if you want to get ahead in that business." He laid out the tie next to his shirt. "How was the workout?"

"Stressful," I said. When he looked up I outlined the conversation I'd had with Hayes. "We need to get something, and we need to do it quickly."

"No argument here," Drake muttered. "I don't like working for that smarmy fucker."

I grinned. "No argument there either."

Drake and I left Izzy and Julian putting the finer points on the surveillance gear I was to be wearing and set out to meet Candi at the spa. I knew just enough about cosmetics and body maintenance to know that my skills were deficient to the task in front of me; I blessed all over again staying friends with someone like Candace.

Candi was sitting in the spa's waiting room when we showed up; her clothes were a black slash in the cool paleness of the spa's chic decor. She looked up and smiled. "Are you ready for this?"

I shrugged. "Ready as I'll ever be."

She stood and hugged me. While embracing me she whispered, "I've explained to them about the bruises...the girls won't ask."

I relaxed a little. "Good," I said. "The last thing I need is some rad-fem cosmetologist taking a shiv to Drake."

"Remember to tip them," Candi said.

"Remember who you're talking to," I replied with a smile.

With that, Drake and I went in different directions; he looked like most men looked when you set them adrift in a place like the spa, and it was work not to laugh a bit at his discomfort. That is, until I realized that in his case the discomfort was bred out of seeing the conspicuous display of wealth. That thought sobered me.

My attendant was a gym-fit redhead just into her twenties, sporting the same polish as the Russian call girl only without the arrogant coldness. Her blue eyes grew wide as I took off my coat; I realized she had spotted my handgun and I dragged out my most reassuring smile.

"Um," she said after a moment, her customer-service training clearly not covering the situation, "I don't know if I can let you have that...thing in here."

"Don't worry," I said. "I'm licensed." I showed her my state CPL.

"...Oh. Wow. I've never even seen one of these

before." She squinted at my license like it was written in a foreign language.

Candi shook her head, still smiling. "*Cherie*, only you would pack a pistol to the spa."

Eventually I got everything sorted out; the staff accepted my concealed carry permit with a sort of nervous tolerance, and I accepted their nervousness with as little disdain as I could manage. My P7 went into the pocket of my spa robe; the cute little redhead did not apparently have the courage to object.

Those who haven't done it have only a sketchy concept of how invasive a full-court press at the beautician's actually is; if I had any modesty before the process began, it surely fled that afternoon. Candi being Candi, she was as relaxed as if she had been sitting in her bathroom at home while the spa girls worked on her. I envied her that.

The girls chatted as they worked, and most of their conversation interested me not at all; watching them work and listening to them talk, I felt like a tourist visiting the country of my ancestors. Which is how I always felt when confronted with classically girly things, especially classically girly things which involved spending lots of money.

I could not deny that the place did a good job,

though. By the time I was done I both looked and felt a good deal cleaner and prettier. Whatever complex chemical treatment they put in my hair actually got it to shine, and my skin looked smoother than it had in ten years. The attendants had thrown in a massage, which did wonders for my stiff muscles. I glanced at my reflection after dressing and smiled; fortunately the mirror wasn't long enough to show me my stomach.

"I could get to like this," I said.

Candi patted me on the shoulder. "Just remember...beauty is a vice like any other."

"Duly noted."

Drake came out, clean and bemused. "Some dude tried to wax my chest," he muttered.

Candi and I both had to laugh.

The last stage took us to Candi's loft, located down in the center of the Pike district. The place was bigger than my apartment and without much in the way of walls; aside from a curtained-off bathroom everything was open and on display. Drake glanced around at the Helmut Newton prints on the wall, the full dominatrix outfit arranged on a stand, and the massive wrought-iron bed in the center of the room. When his eyes came back to me full of questions, I simply shrugged.

There were leather cuffs dangling from the bed's headboard. I didn't think he had noticed and I didn't point them out.

Candi drew a curtain across the front of the loft, bisecting the bedroom from the bathroom. Drake stayed on one side to change into his tux while the two of us got my makeup in order.

"He's quite handsome," Candi murmured as she dusted powder onto my cheeks, "but something about me intimidates him."

I smiled. "Candi, you've got naked women on your wall, handcuffs on your bed and an S & M outfit sitting in the middle of your living room. Do remember that most people are made uncomfortable by that stuff."

"This is one of the things I enjoyed about Europe," she said. "Americans are such prudes." She gave me a devilish grin. "Good thing he didn't look under the bed."

"Probably." I kept my face still while Candi applied some more goop. "Actually...knowing you, almost certainly."

We shared a smile. Hers turned wistful, and she ran two fingers over the top of my head. "Thank you," she said.

"For what?"

"Staying. Listening. Not being bothered. Not judging me. Things like that."

It was Candi's habit to thank me like that, just sort of out of the blue; I'd long since gotten used to it. I patted her on the hand. "Likewise," I said. "Also, risking your butt on a moment's notice with no information."

She picked up the makeup brush again. "What friends are for, if not for that?"

We finished styling me and I got dressed, strapping on the last purchase of the day; a bra holster for Drake's .22 automatic. Candi gave my ensemble a long, measuring look. "Perfect," she said. "No one will doubt you." After a moment, she chuckled. "With that pistol, you look like a Bond girl."

I glanced at myself in the mirror; even all made up in a multi-thousand dollar dress I wasn't seeing the resemblance.

"I'd have to agree with Ms. Estermont," Drake said as he came through the curtain. "I mean, damn."

I eyed him; he had his dreadlocks slicked back and his tuxedo perfectly arranged. After tailoring it did even more wonders for him than before. "Oh, *James,*" I said in a breathy soprano.

Candi smiled and raised her camera. I struck the Bond girl pose; back arched, elbows out, pistol pointed at the ceiling. Behind me Drake folded his arms with a rakish smile, standing with his shoulders against mine. Candi snapped the picture, which was good because our tableau fell apart into giggles after less than five seconds. I enjoyed the moment. It was probably going to be the last honest joke for a while.

"Are we ready for this?" Drake fiddled with his pocket square.

"You are as ready as I can make you," Candi said.

Since I had a chance to do so, I spent a moment familiarizing myself with Drake's little pistol. It was a Jennings J-22, the archetypical Saturday Night Special. It had dinky sights and the stopping power of a slingshot but it was better than depending on bare hands. My P7 was a great pistol but it was too big to fit inside the dress.

I stuck it in the holster and tried a few practice draws. It was a tad awkward but otherwise functionally no different than drawing from a shoulder holster; the drape front on the dress did not get in the way any more than a coat lapel did.

"All right," I said. "Let's go get the surveillance gear and our backup crew."

"Then we go to a party?"

"Yep," I said, tucking the borrowed pistol back inside the dress I couldn't ever afford. "We go to a party."

Chapter 29

The Four Seasons Olympic was a stepped block of off-white stone that loomed over Union Street like a proud and surly beast. Flags rippled in front of the colonnade entryway; United States, Washington, others I could not identify. Limos and European sports cars pulled up to the front in a steady stream. Crowds of people dressed richer than we were milled around outside. They clashed with the tourists and career businessmen entering the hotel to use it for its actual purpose.

I shivered in the cold night air and tried to stay close to Drake as we threaded our way to the entrance. I had forgotten to purchase was some sort of outfit-appropriate overcoat. It was always the small things. The shoes had already started making my feet ache and I had only been wearing them for an hour. I did not know who Jimmy Choo was, but his footwear was apparently engineered by sadists to be worn by Barbie dolls.

Julian had dropped us off a block away and then taken my car to a nearby parking lot; he was under instruction to wait and watch his phone should we need a quick pick-up. Izzy had opted to stay back at the hotel and I had let her without any objection. Besides, I needed her to mind the feed from our surveillance gear.

She had come through on the gear, no doubt about that. clipped to my ear was a Bluetooth headset, doctored to be capable of focusing on conversations at up to twenty feet; I had to turn it on and aiming it was something of a pain but it was just about the smallest version of a directional microphone I'd seen yet. Drake had one too, just so he could catch anything I missed. In my purse was the iPhone, Livestream app loaded and cocked. I'd activate it once I was inside. No sense in wasting battery life.

I kept my eye out for Kasey or anyone who didn't look like they belonged in such a gathering. The crowds of hotel goers made that difficult but not overly so; anyone who could afford a stay at a place like the Four Seasons could likely also afford good dental care and proper hygiene; those were the two things which generally gave away those dressing above their station. I didn't see any gussied-up thugs, so I signaled to Drake for us to cross the street.

"Remember," I said as we hurried across the road, "you're my bodyguard. Don't smile, don't socialize, don't eat, and don't drink. Watch everyone who comes within arm's length and don't let anyone come between you and me."

"I guess I'll have to depend on my charming

personality," he said. I knew what he was talking about; we hadn't been able to get him a carry permit and thus was he unarmed.

"Sorry," I said.

"I'll manage," he said.

The lobby of the Four Seasons was as clean, impressive and crowded as the outside. I started to wonder if buying tickets had even been necessary, seeing as people were mingling and crowding with what came off disorderly abandon. Then I spotted the muscle standing by the elevator door; two hundred pounds of beef in a cheap black suit, martial arts written on his stance like a marquee.

Drake saw him as well. "Guard?"

"You betcha."

I scanned the crowd but did not see anyone I recognized. I looked up at Drake.

"I'm going to use the ladies' room," I said to him. We'd gone over this before we'd shown up; he was to stand near the door, not lean, and look intimidating. I slipped into the bathroom and found a stall. It was the work of a moment to break out the iPhone and get the app updated. Hovering in the text message was the password for the hotel's wi-fi; I keyed it in and fired up Livestream.

You getting this? I texted to Izzy using my personal phone.

Yep, Purse-Cam is LIVE! I got back after about fifteen seconds. **Try to keep the bag as steady as possible and dont put your arm in front of it.**

Got it, I sent back. **Drake's audio working?** We had decided to use the other magic headset to record most of everything we heard at the party. It was a long shot but also a wide one, and sometimes those paid off.

I'm listening to him getting hit on XD

I sighed. **Why am I not surprised**, I sent back before deleting the text thread and slipping my phone back in my purse. I checked the camera eye one last time; from anything other than right close up it looked like a decoration on the purse itself. I slipped out of the stall and used the mirror to check my makeup. Candi did excellent work, but lipstick was still as transient as ever. I had just capped the stick when I felt eyes on me. I turned around.

The girl from Hansen's place stood an arm's length away.

It is work not to react when you see someone you know and aren't expecting; the shock is immediate, suppressing it almost an impossibility. Looking away quickly is the cheap trick everyone uses and therefore a dead giveaway. I instead opted for the next best thing; I jumped.

"Oh!" I said, putting a hand to my chest and taking a breath. "Sorry, you startled me."

She didn't speak or bat an eye. She just brushed into my space trailing a cloud of expensive scent and stepped up to the mirror; I stepped back to avoid a collision. The brief look she gave me was a laser beam of disdain followed by complete dismissal. Thus ignored, I studied her instead; she had on the same thin black gown she'd worn to Hansen's, with the addition of more sedate heels and a scanty thong. She wasn't wearing hose and I was pretty sure I knew why; her legs didn't need any help. I turned and left before she could catch me watching her.

I found Drake outside with two girls trying to talk to him. He wasn't letting them have much luck. One was a pert-faced brunette with the build of a coat rack; it strained to support breasts bigger than my own. The other was a tiny ice-blonde who thought for some reason that coral eye shadow and white lipstick were good colors to pair with skin bronzer. As I stepped out the brunette leaned back and canted her head forward, eyes lidded, touching Drake's arm with two fingers; the flirt-fu opening stance. I cleared my throat with irritated authority;

the two women jumped.

I gathered Drake in by eye and did the same thing to the two girls that the call girl had done to me, which was ignore them with extreme prejudice. I knew they were staring daggers at the back of my head but resolved not to care about it. One of them hissed a nasty word I was too far away to catch.

"Nice girls," he said.

"Virtuous and intelligent," I said.

"What do you suppose they're here for?"

"The same thing we are," I said.

Drake adjusted his tie. "Rich men?"

"Bingo."

We cut the chatter as we approached the elevator door. The guard asked us for our tickets in a flat voice and I handed them over. He barely glanced at them before nodding. He had a square face, a crew cut and eyes like holes in a snowbank. He gave Drake a hard look as we passed, no doubt measuring his competence against a fellow guard. Drake ignored him. He let us into the elevator.

Once the door closed I breathed a sigh of relief. "I saw the hooker in the bathroom. That means Hansen either is here or will be here."

"Guess he takes her everywhere," Drake said.

"She makes a good display piece," I said.

"Good for the guy paying her to spy," Drake said.

"Yeah," I said. I thought about that some as the elevator rose.

The elevator dinged and the door slid open on the fourth floor. I could hear music, some string piece I didn't know. Everyone within sight was just as well-dressed as we were; some of them more so. I took a deep breath and started circulating, Drake at my heels.

There is an art to working a room, especially if you don't belong there and there are people present who can figure that out. Do too little talking, and you look out of place; a spy, a journalist or at the least someone of interest to watch. Too much, and the chances increase that you'll spit out a contradiction. Someone famous once said that no one has the memory to be a successful liar. I don't know if that was true for everyone but it was true enough for me.

I played the social butterfly, flitting from person to person while Drake hung in the background like a cliff face. I didn't learn much of value, but I learned much about the people involved in the development; all of them favored it, all of them spoke in dewy tones about the need for sustainable building and urban renewal. I smiled, nodded and wondered about the implications of what I was hearing. I'd spouted some of the same phrases back in my college years and hadn't given the matter much thought since. I gave it some thought while I listened to what I was hearing.

But despite all my social dancing, I neither saw nor heard a sign of Govrolev or Hansen. I took a break and moved off to a quiet corner.

"See anything?"

Drake shook his head. "A lot of rich white folk wondering what I'm doing here," he said.

"Want me to tell them?"

He smiled. "I like leaving them in suspense."

I looked around. "Good. Now, where the hell is Hansen?"

Drake gave the crowd a glower. "Don't tell me we missed him."

"We couldn't have," I said.

Another five minutes of circulating and my phone buzzed. I pulled it out; a text from Izzy.

Hansen rented a room on the sixth floor. I think you better get up there.

I blinked. **How do you know?**

I broke the hotel's database. I got bored. >:)

I bit back a curse. **Can you get me in the room?**

Hit the front desk I got you the room next door.

I shook my head slowly. **Remind me to give you a raise and then never let you off the leash again Izzy.**

No just don't let me get bored xD

"You clever girl," I murmured.

"What's up?"

I grinned. "Izzy, being awesome as usual." I gave the room a scan; no one was paying the least attention to us. "Come on, I'll explain in the elevator."

It was a short trip back to the lobby. The front desk staff was a little confused at a reservation that had happened less than five minutes ago, but they smiled and nodded and gave me keys all the same. I thanked them and left an unintelligible scrawl on the receipt before collecting my key card.

"Pretty slick," Drake said, "though Izzy's gonna get herself in trouble someday."

I shrugged. "Most of what she does is actually legal.

She just knows how. She likes it when I call her a wizard, so I let her get away with the mystery."

"Girl needs some pride?"

"Yeah," I said. "She's got skill enough to deserve it."

"Still," Drake said, "the bit with the hotel reservations was quick thinking."

"It was that," I said. "Let's hope it works."

I got to the room and unlocked the door; it was one of the nicer setups, with two beds and a big screen television. The decor was a little dated but that was an old hotel for you; big on tradition. I slipped off my heels as soon as the door closed.

"Ow," I said, rubbing my calves.

"Not liking the shoes?"

"Fuck the shoes," I said softly. I could already hear some kind of activity going on next door.

Drake glanced at the wall. "What now?"

"Time to play James Bond," I said.

Hotels vary in decor and quality, but one thing that doesn't generally change is that the nicer ones usually have a balcony; it's a postage stamp affair where occupants can go breathe in some city air, take in the view and - perhaps most importantly for me - smoke without incurring a huge damage charge. The Four Seasons was no exception, and this was part of my hastily conceived plan. According to my research Govrolev was a smoker, and like most smokers probably worked best with a cigarette in his hand. This meant that Govrolev would likely want to conduct business out on the balcony.

It was a long shot, but so far the dice were hot in my hand and anyway it was the only play I could think of. I pulled out my phone and texted Izzy.

Purse-Cam still functioning?

Perfectly. How you gonna get the footage, boss?

I smiled. **Cleverly**, I texted back.

I dug into my clutch to see what I had to work with. It wasn't much; a pack of cigarettes, a lighter, two spare hair bands and a pack of gum, along with my lipstick and compact case. I grabbed the hair bands and the gum and slid the balcony door open.

The night was wet and cold, the wind a sharp bite against my skin; up here there was less to get in its way and it went right through the silk of my dress. I found myself blessing the Spanx I wore underneath it, for another layer if nothing else. I stepped to the right-hand railing, iPhone in one hand and hair bands in the other.

It took me about a minute to get the iPhone strapped to the railing with the hair bands, but looking at the screen I could see the angle wasn't right. I shrugged and wedged pieces of gum underneath the lower edge of the phone until the balcony came into view. The lighting was less than optimal but it would have to serve. Another minute allowed me to tie Izzy's magic Bluetooth headset to the railing the same way.

"Let's hope it works," I said.

I heard activity in the next-door room; I waved Drake back and crouched just inside the doorway, where I could hear but would not be seen. "Come on," I muttered, trying to squelch the feelings of tension in my stomach, "go out, have a smoke, you know you want to..."

After two minutes, I heard the balcony door open.

"...bad for the heart," I heard a voice say. I recognized Hansen's voice.

"As if you would know about having one of those," another voice said. It was deeper and sharper than Hansen's, the Slavic accent as thick as cold honey; Govrolev.

I looked back. Drake was leaning against the door and keeping his body as still as possible. I flashed him a thumbs-up. I heard the familiar *flick-scratch* of a Zippo lighter, followed by a deep inhale.

"I am a busy man," Govrolev said. "So say whatever it is you must and let me go."

"Come on now," Hansen said. I heard the soft thump of flesh on cloth. "We're about to be rich, what's with the -"

"Do you have life insurance, Mister Hansen?"

There was a pause. "What's that have to do with anything?"

"Touch me again, and I assure you it will be relevant."

"Anatoliy, we've been over this." Hansen sounded considerably less friendly.

"Yes Mister Hansen, we have." Another deep inhale. I could smell black Russian tobacco. "That does not change the fact that if I chose to I could render things academic by throwing you off this balcony."

"That...would land you back in prison," Hansen said.

"Your landing would be more permanent than mine." This time the inhale was deep enough that I heard a crackling sound.

"Still wouldn't get you anywhere," Hansen said.

"It would make me feel better," Govrolev said.

Brad's voice grew calmer. "And yet you aren't doing it," he said.

"No I haven't." Govrolev's voice hadn't risen about a conversational tone, but I could detect a faint note of menace in it. "As I said, speak your piece and let me leave. I have things to do."

"Finish your cigarette, Anatoliy," Hansen said. "We'll talk inside."

I flinched and crossed my fingers.

"I am surprised to find you nervous," Govrolev said.

A small laugh. "You shouldn't be surprised to find me cautious."

"As you say." There was a sizzling sound; Govrolev's cigarette butt hitting a puddle, most likely. I heard the sliding glass door open, a quick scuffling of feet, and that was that.

"Dammit," I said. "Dammit, dammit *dammit*."

Drake looked at me. "They went back inside?"

"Yeah." I balled up my fist and resisted the urge to punch something.

"What did we get?"

"Not enough," I said. "Fifteen thousand dollars in

setup costs and I blow it."

"We can tail them," Drake said. "Maybe they'll -"

"What, have an important conversation someplace other than the secure hotel room rented for the purpose?" I shook my head. "We'll try, but I doubt we're going to get anything worth what we spent to get in here."

My phone buzzed. **What now boss?**

I dont know I texted back. After another moment I slipped back out and retrieved my hastily conceived surveillance rig, wondering how Hayes was going to take my miscalculation. When viewed through hindsight it was a pretty risky play. Drake patted me on the shoulder; I made sure not to scowl at him.

"You tried," Drake said.

"Not well enough," I said. I started pacing. "God, this is annoying...getting outsmarted by a bunch of realtors and stockbro-"

I stopped walking and talking as a big chunk of clue walloped me in the brain pan. "Stockbrokers," I muttered, as a bunch of disconnected facts snapped together into a picture as clear as day.

"What?" Drake looked confused but I was already clawing for my phone, punching Izzy's number up on the speed-dial. It took her less than one ring to answer.

"Yeah?"

I spoke rapidly. "Izzy pull up the shareholder list for Ironhorse Construction and tell me what percentage Brad and his friends own."

I head Izzy's mouse clicking. "Okay, each of them owns between ten and fifteen percent -"

I felt a surge of excitement. "No, how much do they all own in total?"

"Checking....around eighty percent, boss. Maybe more."

I grinned. "Bingo. Thanks Izzy." I hung up before she could respond, grinning like a loon. Drake looked more confused than ever.

"Govrolev," I said, "doesn't own his company anymore. Brad and his friends have bought up a controlling interest in it. *That's* what they have on him."

Drake nodded. "Still doesn't prove anything," he said.

"No it doesn't but it gives me an idea." My grin got wider. "Here's what I want you to do..."

Chapter 30

The room Hansen had rented was just down the hall from the elevator. This made what I had in mind both easier and harder. Easier, because I could stay within earshot of Drake. Harder, because the timing would be difficult. I leaned against the alcove wall and watched the big brass-framed mirror mounted in front of the elevator doors, trying to quell the butterflies in my stomach.

After three long minutes I heard a room door open; several seconds later I heard Drake's voice echo down the hall, loud and slightly slurred.

"Brad!" There was a small commotion. "Damn, man, how's it going? I ain't seen you since grad school!"

"Uh, excuse -" Brad's voice, sounding confused.

"Oh hell no, man! You and I are going to get a drink...don't tell me you've forgotten how, eh?"

"But I -"

"Shit, Brad...you got a few minutes, come on."

The sound of Drake's voice grew fainter; I could picture him all but manhandling Hansen down the hall, picture Hansen's very confused expression as he tried to politely fend off a very large and apparently drunk former college buddy he didn't remember. I smiled. *Always talk faster than the other person can think.* A minute later Govrolev came walking down the hallway, face set in a grim mien. I gave it a five-count before stepping out of the alcove and walking up to the elevator.

Anatoliy Il'ych Govrolev was a much larger man in person than his picture had led me to believe; his shoulders were almost twice as wide as mine, straining the fabric of his gray suit. I felt like half a child standing next to him. Up close, it was easier to imagine him in the role of a gangster; I figured it was something Hansen and his cronies were counting on should matters ever progress to the courtroom. He glanced at me with a polite smile. I gave him one back.

"Going down?" I kept my voice light.

He nodded and turned back, obviously lost in his own thoughts. I made sure I did not fidget and mentally urged the elevator to show up before Hansen disentangled himself from Drake. With a musical ding, it did. With one long arm Govrolev gave me the after-you gesture; I smiled again and stepped inside. He followed me.

As soon as the door closed I turned to him. "We need to talk," I said.

His eyebrows went up. "Do I know you?"

I slipped a business card out of my bra and handed it to him. "No," I said, "but you've heard of me."

He glanced at it, and when he looked up I saw shutters come down over his eyes. "I don't know what you're talking about," he said.

"That's okay. I do." I spoke rapidly. "I know about the deal, I know about Hansen and his cronies, and I know that you aren't happy about any of it."

The elevator picked up speed.

"I still don't -"

"Why else would you threaten to throw Brad-boy off the balcony?"

Silence from Govrolev. I glanced at the elevator's control pad; I was running out of floors. "You've got one chance to make a deal, Govrolev. I'm it."

More silence. Underneath the dress my skin was hot. The butterflies became panicky bats, clawing at my insides. The elevator hit the lobby and the doors slid open.

Govrolev's face lit up with a big, friendly smile. "It is so good to see you here," he said, sweeping me into a big bear hug. I played along; in my ear I heard "walk outside and turn right on 4th. Meet me at the end of the block. If you are not alone I will drive right past."

"Understood," I whispered back. He let me go. I smiled at him and waved, walking with brisk but unhurried strides right out the door. Drake had the keys; he was under instruction to turn them in once he had distracted Hansen. Always cover all the angles.

The rain had stopped but the night was still wet and cold, the sidewalk crowded with people. I walked up 4th Avenue to Union Street and found the shadow of a tree to wait in. My phone buzzed; a text from Izzy.

Boss Drake almost got thrown out of the hotel what the heck are you doing??

Something risky, I texted back. **Keep an eye on my phone's location and have Julian pick up the tail.**

KK boss be careful.

"There's nothing careful about this," I muttered. I felt nervous being alone in the dark wearing such rich clothing, even leaving aside who I was meeting; the Jennings was a comforting pressure against my right breast.

I did not have long to wait before a gunmetal Audi sedan pulled up to the corner and slowed. I walked as quickly as my shoes allowed over to the car and got in, reaching for my seatbelt. "Drive," I said.

Govrolev eased the car back out into traffic. "Now," he said, "I would like to know why I shouldn't just take you somewhere and leave you in a ditch."

"Well, there's this to consider." I drew the Jennings, racked the slide and set it in my lap, careful to keep it concealed with my body. It wasn't precisely pointed at him but I didn't take my hand off it.

If Govrolev was perturbed by the gun, he didn't show it. "Are you trying to kidnap me?"

"Hardly," I said. "I just wanted you to know I won't die easily."

"A loaded gun," he said. "Always the best way to begin a friendly relationship."

"I'm off the map," I said. "Here be dragons."

He laughed softly but didn't take his eyes from the road. "You mentioned a deal," he said.

"First I'll tell you a story," I said, "and you tell me if you like it." I leaned back in the seat.

"Once upon a time," I said, "there was a young mobster named Anatoliy. Anatoliy gets busted by the Soviet government in 1984 for selling State-produced gasoline on the black market, a treasonous offense in those days. He's convicted and sent to the Bolshoy Dom...a place people enter, but don't ever leave.

"While inside Anatoliy has a change of heart and Russia has a change of government. He gives the new State - which is fighting a losing war against mobsters - something good, something they can use. In exchange they let him walk, and buy him a plane ticket out of the country. "

Govrolev stared at me.

"Watch the road," I said. "Anyway, Anatoliy comes to America, does manual labor for a couple of years before starting his own little construction company. He wants to go straight, and America's the land of opportunity, and he does pretty well. Well enough that his company goes public. But Anatoliy, he wants to keep his company so he retains a majority share of the stock. He's smart businessman...tough, fair and basically honest. His company keeps raking in the contracts all the way through the housing bubble."

"Two hundred percent growth," Govrolev murmured.

"Yep. But then the bubble pops and everything comes to a screeching halt. Nobody's building, and Anatoliy needs capital.

"Along comes white-bread Brad and his crew of yuppies, with their big development project," I said. "They offer to bankroll Anatoliy's company in exchange for control of it. Anatoliy doesn't want to do it, but he doesn't have a choice. It's that, or go into debt. So he sells, expecting to get forced out. Only they don't force him out, oh no...our friend Brad has other ideas."

Govrolev may have been watching the road but I could tell I had his attention.

"Brad knows about Anatoliy's mobster past, so he gets some Russian gang kids to lean on people - to get things done, sure, but *also* to make sure any cops who start poking around the deal are always looking in the wrong direction. Because no one would believe that white-bread Brad has anything to do with that...not when there's a Russian immigrant with a shady past, stuck out in front where everyone can see him."

"You tell an interesting story," he said. His voice was very soft.

"Oh, it gets better. Anatoliy, he's not the sort of man to take this lying down...and while he may be out of the crime game he certainly hasn't forgotten how it's played. So he starts sniffing around a little, and finds out Brad's got a taste for a certain hooker - a Russian hooker, who also happens to hate Brad's guts. He pays the hooker to steal Brad's files...because he knows where Brad keeps them, and he knows what sort of information he'll find in them."

Govrolev smiled at the rainy streets as he threaded the car through the downtown traffic. "So why doesn't Anatoliy go to the police?"

"Because he knows that Brad's got them in his pocket, probably through the same man who supplied him with the whore," I said. "Anatoliy's got the story - he just doesn't have anyone to tell it to. Stalemate."

"So how does it end, this story of yours?"

"That depends on you." I glanced in the rearview mirror; I didn't see my car, but that didn't mean I wasn't being followed. "I want Hansen's files. I know the hooker took them because I watched her do it. I know you have them because I watched her give them to you - at Sebastian's over on Capitol Hill. You ordered a bourbon and water. She had the house red."

He laughed. "Who do you work for, Ms. Eckart?"

"Someone who can bring these people down," I said.

"How do I know I can trust you?"

"You don't," I said. "But one way or the other, the scheme's going to unravel...your only choice is where you want to be when that happens."

I smiled. "Stockbrokers and realtors, Govrolev. You feel like going back to prison for them?"

There was a long silence while Govrolev drove and I waited. Finally he pulled the car into an alleyway and slowed to a stop. With a sigh, he opened the center console and pulled out a pack of cigarettes. With two thick fingers he extracted a gray object about the size of a fingertip. I recognized it. Hansen's thumb drive.

"I give you the files, you give me back my company?"

"You'll get a chance to take it back," I said.

"I don't think I have to tell you what will happen if you betray me," he said.

"Bradley Hansen may not know who he's dealing with, but I do."

He raised one eyebrow. "Do you?"

I stuck the Jennings back in my bra. "You built Ironhorse Construction out of nothing," I said. "It's all you have, and right or wrong you'll fight to keep it." I looked him in the eye. "And I think we both know that anything worth fighting for is worth fighting dirty for."

He handed me the thumb drive. "I trust you can find your way home from here."

"I'm resourceful," I said.

"I believe it," he said.

I grinned. *"Dosvidanya,"* I said as I got out of the car and shut the door.

He did not reply, but instead drove down the alleyway and turned up the street. I watched the red rectangles of his tail lights recede and disappear as I hefted the thumb drive. It was a feeling better than sex, the satisfaction of a case closed. I stuck the drive in my purse with a smile before turning around and heading out of the alley.

I did not have to wait long before the familiar form of my little Golf came pulling up; Drake got out of the car almost before it stopped moving and hurried over to me. "Jesus," he said. "You and your damn blackjack plays." He sounded more worried than angry.

I walked up and kissed him; the heels let me do it without straining. "Aces and faces, dear." I held up the thumb drive. His eyes bugged out of his head.

"Damn," Drake said. "He just gave it to you?"

"In exchange for the chance to get his company back," I said.

"You sure he's innocent?"

"He's innocent enough," I said.

Julian rolled down the window. "Hey boss...so what now?"

I handed Drake the drive. "Take this back to the hotel. Have the staff lock it and all our case information in the hotel safe. I'll take a cab back to the hotel."

Drake blinked. "Why go separately?"

"Because I don't know if Govrolev's one hundred percent on the level and I want to be seen somewhere other than with you," I said.

He nodded. "Did we just nail the fuckers?"

"The corpse is in the coffin, the lid is on and the hammer is poised," I said. "The nailing will be up to Hayes."

"But we win," he said.

I grinned. "Bet your ass," I said. "Now get moving."

Once they were gone it was a simple matter to call myself a cab. A couple of people looked at me a little funny while I was waiting - a lone woman in an expensive evening dress, smoking cigarettes by a lamp post - but no one bothered me. It did not take the cab a long time to make an appearance.

"Where to?"

"The nearest electronics store that's open," I said.

It took us a little while to find one, but the cabbie was more than willing to drive around on my nickel. I watched the rear view mirrors the whole time but did not catch anyone tailing me. Once we found a store, I went in and bought a thumb drive that matched Hansen's; he had picked a generic model, the better to avoid suspicion, and finding a match was easy. Next I had the cabbie drive me back to my hotel. I tucked the little thumb drive into my left bra cup. The cabbie watched me do it but didn't say anything. I smiled at him and said nothing all the way back to the Doubletree, and he didn't ask any questions.

My room was empty when I got to it; Drake and Julian must have been next door with Izzy, talking excitedly about the case. I figured I should tell them I was back but I wanted out of the finery first. I tossed my purse on the bed and bent down to take off the shoes.

A cold circle appeared against the back of my neck. I froze.

"About time you showed up," a lazy, fake Southern drawl said from behind me. "I was starting to get worried."

Chapter 31

I didn't even think about going for my pistol, especially not when two other figures came out of the bathroom. One was Vadim, the other was a gang kid I hadn't seen yet; the kid might've been handsome except for the blank look in his eyes. Up close Vadim Rodchenko was even uglier, and when he grinned at me I found myself wishing my dress covered more of my body than it did. He had a fedora on, probably to cover the scar on his forehead. Both of them had guns; small automatics of a type I did not recognize. Vadim had my P7 in his other hand, wrapped in a towel.

"You hid in the closet," I said.

"Old tricks," Kasey said from behind me. "They stick around because they work."

"How'd you find me?"

"Later," he said, pushing me up against the wall with his other hand. I put my arms out instinctively to avoid face-planting the sheetrock; he kept me there with pressure from the muzzle of his pistol - suppressed, from the thickness of the barrel - and kicked my feet apart.

"I'm not armed," I said.

"I'll be the judge of that," he said. He ran a hand down both sides of my body and along the outside of my left breast; he was kind enough to use the back of his hand like the cops are taught to. When he checked the inside of my thighs, I twitched.

"That's a little far for a first date," I muttered.

"Actually it's our second," he said. "Now, you know what else I'm looking for."

"Do I?"

He prodded me in the back of the head with his pistol. "Either you hand it over or I let Vadim go digging for it. He's well acquainted with how many hiding places women have."

I had no idea how Kasey could know I had the files so I played dumb. "Look, I still don't -"

"The thumb drive," Kasey said. "The one you took from Hansen's house when you broke in. Hand it over or Vadim goes on a treasure hunt."

"Okay, okay." Very slowly, I reached into my left bra cup and came out with the thumb drive I'd just bought, holding it up between my fingers.

Someone snatched it. With a quick motion I felt my hands yanked behind my back; there was the cold metal feeling of cuffs around my wrists. A second after that the gun left the back of my head and someone draped my trench coat over my shoulders. I turned around.

Kasey had on a three-piece wool suit, a pair of metal-frame eyeglasses with clear lenses, and a brown wig parted ear-to-ear. If it hadn't been for the voice I wouldn't have recognized him. In his right hand he had a Ruger target automatic, .22 caliber, the barrel shrouded by the thick cylinder of a suppressor. As I watched he dug my phone out of my purse and stuck it in his pocket after fiddling with it for perhaps thirty seconds. He took the cigarettes and lighter out as well, but stuck those in my left-hand coat pocket.

"Let's go," he said, draping a coat over his gun arm. "I even think you're going to do anything like make noise and you get it right in the heart."

"That suppressor won't do you much good in here," I said.

"It's good enough. Move."

I didn't have much choice; I let them lead me out the door, down the hall and down the stairs to the back wing exit. We passed three people in the hallway, but none of them looked twice at the group of us.

 I was led to a dark green Ford sedan with rental-car stickers on the windshield. Kasey opened the rear passenger door for me and helped me into the car in such a way that no one watching would notice my hands were cuffed. Vadim got in next to me. His lackey took shotgun. Kasey got in behind the wheel. I watched him stick the Ruger in the glove compartment, careful to keep it below the dash.

Once all the doors were closed Vadim leaned over and fastened my seat belt. On the way across he gave my breast a squeeze. I willed myself not to react; his other hand had a pistol pressed against my ribs and I did not feel like getting shot over the matter. I just thanked my lucky stars he had groped the left one.

"Behave yourself, Vadim," Kasey said from the front seat.

"What's wrong with a little fun?" He grinned.

Kasey started the car and pulled it out of the lot. "You'd know better than I would," he said.

Vadim shot the back of Kasey's head a look of pure venom, but leaned back in his seat and other than the gun in my side didn't touch me.

"So," I said, "how's this going to play out?"

Vadim jabbed me with his pistol. I ignored him.

"You tell me," Kasey said.

"Ah," I said. "I'm going to try and blackmail Hansen.

Except it won't go well...and you, being a security guard on his payroll, will fill me full of holes."

"That's just about the way it will happen," he said.

"What about my associates?"

"You just told them to back off, that you were chasing down one more lead. It'll come out that you've been playing them the whole time, looking to get rich off Hansen by scamming him."

I nodded. "You sent my people a text from my phone," I said.

"Technology's a wonderful thing," he said.

"What about all our files?"

Vadim jabbed me with his pistol again. I kept ignoring him.

"The cops will seize them as evidence and the relevant parts will find their way to the jury," Kasey said.

"Relevant parts," I muttered. "Cute."

"Yeah, your employees will get a public defender...who'll encourage them to plead, once he gets the shit scared outta him by Hansen's superstar attorney. They'll be out with good behavior in a couple of years - less than that if they decide to testify against you, of course." He handed my phone to the kid in the passenger seat. "When we go over Green River, toss this in."

"That's a five hundred dollar phone," I said.

"Bill me," he said.

Vadim prodded me with his pistol a third time. I turned to face him.

"Look," I said, "we both know you aren't going to shoot me. So put your thing back in your pants, okay? It's pretty small anyway."

"Yob' vas," he snarled.

"Idi na kluy, suka."

He leaned over and slapped me hard enough that my head bounced against the glass. It hurt.

"Got anything else to say?" His voice was hot.

"Yeah," I said. "You hit like a *pidoras*."

He balled up his fist with a snarl, and I tensed.

"You kids better behave yourselves," Kasey said. There wasn't any lazy mockery in his voice anymore. "Somebody's gonna get a spanking."

"I got to listen to this bitch run her mouth?"

"She'll be dead in another hour anyway," Kasey said. "And she knows it. So relax."

Vadim sat back, doing his best to glare a hole in the side of my head. I let him without further comment. My head hurt enough already. I settled for watching where we were going.

Kasey took us up 188th and connected with Interstate 5, heading north; I wondered where the shooting was going to happen. I thought about asking but didn't feel like getting manhandled by Vadim any more. Once the freeway went over Green River the kid did indeed toss my cell out the window. I wondered if it would make it all the way into the water or if someone would just run it over.

We got off I-5 heading towards downtown; I thought it was funny that I had just been here, but I kept the thought to myself. When we passed the big First American building downtown, I knew where we were going.

"The bank parking garage," I murmured.

"Smart girl," Kasey said. "Maybe that's why you're such a pain in the ass."

"Probably," I said.

It made sense, really. A parking garage was out of the way, Hansen could use his influence to make sure the place was deserted, and with all the traffic noise it was even money that no one would hear or see anything and call the police. I guessed that

Hansen would put in a ring to whatever tame cop he had on his payroll once the proper scene had been set. I tried not to think about it too hard. My arms burned and throbbed from me having sat on them for around an hour. I flexed them, but it didn't help much.

Our car pulled into the back entrance of the parking garage; I noticed the security guard booth was not manned. Round and round the ramps we went, all the way up to the top level. That made sense too; more time to get everything straightened out. There was only one car in the lot; I recognized Hansen's Mercedes, sitting near the door to the staircase. Kasey parked our car nose-to-nose with Hansen's and got out. The kid in the front seat did likewise. I sat very still, trying to ignore Vadim's slimy grin as he undid my seat belt. His breath smelled like a bus station bathroom. My heart pounded, beating against my ribs like it wanted to get out.

Kasey leaned down and yanked me firmly but not roughly out of the car. I made sure to keep my face as neutral as possible. It wasn't easy.

In front of me both doors on Hansen's car opened; Brad himself got out of the driver's side, his pet hooker out of the passenger's. She was wrapped up in an ankle-length coat of black fur; I had to shake my head a little at the retro trashiness of it. No one wore fur like that anymore.

"So this is her," Hansen said as he walked up.

Kasey nodded. "One PI, packaged for delivery."

He gave me a look that was probably supposed to be hard. "Do we know who she's working for yet?"

"We will," Kasey said.

"You're going to kill me," I said. "Not much motive for me to be helpful."

Vadim's hand dipped into his jacket came out with his switchblade. The edge flashed in the harsh lights of the garage as he flicked it open.

"Fast or slow," he said. "Your choice, bitch."

I laughed and looked at Kasey. "A bunch of knife cuts all over me will poke a big hole in that pretty plan of yours," I said.

"So they will," he said. He waved at Vadim. "Put your thing back in your pants."

I made sure not to snicker as Vadim turned dark with anger. I did smile, which almost set the man off again.

Hansen looked at me. "You have a talent for irritating people."

"It's what I do," I said.

"Not anymore," he said.

I found myself regretting wearing the Spanx. My stomach felt like it was full of molten lead and fireworks and having it all squished down flat wasn't doing me any favors. I dug deep and came up with a smile that I hoped looked defiant and relaxed; inside was quite a different story, but I saw no reason for anyone else to know that.

Hansen looked me over, examining me like a product he'd heard about but had no intention of purchasing. "There's no need to torture her," he said. "We'll find her employer's information among her files once her employees are arrested, I'm sure." He turned to Kasey. "I trust you know where they are."

"Same place she was," Kasey said. "Don't worry, they're all still in the dark."

"Did you recover the files?"

"Yeah." Kasey produced the thumb drive and handed it over.

"Good," Hansen said, taking the thumb drive with a smile. "You've done well, Charles. I'm grateful."

"I'll take my money now," Kasey said.

"Payment on completion," Hansen replied.

"Then let's get on with it."

Hansen dug out his keys and hit a button on the fob; the Mercedes chirped and I saw the truck twitch. Kasey walked over and opened it, coming back out with what looked like a stack of papers, along with a Glock automatic. He checked the action and inserted a magazine. Vadim produced my P7, all neatly wrapped in a square of cloth. I noticed he was careful not to touch the metal as he put it on the ground. Looking, I saw the gun had a magazine in it, but it was out of reach. I also saw that no one was really watching me but Kasey. I wiggled my fingertips, trying to put feeling back into them as I made them do something else.

Hansen looked over. "So where should I be standing?"

Kasey shrugged as he set the stack of papers on the hood of the car. "Doesn't matter," he said. He took the Glock in a shooting grip. It was hard to breathe; I watched the little black eye of the pistol's muzzle come up.

"Wait," Hansen said. "Let me do it."

Kasey looked over his shoulder at him. "You sure?"

Hansen gave me a nasty smile. "For what she's cost me, It'll be satisfying."

"I bet you've got a cool line all picked out," I muttered.

He laughed. "Would it be chauvinist of me to call you an insufferable cunt?"

I came up with a brittle laugh in turn. "Take off my cuffs and we'll discuss it."

Vadim sighed. "Just shoot her," he muttered. "I'm sick of her mouth."

Hansen put on his suit gloves and Kasey handed him the pistol, butt-first. Vadim moved his pistol from the small of his back to the front of his pants, keeping one hand on it. Hansen flexed his hands around the grip of the Glock, something sick and hot in his gaze. I let my eyes go unfocused, trying to take in everyone around me.

The kid stood fidgeting near the front fender of Hansen's car, the hooker off to his left; she had her left hand in her coat and her right in her purse. Vadim leaned against one of the concrete pillars to my right, one hand on his gun, lazy arrogance written all over his face.

Hansen stepped back and pointed the pistol at the back of Kasey's head. "Don't move," he said.

Kasey didn't even twitch. "I knew it," he said.

He smiled. "The gun's registered to me, Charles. You and this bitch just became co-conspirators. This deal's over."

Neither Hansen nor Vadim could see it, but I did; the tombstone grin that flashed across Kasey's features for just an instant. "You gonna do us both?"

"Of course I am," Hansen said. "I'm an armed citizen, and you two are trying to blackmail me. It'll be self-defense with a witness." He gestured to the hooker. "Open and shut."

"I'm going to enjoy this," Vadim said.

"We'll see," Kasey said as he turned around.

Flex, flex flex went my hands. The blood in my veins was a hot, fierce roar as Hansen leveled the pistol at my face. I stared into the little black eye of the Glock's muzzle and didn't blink as he pulled the trigger.

Click.

Time froze into an absurd, awful, wonderful moment.

My perception flooded with a rush of adrenaline; the world was brighter and sharper than it had ever been as a dead-eyed doll and three degenerates convulses in shock, reached for weapons in slow motion. Four against two; the odds were ridiculous and the clock had run down to zero.

But the trick handcuffs - they had worked. Just like Kasey had promised.

Eric Plume

Chapter 32

I didn't go for my gun but instead I dove for cover behind the rear of the rental car. Five other people all thought they could draw first but I wasn't so ambitious. I didn't know what Kasey's first move was and I didn't care as the Jennings came out of my bra as fast as I could yank it free.

Gunfire exploded around me.

Sound vanished in the bad-static shriek of tinnitus. I felt a *thunk* in the car body and a hot sharp chunk of metal smacked into my cheek. My head snapped sideways with a stinging smack. *You've just been shot,* some rational part of my brain reported.

A blurred man-shape in all black darted past me. I brought my pistol up and fired four rounds as fast as I could pull the trigger, screaming *fuck* with each shot like punctuation. The *pop* of the little gun sounded like a toy. My target folded up on himself and hit the ground. I pulled the trigger again but nothing happened. That made me mad and scared and I swore. More gunshots registered through the ringing in my ears, *bang bang bang*. I saw someone running for the stairs and pulled the trigger three more times; still nothing happened and I realized there was an empty cartridge stuck point-first out of the chamber. I yelled *shit* and clawed at the slide, just like I'd seen a redneck do several days and a lifetime ago. I heard a male voice screaming ugly words I couldn't understand. I tried to make my fingers fit around the goddamned ridiculous tiny slide on the Jennings while *goddamn motherfucking piece of shit* yammered through my mind. There was one more shot, then no more noise except screams.

The jammed casing popped free of the chamber and the slide clacked forward. I took the little gun in one hand and scrambled forward on my knees towards the person I'd shot, swatting his pistol away from him with a sweep of one hand. It was Vadim; he'd taken one of my bullets in the hip and was curled tightly around the wound, air and animal whines hissing out through clenched teeth. I looked around.

It was over.

Bodies littered the concrete like discarded mannequins. The teenage thug was sprawled out with two bloody holes in his chest, eyes wide and staring. Something twitched in the corner of my vision.

It was the hooker's foot. She lay in a red pool of glistening blood strewn with chunks of something I couldn't identify. A pistol was near her hand, a chrome-plated pearl-handled twin to mine complete with a jammed casing stuck crosswise in the chamber. She had a hole in her wrist and another in her cheekbone. I realized the chunks were skull and brain and I swallowed hard on a throat full of bile. The air reeked of blood and gunpowder and sweat.

Kasey stood from the crouch he'd dived into. He had torn one knee on his suit but other than that he was uninjured. His right fist held a snub-nosed revolver.

My cheek throbbed. I touched it and found a piece of metal stuck in it. I pulled on it and it came free but it hurt to take the thing out. I looked at it; after a moment I recognized a piece of copper jacket. I tried to get to my feet again, stumbled and looked down. My right heel had pierced the hem of my dress and destroyed shoe and gown; the heel had snapped off and there was a long tear in the gown from the hemline almost to the bottom of my ribcage.

"Well fuck," I muttered.

Vadim whimpered some more, squeezing the wound on his hip.

"Hansen got away," Kasey called out. "I don't fucking believe it."

"Forget him," I said. My brain went into lock as I tried to figure out what to do next. There was no way I could think of to explain the total shit-show around me that wouldn't involve us going to jail for a long time.

Kasey flicked open the cylinder on his revolver, looked at it and closed it. He walked up to where Vadim lay. I knew what was coming and I didn't say a word. Vadim looked up with fear in his eyes.

Kasey smiled down at him over the sights of his revolver. "You enjoy it?"

I closed my eyes; I knew what was coming but I didn't want to watch. One final shot echoed through the garage. When I looked, there wasn't much left of Vadim's face either.

"Jesus," I whispered.

"No witnesses," he said.

I closed my eyes again, the adrenaline barreling through my system like a freight train.

"Give me that piece and get out," Kasey said. "I'll clean up here."

"You will?"

He nodded. "All part of the service," he said. "Give me the gun."

"Piece of shit jammed on me," I muttered as I handed it over. My voice sounded far away.

"Katya's jammed on her too." Kasey said.

"Didn't know her name," I said.

"Now you do," he said. "Get out. Don't forget your other gun."

I took a deep breath and tried to put a choke valve on my emotions. My head was a song full of bells and so much blood coursed through my body I felt almost aroused, excitement and fear molded in a fist of adrenaline. I shook my head to clear it, which only sort of worked. My ears still rang.

I picked up my trench coat and put it on, grabbed my P7 and stuffed it into the pocket of my coat. With shaking fingers I undid my shoes and scooped them up. Kasey was in the process of swapping my little .22 for the one in the hooker's hand. He stuck hers in his coat pocket. That was the last thing I saw before heading into the stairwell.

I took the steps two and three at a time as the blood rush crumbled and awful fear rose in its wake; shadows grew horns and teeth and jumped at me until I ran as fast as I could. I fell down and skinned my knee on the concrete, scrabbled back to my feet and kept running and didn't stop until I found a doorway in an alley to curl up in. I didn't know if anyone saw me and I didn't care, not with the shadow monsters all around and hard-edged images slicing into my mind.

I pitched forward and bile spewed out of my mouth like rabid froth. One image that kept coming back to me; the hooker's head opened like a rose five days past due, clear fluid running down what was left of her face lie tears from wet red holes where eyes had once been. I vomited again but I couldn't spit the picture out.

"Vitreous," I muttered to the wall in front of me. "Vitreous humor." The juice eyeballs are made of. I had learned that, but I couldn't remember where. I wiped my mouth on the sleeve of my coat and spat on the asphalt as the world reverted to normal around me. My head felt like empty space, the wet alleyway cold and slimy against my bare feet.

I was alone, and it was time to go.

I buttoned my coat all the way and turned up the collar before doing a quick inventory of my pockets; I had a full pack of cigarettes, a lighter, two receipts and forty seven cents change, along with my room key. Plus my automatic, which was useless in my current situation as long as my luck held. No phone and no car keys. It was a long walk from where I was to the Doubletree Hotel, but waiting wouldn't make the walk any shorter.

I lit up a cigarette, stuck my hands in my pockets

and started walking, careful not to look back.

The cellular age meant that pay phones were a thing of the past; I had change, but no way to use it. I did not dare stop in anywhere and ask to use the phone, seeing as I looked like a suspect of something, so I just walked. My feet stopped hurting about an hour in. They went numb and stayed that way. I rested here and there at bus stops and park benches, watching the late-night denizens of Seattle go by. Some people gave me funny looks and I didn't blame them; an empty-eyed woman in a stained raincoat with a burn on her cheek, walking barefoot on a cold winter's night. Yeah, you didn't see that every day, even in a big city. No one bothered me and I didn't bother anyone. I had plenty of time to think.

The only evidence I had left behind was one heel from a Jimmy Choo pump and five .22 shell casings. The gun that produced those shell casings would soon be at the bottom of Puget Sound or melted into scrap. The shoes I would dispose of. That would sever my link, as long as I could get somewhere to wash off all the blood and cordite before the cops found me. Hansen had seen everything but he had as much stake in keeping quiet as I did. That assumed, of course, that Kasey did not find him before the police did. I wouldn't have laid odds on the situation either way.

Eleven blocks from the parking garage I pitched the broken shoes into a dumpster; the two receipts went into a similar receptacle two blocks after that. The cigarettes vanished one by one as I smoked them, leaving the butts in a trail all the way down 4th Avenue, like breadcrumbs. Someone could've followed them if they had known what to look for.

I grew cold, then warm, then sweaty and thirsty and hollow and tired. Eventually moving just became a habit; stopping would have meant curling up and sleeping, possibly dying, so I didn't take any more breaks as 4th gave way to East Marginal Way and the Georgetown district. By the time I reached Pacific Highway the night sky had given way to false dawn. The last stars had gone out and the traffic had increased when I could make out the big glowing sign of my hotel. I walked the rest of the way; it was all I could do not to weave like a drunk. Fortunately it was early, early morning and no one saw me go in one of the side doors. Compared to outside the hotel felt like a sauna and it made me sleepy.

My employees were deep into what looked like a war council when I walked through the door. They all jumped up and Drake came over and hugged me and I just sort of stopped standing up, but no one let me fall. Everyone started talking at once and I let them. I was too tired to try and talk over them. Drake guided me to a chair and I let him; I was done being tough. I let them all babble at me until they were done.

"Jesus," Drake said as he looked me over. "What the hell happened?"

"The balloon went up," I said. "Hansen tried to frame me for blackmail and bump off his enforcer in the bargain. We all argued about it some."

"What happened to your face?"

I looked at him. "A bullet hit me in the cheek."

That shut everyone up. Izzy, Julian and Drake all stared at me.

"Well," I said, "part of a bullet anyway. Or maybe a piece of car bumper. I'm not really sure."

"Holy crap." Julian ran his hands through his hair, still staring at me. "Are we in trouble now?"

I sighed. "I don't know, Julian."

Izzy came over and knelt by my chair. Her face was puffy with tears and worry. "I got your text, but I didn't really believe it. I knew something was up when you didn't answer me."

"I didn't answer because my phone's at the bottom

of Green River," I said.

Izzy's eyes were very wide. "Boss, there was a breaking story about a triple homicide at a parking garage downtown. Was that...you?"

I shook my head. "Mostly Kasey," I said.

"And he just let you go," Drake asked.

"I paid him to," I said.

Drake blinked. "What? When?"

I smiled. "The night I met him at the Gridiron Bar....ten thousand dollars, in exchange for his help. He knew that Hansen wouldn't need him after all this was over. He's been looking for a profitable way out and I gave him one." The smile faded. "Sorry I didn't tell any of you, but that was part of the deal."

Izzy looked over her glasses at me. "Boss, how would he have known if you'd told us?"

"He wouldn't," I said, "but I had to keep my word to him. It was part of the deal."

She shook her head. "I don't get it."

I coughed a bit before responding. "Kasey is the sort of man who expects everyone to turn on him, thinks he's the last honorable son of a bitch on the planet, that kind of thing. I paid him up front, which said I trusted him. He wasn't used to that, I'm sure." I tried to run my hands through my hair but the tangles defeated me. "I paid him to back me up if they turned on him. Well, they did, and he did."

"Go put your creed into your deed, nor speak with double tongue," Drake intoned.

"Exactly," I said.

Julian raised an eyebrow. "So, you gave ten thousand dollars to the guy who almost put you in the hospital and trusted that he'd save your life?"

"Basically."

"That's nuts," Julian said. "Sorry boss, but that's bug-fuck insanity."

"No," I said as I stood up, "it's what we call 'a backup plan' in the industry."

I was shaky on my feet; they had started to throb. "Look, I'm beyond tired. I'm going to go get a shower and pass out for twelve hours or so. Everyone try to get some sleep...tomorrow we pack up and get the hell out of this hotel." I walked into the bathroom before anyone else could ask me questions.

Once inside the bathroom I made the mistake of looking in the mirror. The Chanel gown was ruined; two long tears and several bad stains ensured it was fit only for rags, if even that. The chunk of hot shrapnel had left a burn on my left cheekbone right below my eye, surrounded by a brown crust of blood. Another inch upwards and I would have been like that Russian hooker, dripping vitreous fluid all down my face. My makeup had run in inky streams over my eyelids and cheeks. Underneath that my skin was pale and my eyes were fever-bright. There was still a yellow bruise on my temple. My hair was a wet nest of tangles.

"You," I told the walking disaster on the other side of the glass, "need a vacation."

I turned up the shower as hot as I could stand it and scrubbed all the blood and cordite and makeup and sweat off of me, working with soap and washcloths until my skin turned pink. By the time I was done I could barely keep my eyes open. When I came out, Izzy and Julian were gone and Drake sat in one of the big armchairs, a glass of whiskey at his elbow. He looked about as tired as I felt. We met halfway across the room and folded into a tight embrace. It felt good beyond words to be held.

"You scared the hell out of me," he murmured into my hair.

"Sorry," I said.

"I know."

"Had to be done," I said.

"I know that too."

He squeezed me tighter. "Tell me this shit is over."

"Almost," I said.

Eric Plume

Chapter 33

I met up with Hayes two days later at Gas Works Park to complete our deal.

Getting out of the hotel had been much less problematic than getting in; there was a similar bit of tension smuggling Zork out but he seemed to know to be quiet and once again no one noticed the suspiciously cat-carrier shaped box. I dispatched Julian to Carter Burton's office with the missing files and a note giving an explanation of what happened...more or less.

I sent Izzy home but told her I wanted her to work on one final project; tracing the money we were to be paid with. I told her to get it done, cover her tracks and spare me the details.

My apartment looked about as it had when I'd left it, except for a couple of things; all the perishable food in my fridge had spoiled and there was evidence that someone had been through it. There were scratches on the door lock and some of my papers were out of place on my desk. Whoever had done it had been careful and thorough about it; I figured it had been Kasey. It was the sort of thing I might have done in his shoes. I sent Drake out for groceries and tried not to think about how much I hurt.

I was still in a good deal of pain once I made my way to Gas Works, but most of the bruises had faded and thanks to long pants and a coat, most of the other evidence of rough use was hidden from view. Only the butterfly bandage on my cheek and my skinned knuckles gave any indication regarding the events of a couple of nights ago.

It was a nice day out, one of those cold clear afternoons we get once in a while in the Northwest; the sun shone against the waters of Lake Union, and the air was clean and crisp. I sat on a bench and watched the lake ripple. My phone buzzed; I took it out and looked at it. There was a long text from Izzy, detailing just where the money was coming from. I smiled and put my phone away.

"Good afternoon," I heard from behind me; I recognized Hayes' friendly courtroom voice and turned around. He was casually dressed this time; blue jeans and a dark navy windbreaker, his eyes hidden by flat black sunglasses.

I looked him over. "We seem to have switched bodies," I said.

He sat down and watched the water for a minute. "Tell me you got something good," he said.

I passed him a thick manila envelope. "There's

everything we found," I said.

"Give me the short version," he said.

"A group of rich assholes decided to get a massive development deal pushed through by cutting corners," I said. "They hijacked Ironhorse Construction via the stock market and blackmailed the owner into going along with the whole deal. I've got you proof of a conspiracy, plus all the financial records the group used - including all the bribes they paid."

"So Ironhorse was clean," he said.

"The owner," I said, "would make a much better witness than a defendant."

"So who was running the show?"

"A banker named Hansen," I said. "He was the one who turned the gang kids loose on Kitsmiller...and he's the reason why Andrew Stark was killed."

Hayes blinked. "How does a downtown banker end up running gang kids?"

"All in the report," I said.

He took the envelope and hefted it in his hands. "Banker's name was Hansen? Bradley James Hansen?"

"Yeah," I said. "Why?"

"Seattle Police fished him out of Elliot Bay yesterday morning." Hayes said.

"Dead?"

"Very," he said. "Almost wasn't enough left for an ID."

"Jesus," I said, wondering who had done the work.

"The cops are convinced he had something to do with a triple homicide over at First American's parking garage...a real mess." He paused. "What happened to your face?"

"Bizarre gardening accident," I said.

"You live in an apartment," he said.

"That's what makes it bizarre."

Hayes frowned. He waited for me to elaborate but I didn't. After a second he looked down at the envelope. "Will the case hold together without Hansen?"

"Like I said, all Hansen's financial records are in there," I said. "Including the payment to a trigger-man to bump off Stark and several bribes to SPD officials."

"Is any of it admissible?"

I laughed. "I'm sure you can make it so," I said.

"Come on Hayes, I couldn't do it all for you."

"This isn't how I wanted things to get done," he said.

"But you'll take it," I said.

"Guess I have to."

"I'd like to get paid now," I said.

He reached into his jacket. My own hand was on my pistol and popping off my holster's safety strap before I was even consciously aware of the act. I forced myself to relax as Hayes pulled out an envelope and handed it to me.

"Maturation paperwork," he said, "for both loans. Technically it is within our contract...you can put it all on your tax form and no one will question it."

I took the envelope and opened it, giving the contents a quick scan. Everything was as he said it was; several loan payoffs, courtesy of the Davis-Callion Corporation. I closed the envelope back up and stuck it in my purse. "Pleasure doing business with you," I said.

"As long as you forget it happened."

"I plan to," I said. "Speaking of which, I should probably forget this ever existed as well." I passed him the expense card. He folded it into his palm; there was a small snap of breaking plastic as he stuck the remains in his pocket.

"You did good work, Eckart," he said. "Better than I thought you would, and I had high hopes for you."

"Really? You don't even like me."

It was his turn to smile. "I don't have to like you to see the skills you possess," he said. "You're a cast-iron piece of bitch meat...and that's why you got the job done."

"You're going to make me blush," I said, but inside I was on my guard. Something about his tone told me his comments were a setup for something else.

He took a card from a case on his belt and held it out to me. "You," he said, "would have been wasted on a small-town police force and you're wasted in private practice. If you want I can put in a good word for you, get you enrolled at Quantico."

I didn't reply right away; I didn't trust myself to keep my game face on. Instead I looked at the card, a simple rectangle of white paper and script. I thought about what it might mean.

"It's a straight offer, Eckart."

I nodded. "I'm a little old to enter the FBI Academy."

"But not too old," he said. "And besides, I know why the Lynden police didn't take you...it was silly bureaucratic nonsense, easily overlooked."

I could hear people approaching and I looked over my shoulder; a group of kids, maybe eight at most, in the company of two middle-aged ladies. A school field trip, or perhaps some short of church event. They barreled past us in a burst of noise and commotion. I closed my eyes and took in the harmless sound of children laughing. When they were gone I opened my eyes and reached into my purse.

"You," I said, "might need my help again." I slid one of my business cards into Hayes' hand, right over the one he had intended to give to me. "Besides, I've got people who depend on me. I appreciate the offer though."

"You'd work for me again?" Hayes cocked his head. "But...you don't like me either."

I smiled. "I don't have to like you," I said, "to take your money."

He laughed. I didn't.

"Speaking of, I ran down the Davis-Callion Corporation and I have just one question." I leaned forward. "How does an FBI agent get access to a DEA slush fund powered by drug seizures?"

Slowly, Hayes took off his sunglasses. "You don't

know when to quit, do you."

"Hayes," I said, "some people might object to getting their pay this way, but at the moment I'm not one of them. So the government puts drug seizure money to work off the books...so what? I'm just curious how you got access to the DEA's gray accounts, but I doubt you're going to tell me that."

"Why dig at all? You want more money or something?"

"Nope." I smiled. "I just wanted you to know that I know what you're up to, in case you get the bright idea of putting me in court."

"...And if I try to silence you, the whole thing goes off on a dead man switch." He put his sunglasses back on. "Maybe you *aren't* wasted on private practice, Eckart."

I stood up. "You need me again, you know where to find me."

He nodded. I left him staring out over the sun-struck waters of Lake Union, contemplating a great many things that I didn't need to know. I walked back over to the massive power plant structure that gave the park its name; Drake stood near the fence around it. He smiled as I approached. His dreadlocks were hidden under a wide-brimmed hat and his clothes were new. One last purchase courtesy of the Davis-Callion drug money. I smiled at him.

"How'd it go?"

I shrugged. "About as well as I could have expected." I tapped a cigarette out of my pack and lit it. "He now has about five reasons not to want to reveal me, not the least of which is that I could do such services for him in the future."

"You'd work for him again?"

I nodded. "Of course. The money's right. Besides, he's an attack dog...that's a useful thing to have if you can keep it on a tight enough leash."

Drake glanced over to where Hayes was sitting, about two hundred feet off and barely visible. "You know he views you the same way, right?"

"Of course he does." I flicked ash off the end of my cigarette and took another drag. It didn't taste all that great and I remembered why I'd quit in the first place.

"So which one of you is wearing the collar," Drake said, "and which one of you is holding the leash?"

I ground out the cigarette under my foot, took out the pack and tossed it in the trash. "That," I said with as little irony as I could muster, "remains to be seen."

Drake did not have a response to that, but then again neither would I if I had been in his shoes. I smiled at him and looped my arm through his elbow. "Come on," I said, "let's get the rest of our business concluded."

I drove over to Kitsmiller's house and gave her a heavily-edited recounting of what had happened, leaving out most of the shady dealings and all of the violence. She accepted the news with no small measure of relief, hugged me and gave me a box of freshly baked cookies. There was no way I could turn those down. I gave her a business card and told her she could contact me if there was any more trouble.

"Of course, dear," she said. "If I may ask, what happened to your face?"

"Oh, just a little kitchen accident," I said. "I'm not much of a cook."

"I see." I could tell she did not completely believe me but also that she was too polite to inquire further. I was glad of it. "Ms. Eckart, I have to thank you for all that you've done...but would I be out of line in saying that I wish none of this had ever happened?"

My mind's eye filled with blood and death and it was work not to shudder. "No, ma'am," I said softly.

"No you wouldn't. In fact I agree with you."

We exchanged a bit of small talk before leaving; I dropped Drake off at home and told him I needed to make my final stop all by myself.

"Kasey," Drake said. It wasn't a question. I nodded.

"Last bit of business," I said. "I'll be careful."

The Gridiron was almost empty when I got there; a couple of bored-looking waitresses and a thin crowd of mostly silent drunks kept the place just to the right of closed. Kasey was leaning at the bouncer's podium when I walked in; he gave me a smile that said he had no idea who I was. I returned the gesture as I showed him my ID along with a note. *Meet me out back,* the note said.

"Sorry lady," Kasey said, "I can't let you in. Your ID's expired."

I made a small pretense of kicking up a fuss before sighing disgustedly and walking out of the bar. Once clear of the door I turned and walked around the block, sliding down the alleyway after a quick check for anyone following me. The alley behind the bar was surprisingly clean; no bottles, no puke, only a little rubbish here and there. I did not have to wait long before the back door opened and Kasey slipped out.

"I thought our business was done," he said.

"It is," I said.

He leaned up against the wall. "So what are you doing here?"

"Making sure you didn't get caught."

I didn't." He glanced up the alleyway. "Cops ain't got a clue what happened...as far as they're concerned, a couple of assholes shot it out over a hooker. Case closed."

"And Hansen?"

He shrugged. "The gang kids didn't like him getting poor old Vadim killed," he said.

"And the kids?"

"Cops picked three of them up. Probably gonna charge them with the murder."

"That's convenient," I said.

"Not for Hansen," he said.

I glanced up the alleyway in the other direction. "I've got one more thing to give you. Call it a bonus." I reached into my purse with my left hand and came up with an envelope, flapping it in the breeze and making it make noise while my other hand went for something else.

Kasey glanced at the envelope. "Thanks, but what is this-"

An expandable baton packs quite a wallop, especially when you don't open it before you swing. My shot caught him right in the side of the nose; all four of his limbs shot out and his ass hit the ground as blood sprayed from his face in a hot arc. I had already let go of the envelope; when he looked up he found himself staring down the business end of my H & K. His eyes were wide with shock and sudden anger but he didn't move. With the tip of my baton I tapped the side of my head twice, slowly. "I worked with you because I had to, Kasey. Don't get to thinking we're friends."

"Wouldn't dream of it," he said. He probed the side of his nose and winced. "Damn, three places."

I snapped the baton shut. "Should be more careful next time."

"I will be." He stood, slowly, one hand holding the ruin of his nose. "You think I'm going to let you get away with this?"

I took another two steps back and holstered my pistol. "Yeah you are," I said, "but just this once."

His laughter followed me out of the alleyway, cold and bright like the steel of a knife.

Chapter 34

I gave everyone a three days off, myself included. For one it seemed wise to close the office while events sorted themselves out around us; for another, I was too damn tired and sore for much of anything except lazing about on the couch. I let Julian use his phone-etiquette magic on our two prospective clients and tried to let myself relax.

A trip to the doctor's office was problematic, but Drake insisted that I go. They found evidence of a mild concussion and I spun a story about falling backwards on a stool; they admonished me for not showing up sooner and put me in for several expensive tests, some of which I consented to. Fortunately my general physician wasn't sharp enough to guess the provenance of the burn on my cheek, but instead stitched it up and told me to keep it clean. Even if he wondered where all my scrapes and bruises had come from, he didn't think to inquire and I didn't volunteer any information.

Nights were tough to sleep through. The nightmares were always real and sharp; clear fluid dripping down a pale smooth face, wet red holes where eyes should have been, the bang of gunfire and the screams of men in mortal terror. I woke up sweating several times but always Drake was there for me with hugs and soothing words. I found I couldn't eat strawberries anymore. Sudden noises and movements out of the corner of my eye made me jump. I wondered how long it would take to go away and hoped it would be soon.

Information came in, courtesy of the evening news. The shootout was being termed by the police as a "crime of passion"; apparently their theory was that the hooker and the two men had shot it out in a dispute over money and Hansen had been involved in the shooting. This was corroborated by the discovery of a handgun in Hansen's car. The details of his demise were gruesome enough that even the nightly news didn't elaborate.

I turned on Netflix and blocked out the world.

It was the third day of my vacation. Drake and I snuggled under a nest of blankets we'd made in the living room. *Doctor Who* played on the television and we munched on popcorn. Neither of us had a stitch on, a state I'd been in more often than not over the past three days.

Since the shootout, I'd found myself in a dizzy, childlike state of mind. All I wanted to do was taste delicious food and have orgasms and snuggle.

I wanted to feel alive.

"Maybe," I said around a mouthful of popcorn, "I'll

take another day off."

Drake toyed with a lock of my hair. "I think you'd better get back to making money," he said.

"If ever I wanted to be a Time Lord it'd be now."

"Sorry I'm not David Tennant," Drake said.

"Don't be," I said. "You're far better looking."

He laughed and I swallowed my popcorn so he could kiss me properly, which he did. Afterward he simply lay there and looked down at me.

"So," he said.

"Yeah," I said. "About that thing."

"The thing we were going to talk about when people weren't trying to kill us?"

I nodded. "That one."

"Okay." He shifted position and sat up. I did the same, not bothering to keep the sheet around me. Drake's eyes followed my naked body; I liked him looking at me. I usually didn't care for being naked but something about the way he did his looking made it different.

"So," he said, "what happens now?"

"Well you probably shouldn't keep working for me," I said. "Don't get me wrong, you did a great job...but it's bad office etiquette for the boss to be boffing one of the employees."

Drake grinned. "We could always stop with the boffing."

"That's crazy talk," I said.

"Amber," he said, "are we dating?"

I reached out and toyed with one of his dreadlocks. "Yeah, we are." It felt strange to say it, like trading one heavy weight for another one, but the new one was easier to bear. I just didn't know how heavy it'd end up being yet.

"I guess I'd better start looking for work or something," he said.

"You could always be my house-boyfriend," I said.

He ran a fingertip over my cheek. "Like that idea?"

"Oh yeah," I said.

We both had a good laugh as I snuggled into the crook of his arm. Outside, a car horn blared and I jumped, hand slapping down towards my left hip. Drake saw it and frowned. "Still there," he said.

I took a deep breath and nodded. "Sorry. I hope it goes away soon."

"It won't," he said. "But you will get used to it. I had

a friend who was in Afghanistan, he saw-well, he saw something he couldn't forget. Used to make him wake up screaming every night. There were places he didn't want to go, things he couldn't eat. Eventually he got used to it, but not until he got some serious therapy."

"Post-Traumatic Stress Disorder," I muttered. "Jesus."

"Amber, you watched three people die. It happens."

"I know. I just want it to be over."

Drake spread his arms, hands palm-up as if to frame a picture. "This just in...Amber Eckart is not invincible. We will have more on this late-breaking story as it develops."

I gave him a wry smile. "Har, har."

"Seriously...you should go talk to someone about this."

"I can't, Drake. Not for a while." I watched Zork play with one of my shoelaces for a moment before answering. "I can't tell anyone this happened...it's too risky."

Drake nodded. "Okay. Just, you know, someday."

"I will." I leaned up and kissed him. "But for now," I said between kisses, "help me forget, okay?"

He smiled. "Easily done."

I pulled his head down and kissed him some more while *Who's* credits rolled. Things started to get more intense, but then he broke off with a laugh. I cocked an eyebrow at him.

"Sorry," he said, "nature calls."

"Don't be gone long," I said.

"What, you'll lose interest?"

"No, I'll kick down the door."

He stood up. "That would be hard to explain to the apartment manager," he said over his shoulder as he made for the bathroom.

I chuckled to myself as I rearranged the sheets. After I had the nest prepped I got the urge for another glass of wine; I'd been several kinds of bad all weekend and it showed in the scatter of bottles and shucked clothes cluttering up most of the available surfaces. I made sure to grab my robe before venturing into the kitchen, on account of the fact that my curtains were less than perfect at blocking the windows. While digging out my bottle of Riesling I happened to glance out the crack between the curtains.

There was a car parked at the curb, right beyond the apartment parking lot. I could just make out the front half, see that there was a person sitting in the driver's seat doing their best to look inconspicuous. I stood there for a good ten seconds and watched.

He had a camera.

I put the glass down and the bottle back in the refrigerator. I turned around and walked back into the hall. The bathroom door opened and Drake stepped out smiling, a smile that died when he saw the look on my face.

"What's up?"

"Someone's outside," I said.

"Huh?"

"Sitting at the curb. Watching my apartment and doing their level best to pretend they aren't."

"Oh shit," he said, "Cops?"

I shook my head. "No. The car doesn't have government plates." I looked at him. "Another PI."

We both stood in the hall for a good long moment without talking; there were a good many things I wanted to say and do, but nothing that crossed my mind was worth doing or saying. I closed my eyes and felt his arms around me. It was work not to cry but I didn't.

"They found me," he said.

I nodded.

"You know," he said, "I'd almost forgotten about that."

"I did forget about it," I said.

"I don't want to leave," he said.

"I don't want you to go," I whispered. "But if you stay, they'll find you...and you still don't have the money to go to court, do you?"

"Nope," he said. "Halcourt's lawyers would eat me alive. Again."

"Yeah." Anger was a hot heavy knot pressing against the base of my throat. Instinct kept trying to get me to swallow but I knew if I did that there might be tears and I didn't want to cry. I could still taste the rage and it was foul, but there was no one to vent it on, no one who deserved it anyway, and so I just sort of held onto it along with my brand-new boyfriend who was about to go away.

"What happens now?"

I took a deep, long breath, held it in and let it out slowly. *One, two, three, four,* I thought to myself. *Five, six, seven, eight.* "I'll go out there and distract the guy in the car. You slip out the window in the bedroom...there's a big bush next to it you can hide under. Crawl from there to the ravine next to the road. You should be able to make it all the way up to the metro station without the guy out front seeing anything."

"Amber..."

"Drake, we both know what has to happen now."

*Nine, ten, fuck, fuck, **fuck**.*

He shook his head slowly, once. "Okay," he said. "Okay. I'll go pack."

"Not yet you won't," I whispered.

I reached up to kiss him. I didn't stop kissing him all the way to the bed, not throughout the whole time we shared each other the same way we had on our first night; no restraint, no artifice. I could taste tears in our kiss. I didn't know if they were mine or his. Afterward I leaned into his embrace, savored its feel.

"This isn't over," I whispered into his neck, my voice bruised. "You're still my boyfriend...I don't fucking care that you have to take a leave of absence."

He brushed gentle fingers across my cheekbone. "Long distance it is," he said.

We both dressed and I helped him get his things ready. Out of habit I slipped my pistol into my waistband but then changed my mind and stuck it back in my nightstand drawer; it would not do to shoot the poor bastard parked outside and some part of me very much wanted to.

"I'm sorry about this," he said.

I found a smile for him. "You didn't do it," I said.

"Is this goodbye?"

"No," I said. "It isn't."

I put on my coat, collected my keys and took another deep breath before stepping outside. The air was cold and damp; not raining, but everything was wet enough that the drips off the trees felt close enough to rain that an outsider probably wouldn't know the difference.

The man in the car was a pro; he didn't stare at me as I walked up the steps and across the parking lot, but instead studiously focused on what appeared to be a magazine. I could only make out the top part of his head, encased in a stocking cap. I wore the things myself on stakeout. They were great for hiding hairstyles and head shape. Take them off and you become a whole new person when following someone.

He did, however, look up when I rapped on his car's window. His smile was a perfect blend of politeness and faint confusion. If I hadn't been in the trade I would have bought it. It was too bad for him that I recognized him; there are downsides to attending industry conventions.

He rolled down his window. "Can I help you miss?" He was an average-looking sort with a round face and dark eyes, wearing jeans and a green Patagonia fleece.

"Dave Stavros," I said. "Tell me, how's business? Mine's booming."

"Jesus, Eckart...what're you doing?" He put the magazine down. "I'm on fucking stakeout here."

"I know," I said. "You're watching my building. You're watching my apartment."

"I'm here on a divorce case -"

"Stavros," I said, "I'm not a mark, okay?" I turned. "From here the only apartment you have a good view of is mine. If it was the people above me you wanted to see, you'd be a hundred feet down that way." I pointed. "And if you were looking for the people next to me, you'd be fifty feet up the road that way." I turned and pointed again. "I'm not married and I haven't made an insurance claim since some drunk driver tried to park his car in my backseat. That was eight years ago."

He stayed silent. I could see the gears turning inside his head, so I kept talking. Always talk faster than the other person can think.

"Now, unless you level with me I'm going to call the cops and report you as a peeper," I said. "It's hard to do surveillance work from jail, y'know?"

He let out a sigh. "I *told* my boss this was a dumb idea."

"Drew the shortest straw, did we?"

He gave a rueful grin and nodded. "Okay, you got me. I'm watching you. You know I can't say why, right?"

"I'm not even going to ask you," I said. "In exchange for ruining your day, go ahead and ask me some questions."

"You know a guy named Drake Albie?"

I made like I was thinking. "God, it's been years...I think I went to school with him. Let me see...tall, skinny, curly hair, dark-ish skin?"

"He is tall," Stavros said, "but these days he's packing around serious muscle. Dreadlocks, too. A clerk down at the grocery store saw him, and said they saw someone who looked like you, and since you two went to school together the boss figured you might know something." He paused, and I could tell he wasn't buying my ignorance completely. Playing a player always cut both ways.

I shrugged. "I haven't been down to the grocer's in a couple of days," I said. "I've been home, recuperating...I wrecked my bike." I pointed to the mark on my face and held up my hand so he could see my half-healed palms.

"So you haven't seen Drake Albie."

"Not for a while," I said.

"You mind if I sit out here, take some photos?"

I shrugged like I didn't care. "Knock yourself out, but stick that lens in my bathroom window and our next talk won't be so pleasant."

He laughed. "Come on, Eckart, I'm married."

"You and I both know that doesn't really matter."

He kept laughing and I made myself join him before I walked back inside. Drake was gone, along with his stuff; there hadn't been much of his to begin with but it was amazing to me, how big a hole it all made now that it wasn't around. The apartment just seemed messy and big without him in it. Messy, big and cold. I closed the window and looked out of it; there was no sign of him but then again I had not expected there to be, I only looked because that is what you did.

After that I went to fetch my wine. Zork hopped up on the counter; I petted him some and he purred, butting his head against my chin. I finished the glass but did not pour another. Instead I set to cleaning up my apartment, putting all the spare sheets away and taking out the trash and doing some dishes I hadn't gotten to. While tidying up my nightstand I found a little paper crane. I hadn't known Drake could make those. He was full of surprises.

I opened it. *Gone far,* it said inside, *but back someday.*

I closed my eyes and planted my lips against the paper. "You better be," I said softly as the tears came out for real. "You goddamn well better be."

Epilogue

I did indeed take one more day off from work, but not to relax.

I spent the rest of the day out jogging; I hadn't ever really been one for working out but I knew the only way I would get any sleep at all was if I was exhausted, or drunk. I didn't want a hangover and I didn't want to become an alcoholic, so I strapped on some tennis shoes and some shorts and ran. I jogged all over the wooded parts of Des Moines until my legs felt wobbly and the sun dipped low on the horizon. Full dark had come before I made it back to my apartment. Stavros was gone, and I did not give a bent hangnail if he returned. In fact, I kind of hoped he did. Let Halcourt waste the money looking where his quarry wasn't.

The exercise did a good job of knocking me out; I fell asleep with only an hour of tossing. The dreams still came and I still woke up sweating at 2 am, but I did manage to fall right back asleep. You take what you can get in this life.

The next morning I rose with the dawn, somewhat stiff and sore but no worse than I had been after getting beat up. A hot shower and a cup of coffee helped, and after a good light breakfast I actually felt human. As much as I did not want to admit it, exercise beat booze as a way to relax. I did not, however, feel up to jogging that morning.

"Next week," I told myself. "Next week, jogging in the morning." Unlike the last five dozen times I'd had this conversation with myself, I actually planned on doing it.

My first stop that morning was at a local gun range. Up until recently I had gone there twice a month to stay current, but the last few weeks had given me cause to believe that not to be sufficient. I asked the clerk if it was possible to talk to the range master; he smiled, pointed me to a chair and got on his phone.

The range master turned out to be younger than I was, a clean-cut Army boy with blond hair and a smile that blended calm confidence with just the right pinch of shyness. I stood and shook his hand as we exchanged names. His was Vickers.

"What can I do for you, Miss Eckart?"

"I'd like to sign up for some pistol training," I said.

"Well, we've got a range class -"

I pulled out my investigator's license and my state CPL. "I'm not looking to make tight groups in a paper target," I said. "I'm looking to survive if someone starts shooting at me."

I could see him re-evaluate me in the blink of an eye, which made me like him a bit more. "I teach a security class every Friday, five to seven," he said. "You figure you qualify for the Intermediate section?"

"Put me in with the newbies," I said. "There's no harm in learning the basics again."

"Always wise," he said.

"There any spaces left?"

His smile deepened. "I'll make sure there's one."

"I'll be here, check in hand."

I bought two boxes of generic lead-nosed 9mm and spent a couple of hours finding out how bad my marksmanship was. "Not terrible" was the answer; however, I had to keep shooting or I started getting twitchy. The gunfire from the rest of the range put me into a cold sweat unless I had a loaded pistol in my hand. Once I was done I walked off the range as quickly as I could manage without running. The shots mirrored the ones in my own head. At least there were no screams.

I spent the rest of the day looking up gyms and martial arts instructors. The range had been an easy choice; I'd been there many times and I felt comfortable with it. But for the other instruction I would have to take my time. My legs were still sore from the jog last night but I made myself do it again anyway, working myself into that numb place where wanting things like food and sleep eclipsed higher cares like loneliness and nameless fears. I was pretty sure I slept through the night that time, but I was also equally sure my dreams weren't the pleasant kind.

Julian was happy to see me when I walked through the front door on Tuesday. He had gotten his hair cut since the last time I had seen him; it was short and spiky, shiny with gel. A new set of studs gleamed in his ears. He was, however, wearing a nice set of slacks and a button-down shirt.

"Hiya boss," he said. "Vacation go okay?"

I shrugged. "It went," I said. "Any calls?"

"Izzy's already deep into some insurance work." He grinned. "Also, that crazy Winchell lady called again."

I shook my head. Alicia Winchell was a perennial client; her requests stemmed from a strange cocktail of paranoid delusions. "Is her postman trying to steal her mail, or did she see Elvis at the supermarket again?"

"She didn't mention them, but apparently her husband might be cheating on her."

I sighed. "Write her up an invoice, I'll add Mister Winchell to my to-follow list."

"But boss, hasn't she asked you to do this like, three times already?"

"Four," I said.

"She's a nut-bar," Julian muttered.

"No argument, but the dollars in her pocket are still worth a hundred pennies each. Write it up."

"Sure thing," he said, chuckling.

I walked back into my office; Izzy was in her accustomed place, mouse zig-zagging this way and in time with the click of various keystroke shortcuts. She had gotten her hair dyed again; this time it was a mess of blue, red, black and peroxide blonde, in stripes and splotches. I shook my head and grinned.

"I didn't know Manic Panic did drive-bys," I said as I sat down.

She swiveled her chair around. "I don't deal with customers, so I figured it'd be okay." She looked me up and down. "It is okay, right?"

"It looks great," I said. "Very you."

She beamed. "So, I've got two due-diligence reports and a slip-and-fall," she said. "An old lady tripped on a curb up in Kirkland, claimed it crumbled under her walker. She's asking for a couple million."

I whistled. "What's the damage on her end?"

"A seriously traumatized Shi-Tzu."

I blinked. "What?"

"She was carrying her dog and landed on it when she fell," Izzy said, "then couldn't get up. Apparently the poor thing was almost smothered to death."

"Whose side are we on?" I cracked open my coffee and added more sugar. I had tried to be good over at the Starbucks but after a half-dozen sips my sweet tooth got the better of me. One thing at a time.

She shrugged. "We're the bad guys. The insurance agency for the gas station thinks two million is way high for a scared dog, says it isn't the clerk's fault he couldn't see her fall."

"Only a lawyer would disagree," I said. "Get me the pertinent facts and I'll go run it down after lunch."

"You doing okay?" She took off her glasses and wiped at them.

I took a sip of coffee before opening the door. "Julian, could you come in here please?"

One of the nice things about a small office is that

getting everyone together took less than fifteen seconds. Julian walked in and I closed the door behind him. "Okay," I said, using my best boss voice, "I'm only going to talk about this once and then never again, so I hope you both are listening."

Julian fidgeted with the hem of his shirt. Izzy just sat and looked at me, eyes unreadable behind her glasses.

"What we just did, you guys can't ever talk about it. Ever, at all. Not with each other, not with me, not with your girlfriend or your boyfriend, not even with God if he happens to ask you. From now until the end of the world, you two don't know anything about any shooting, you don't know anything about John Hayes the FBI agent and this company sure as hell did *not* profit off those events. You understand?"

They both nodded.

"And in case our relationship changes, I want both of you to know something...some people, like a court of law, might consider you accessories - maybe even conspirators should you try and come forward with this to get back at me for something."

Julian shook his head. "Boss, I'd never-"

"What if I fired you?"

"But...you wouldn't. I mean, you aren't planning to, are you?" He looked confused.

"I'm not," I said, "but if you don't work hard I might. Or the company might go under. Or someone might try and bribe you, and maybe that day I was hard on you and you might be a little mad at me. No matter what, you can't tell. Telling puts people at risk and will probably get everyone arrested. You, me, Izzy, Drake, the old lady we helped, everyone. Don't do it." I looked at both of them in turn. Julian flinched a little, but Izzy didn't.

"You both volunteered," I said. "This is part of what volunteering meant. This is why I asked you if you wanted to stay."

Julian met my eyes. "I get it, boss."

"You won't tell?"

He blinked. "Won't tell what?"

I smiled. "Exactly."

Izzy nodded. "What he said. I know what'll happen if I do."

"Okay," I said, "I'm done being a hardass now." I reached into my purse and pulled out the maturation paperwork Hayes had given me. "I wanted you guys to see this," I said as I signed everything off. It was just a simple signature, but I felt the weight of debt lift from my shoulders as I handed the envelope to Julian. "Mail that off," I said. He nodded.

"Drake should have been here to see us do that," Izzy said.

"Speaking of Drake," Julian said, "where is he?"

I had known the question would show up eventually, but hearing it didn't make answering much easier. "On a bus to Utah," I said. "Or California maybe. I don't know."

"What?" Izzy and Julian spoke almost simultaneously.

"What happened," Julian said.

I took a deep breath and gave them the short version of Drake's troubles. I got as far as the PI in my parking lot before Julian exploded.

"What a bunch of bullshit! We can't-"

"-do a damn thing," I said. "There's nothing we can do, Julian. Not now." I tried to keep the anger out of my voice and was more or less successful.

"But...I don't -"

Izzy's voice was quiet, but very firm. "Let it go, Julian."

He looked from me to Izzy and did not seem to know what to think. Finally he walked back to his desk, face a mask of confusion. Izzy stood up, walked over to me and gave me a hug. I hugged her back. "Sorry boss," she said.

"You didn't do it," I said. "Now, I've got work to get to."

She smiled at me before sitting back down. "Life goes on?"

The phone rang in the background.

"When you're lucky," I said.

Made in the USA
Coppell, TX
08 April 2020